REY DE LA GARZA

The Oracle

Foundation

To my inner child, I whisper, "We did it."

So much of life we spend thinking we are the roots of a tree. Living from the limited view of the roots. Strong, solid, growing down and out. The lucky ones instead, realize we are the leaves. Caressed by gentle breezes, kissed by the sun, ever-changing with time fleeting.

Rey De La Garza

Chapter 1

Deyanira woke to a loud, panicked banging on her door in the middle of the night. The room was blurry and out of focus as she sat up. Squinting and rubbing her eyes, she placed her feet in her sandals. Deyanira, with a hand on her knee, slowly rose from her bed. It wasn't the first night that loud, erratic banging on her door jolted her out of bed.

The curiosity of a child caused her daughter Calida to rise before her body had fully woke up. Calida stumbled clumsily out of her bedroom and met Deyanira in the hallway.

"Go on back to bed, *mija*. I'll call if I need you," Deyanira said in passing.

Deyanira opened the door to one of the kiosk owners she often purchased from. His wife was crying and trying to explain. Their daughter laid in his arms unconscious and drenched with sweat. They were an older couple, and their child came later in life. The daughter had fallen ill a month ago. They took her to the hospital earlier that day because she hadn't gotten better. The doctors told them she was sick with pneumonia, but the child was too far gone to survive. They were instructed to take her home so she could pass in the comfort of her family.

There knelt the mother in Deyanira's doorway, consumed with grief. The father was silent and stoic. He held his child, rocking her and kissing her forehead. His tears escaped from his eyes into her hair.

Deyanira let the mother finish her story and then pitch her plea for help. Deyanira was known as a healer to some locals on the island and a *bruja* to others. Mostly she was only sought after in desperation. Deyanira knew the mother's emotions were huge and if locked away in her body, they would burrow into her stomach and manifest later as a debilitating illness. The mother finally fell silent. Deyanira bent down to the kneeling mother, both hands placed on each side of her head, and gently kissed the top of her head, signaling for the mother to stand.

As the mother rose, Deyanira whispered, "I'll do what I can, *amor*. What is her name?"

The mother shuttered and whispered, "She is Solanine. I am Halima and this is Adan."

Before entering Deyanira's house, there were rules. Halima removed her shoes outside the door and begged Deyanira to waive the remainder rituals of entry because they were wasting valuable time. Deyanira understood Halima's concerns, but there can never be exceptions–protecting the home from outside forces was top priority. Deyanira took the weary mother's hand and helped her. Guiding her to the washing basin filled with salt water, Deyanira placed Halima's hands in the washing basin, rinsing her hands and then shaking them off. Deyanira took her own hands and ran them over Halima's head, then down Halima's back and down to her heels. Deyanira pulled out Halima's erratic emotions and placed them in the woven basket that lay to the right of the doorway on her porch.

Halima entered the home when the ritual was complete. She

felt light, and she could think clearly. Her grief was absent. Deyanira repeated the ritual on Adan and their child.

Deyanira glanced up at Halima to see her face twist with guilt. "Your grief is in the basket, mother. It will return to you as you leave. You will need your wits tonight, so focus."

Relief moved like a wave across Halima's face.

Adan laid Solanine on the couch while Deyanira dressed the table. She removed her bowl of dried flowers and rosemary from the center of the table and wiped the table with Florida water. Once complete, she dressed the table with a fresh white linen cloth. She instructed the parents to remove Solanine's shirt and place her on the table lying on her back. At Solanine's feet, Deyanira placed a glass bowl of water. She walked over to her shelf and took down a bottle filled with lavender tincture.

She told Halima, "When the time is right, you'll need to spread this on her chest, and then we will repeat the same thing on her back. I will give you instructions, and you must follow all of them."

Halima and Adan nodded silently.

In Deyanira's *pilón*, she ground corn, yerba santa, wood betony, cypress, a pinch of xanthan gum, dried yew, a sliced piece of yucca, a dried violet, some fresh vervain flowers, and spearmint.

Calida, peaked into the room from the hallway, ready to assist with whatever Deyanira needed. Disregarding her previous instructions to return to bed, Calida fiddled with her curls to stay awake.

Deyanira waved Calida over into the kitchen from the hallway. "I need you to go out and get an adolescent hen, *mija*. Not a chick or an egg layer, but a young hen. Ask the ancestors for their guidance on which one to pick. It is very important to listen to your *knowing*. Hear them with your sight. Let them guide you. Go now, *niña*, and take Bassat with you."

Bassat was their cat. Calida's cat. When they first returned to Puerto Rico, they rented an apartment temporarily, and Bassat found them there only three days before they moved into their forever home. The young black cat was extraordinarily vocal, and in Deyanira's opinion, a pain in the ass; however, Bassat chose them. She protected Calida from things unseen. Calida ran to the back door, pausing only to look towards the hallway and call Bassat telepathically. The black cat emerged from the bedroom with a loud cranky meow and sprinted for the back door. Halima nervously questioned Deyanira if she should trust such a young child with the task.

Deyanira replied without even looking up from her *pilón*, "She is more powerful than you could ever imagine. It is a gift to your family that she woke and is choosing the vessel for this ritual. Trust the process, or it will fail. Now prepare Solanine's body."

Deyanira rubbed the grainy concoction generously across Solanine's chest. For the first time since they arrived, Solanine moved and coughed, briefly showing signs of life. Quickly, the paste hardened on the girl's chest, and Deyanira scraped it off into a container. She then repeated the process on Solanine's back.

Calida emerged from the darkness of the backyard with a young hen cradled under her arm, Bassat not far behind her loudly meowing opinions. Deyanira took the hen from her daughter's arms and held it up to examine it. She trusted her child's gifts better than her own most days, but she knew Calida needed the encouragement.

"Perfect *mija*, you did good." she said.

Calida smiled and skipped down the hallway to her bedroom.

Deyanira spoke to the young hen with soft words of gratitude and love. She told the hen it would come back elevated as a hawk, the animal guide of Deyanira's bloodline. She then held the container up to the hen so it could eat the contents.

Once the container was empty, Deyanira handed the hen to Halima. "This hen is your child for the next three days. You will bring it into your home, give it comfortable bedding, read to it, sing to it, feed it, and love it. On the third day, the hen will die. You are to have a funeral and weep as if your daughter has passed. Because a piece of her essence has. You must do these things, both of you." Deyanira looked towards Adan for acknowledgment. "If you treat this hen like a regular chicken, your Solanine will not heal, and you will lose her. You will lose her between the land of the dead and the living," Deyanira reiterated.

They understood. Deyanira reached into a drawer for a recipe for oxtail stew. "You will make this tomorrow and bring it for my daughter and sister as payment. I will be at the crossroads waiting for the piece of Solanine's essence traveling with the chicken's spirit. Calida will need a home-cooked meal because my sister can't cook. Now go home. I need to rest."

Adan was silent for the entire ritual. Deyanira frightened him, and he only brought Solanine because Halima insisted. Stealing his daughter away from death felt like evil.

"I know you fear me, Deyanira said. "I know you don't think my gifts are natural. I promise I am not evil. There is evil out there, but not here."

Adan didn't want to offend Deyanira, so he nodded and then dressed Solanine, cradling her to his chest. Halima folded the recipe into her pocket and wrapped the hen in her jacket for comfort. They exited out the front door as the sun peeked out behind the hills, providing a physical manifestation of hope.

Deyanira, exhausted from the working, washed her face and hands after using the restroom. Her body moved like an elderly woman walking to bed– shuffling her feet instead of picking them up and slightly hunched with a dull pain radiating throughout her muscles.

Deyanira laid back in her bed and reached for her lamp, but was startled by the sight of Calida creeping in the doorway, leaning on the door frame.

"Come here, *bebé*, you did so good today." Deyanira scooted over, and Calida nestled into her mother's body for comfort.

Calida always felt safest from the world and its pain in Deyanira's arms, even when those pains were worries about Deyanira's health.

Deyanira turned the lamp off and ran her hand over her daughter's big curls. "Oh my *bebé*, do not worry about *tú* mama. I am young and have a long life ahead with you. I have many things left to do and so many cuddles to give you. I just have to go to the crossroads to help that little girl find her way home to her Mami. I'll be better soon, I promise. That working just took a lot out of me because I didn't have Titi Camila here to help. I am not going anywhere anytime soon. You're stuck with me."

Calida huffed in disapproval. "You should've called Titi Camilla, Mami. She would've helped and made sure you were okay. I need you. You are all I got."

Deyanira nodded and apologized with a barrage of kisses on Calida's head and face. "Remember you can only sleep with me now and no more until I return from the crossroads, you know that, right? You call Titi in the morning to stay with you, okay?"

Calida had already drifted into slumber safe in Deyanira's embrace.

Chapter 2

Deyanira prepared for her journey to the crossroads.

It was all about the intentions set when falling asleep or in meditation. One of Deyanira's many gifts, or curses depending on the day, was dream walking– but also astral projecting into the crossroads.

Calida also had the gift of dream walking, which was a curse at the moment. She had not entered the crossroads yet, and it was unclear if she would gain access in the future. Calida often hopped into other people's dreams unintentionally while she slept. It might benefit her later in life, but right now it was dangerous. Calida preferred to sleep close to her mother physically, because if she ventured away into a person's dreams, Deyanira could retrieve her.

There was an instance where Calida stumbled into a neighbor's dream when they lived in Chicago. Calida abruptly pulled in her mom. Deyanira wasn't sure what was happening at first. The experience had disorientated her.

There, Deyanira stood in a large entertainment room with one wall dedicated to a movie projection. There were people talking in the room, as if it was a friendly get-together. Deyanira didn't know any of the people in the room at first. She scanned the room for familiar faces to understand what was happening. Deyanira focused on the people, trying to understand how she got there. She didn't even see what was playing on the movie screen at first, until the woman on the screen started screaming in pain. It was at that moment Deyanira turned to the screen and saw a woman being cut open slowly. There was a man, also in the movie, watching her being cut open alive begging for her life. That was when Deyanira saw him. Her neighbor was on the couch pleasuring himself, laser focused on the screen.

Deyanira felt her ancestors' push to turn her head towards the back of the room's doorway. There she saw her child, Calida, frozen in fear, eyes locked on the screen. Deyanira's eyes lit up golden and her body filled with storm of rage, fear, and panic. Those emotions then erupted out her mouth with such force that her words cut through the air, knocking people, chairs, and tables over, like a tornado-worthy gust of wind, until it reached its designation.

"GET OUT," Deyanira roared with her right hand outstretched towards Calida.

Once the force connected with Calida, Calida's torso flew backward. The force lifted Calida's feet and legs off the ground. Calida flew backward through the doorway of the dream room, pushing her out the door in the dream and straight back into her body. Calida's physical body shook; the aftershock rattled the bed and she woke up gasping.

Once Calida was out of the room, Deyanira turned back towards the movie screen, but when she turned around, the neighbor was no longer on the couch. He was walking towards her with a sinister smile that scared her. Suddenly, her body froze. He wasn't powerful enough to freeze her, but sensing his intentions stunned Deyanira; her fear froze her. Her hand felt a sensation. She felt Calida's hand squeeze hers in bed, and it was enough to pull Deyanira out of the dream and back to her body.

Deyanira woke up terrified, gasping for air with tears in her eyes. She was very groggy. Deyanira's spirit had not settled back into her body yet. It was dangerous for them to return to sleep too quickly. Calida was already laying back down. Deyanira had to carry her daughter into the bathroom and talk to her about her favorite cartoons. She had to give the spirit time to anchor back into the body. Falling back to sleep too quickly could mean returning to the neighbor's dream. While in a scattered and weakened state Deyanira and Calida could unintentionally disconnect their spirits completely from their bodies.

A powerful medium on the island of Puerto Rico trained Deyanira as a young child. The strongest psychic in Louisiana later picked up where her training on the island left off. They taught her about the crossroads. The crossroads are the place where everything and nothing meet. It was where Deyanira learned that time was not linear, but happening simultaneously. All past lives were current lives, and all timelines were current timelines. Spirits were infinitely larger than one's physical body. Spirits were cast into bloodlines to learn the lessons of humanity, and clear karmic debts *and* generational curses. The crossroads are where a person's spirit returns to itself. The crossroads are where gods, deities, Lwa, and Orishas come to meet with a person's guides and ancestors.

Deyanira entered the crossroads in spurts, mostly through her mind in meditation or in sleep. Occasionally, her ancestors also pulled her into the crossroads. One of Deyanira's gifts wasn't just having permission to enter the crossroads, but when at the crossroads, she could also time walk. She could go to any point in her timeline or any point of anyone's life on her timeline. She could witness that moment and reflect on it. She could use any knowledge gained during that time walk to help her in the present day.

The gift of time walking didn't unlock in Deyanira fully until after Calida's birth and surgeries. Deyanira's gift of time walking was limited and also blocked because of her loved ones. Her ancestors knew Deyanira loved hard and would use her powers to alter *and* save those she loved from themselves. Staying at the crossroads for the time required to bring back the piece of Solanine's spirit was dangerous and taxing for Deyanira. Potentially, Deyanira could get exhausted, weakening her spirit's connection to her physical body, and causing her to become lost. Deyanira had to wait the three days so her energy was no longer a disruption in the energetic field of the crossroads. Resting would make it easier for her to swoop up Solanine and return with her.

While waiting for Solanine at the crossroads Deyanira would dip into different times and return to moments in her life that would bring insight and wisdom. It would give her time to grow, heal, and the tools to fight the war to come.

Chapter 3

Deyanira loved the island of Puerto Rico, through the eyes of her eight-year-old self; it was magical. She woke up early most days and walked down to the Rio de Tanama and sat listening to the water carrying leaves and sticks that passed her. The hills of Puerto Rico were steep and the trail to the river was slick with dew in the morning, so she always took her time walking.

Deyanira listened to the birds on those early mornings. Their songs were unlike any bird she'd ever heard anywhere else. As a child, those songs connected to her spirit. Maybe it was the child-like wonder or maybe it was the absence of trauma at that age, but the island was a wondrous place back then. The island felt alive to her like something connected her to its pulse. Everything on the island was alive *and* a bounty of life. Deyanira could always feel the energy on the island pulsating at a frequency that Chicago had been void of for centuries. Her slow pace down to the river was a journey of connection for her. As a child, each blade of overgrown vegetation, each smell, each butterfly and bee connected her deeper with the land. She carefully reached the bottom of the hill. Her spirit was completely immersed and connected with the spirits of the land. She touched everything on the way down, intimately connecting and waking up the land or– allowing the land to wake *her* up; she wasn't sure which, if not both, were true.

Deyanira would sit by the water for hours, watching the water bugs and fish in their separate world. She would wonder if they realized there was a world outside of their water, full of people and other animals. Listening to the birds, she wondered if the fish heard their songs. She pitied them. They lived in such a magical place and couldn't hear the songs of the birds. She would giggle, asking herself, *do they even have ears?* She had entire conversations of reflection in those moments. Just a girl and her thoughts, feeling the wind in her hair and down her arms. Like a mother's touch, caressing and tracing her baby with her fingertips. On Deyanira's skin, through the leaves, on the surface of the river, it was a love song of the Semis. Words only her spirit understood and took in. Words that were lost to her mind at that age.

Hunger pulled Deyanira out of her trance of the river. It triggered Deyanira to return home. She began the journey back to her home, climbing the hill back up to the road. The grass was dry now from the heat of the sun at its peak. The walk home was always shorter and somehow less magical with hunger pains. By then, she was hot and hungry, so the grass was just grass on the way back home and the bugs were no longer companions on a journey of connection; they were a nuisance, causing her to fuss on her way up the hill.

As Deyanira reached the road that day, a woman walking with a jug filled with oil and herbs met her. Deyanira knew her as the local healer but avoided the woman most of her life. Her complexion was a beautiful golden bronze.

Deyanira was not like her classmates. She honored and loved the beauty of tanned skin. She wore it proudly. Her father and *primos* had a dark complexion, and everyone made a fuss about how beautiful her youngest sister Alma's pale ivory skin was. She hated it when they did that. Deyanira stared too long at the woman's beauty, admiring her radiance; they made eye contact. The woman's Spanish was the most sing-songy she had heard on the island, but there were some words she didn't recognize. She knew those words were the words of the ancients, the ancestors, the Tainos. Immediately frozen with intimidation of misunderstanding, she stared wide-eyed at the beautiful woman.

The healer could tell by the look on Deyanira's face that she needed to speak slower and use more Spanish words than Taino. The woman spoke slower Spanish to Deyanira and complained that no one knew the language of the Tainos anymore; they only knew Spanish. Through her fussing, she asked Deyanira to carry the jug for her. Deyanira took the jug silently.

They approached a small dirt path from the road and the woman wandered down the path, touching the flowers and trees and speaking sweetly to them. At the end of the path was a small house colored bright green. The woman walked into the home with Deyanira waving toward the table for her to set the jug down. The woman glanced toward Deyanira as she set down the jug. She yelled, frightening Deyanira.

"Aye!"

The healer walked quickly towards Deyanira, grabbing her arm. "This! This! How long have you had this!" She pointed to Deyanira's forearm.

On Deyanira's right forearm was the big dipper formed by freckles. Startled, Deyanira said she wasn't sure. The woman then turned Deyanira's hand over to feel the lines on her palms. Quietly, the woman spoke words Deyanira didn't know. She then looked into Deyanira's eyes, but the healer wasn't looking at Deyanira's eyes at all. The woman seemed to be listening to something, or someone, beyond Deyanira. The spirits around her and maybe even Deyanira's spirit itself.

Then she broke free of her hands and asked, "Are you hungry?"

The woman intrigued Deyanira, and Deyanira was starving. She had so many questions about what had just happened, but also a soothing feeling that the woman would answer them.

The woman waved for Deyanira to follow her outside. "My name is Marina. You can call me Doña Marina."

There was a fire pit roasting a chicken and a pot cooking something. "*Comes arroz con gandules?*"

She pointed to the firewood and told Deyanira to bring her two logs for the pit to finish cooking the food. Fright and uncomfortable feelings suddenly overcame Deyanira. She knew she was safe at Doña Marina's house. Island life differed from the rest of the world. They were a community. It was nothing for kids to be at neighbors' houses eating. She felt that Doña Marina was going to tell her things she didn't want to hear. Many of the children in the community feared this woman. They had no desire to connect to the old ways or anything spiritual.

Deyanira realized her curiosity may have gotten the best of her, and panic flooded her mind and body. Staying longer would only make her more of the "weird kid" to everyone. "Maybe I should get home to help with my sisters."

Doña Marina listened without eye contact as she stirred the rice, nodding silently. Deyanira trailed off because there wasn't much confidence in that statement. Doña Marina turned from the fire pit and grabbed Deyanira's shoulders and gave her a slight shake, then spoke to her but also over her. "You are exceptionally powerful. You will speak to deities, spirits, even Semis. *Amor*, you will heal many people, guide them towards their ancestors, run off bad spirits, curse some people that deserve to be cursed, heal others, and birth the most powerful being the world has seen in a long time. Do not let anyone treat you like they are more of anything than you. Now go wash your hands and sit at the table."

Most children would hear those words and be excited, ready to step into that power, but Deyanira, however, was terrified of the idea of power that strong. It all sounded surreal and it didn't make her feel more seen at all. She had only seen things like this on TV and in books she had read. She was terrified. Her thoughts were swirling around her head. The heat, the thoughts, and her low blood sugar made Deyanira dizzy sitting at the table. She was worried she would fall out of the chair. She ran for the bathroom as she felt the vomit rise in her throat. Deyanira emerged from the bathroom and Doña Marina was in the kitchen with a pot of rice and a roasted chicken on the counter. She slid back into her chair, embarrassed.

Doña Marina spoke with her back turned. "You scared?"

Deyanira nodded her head yes as if Doña Marina could see her. Doña Marina spoke to Deyanira, "*Bueno*. Being scared makes you the right person to hold this power. If you wanted it and it didn't scare you, we would all be in danger from you." She turned to hand Deyanira a plate and a cup. The cup had sugar cane and another herb in it. She told Deyanira to drink the cup first, it'll help her feel better and then she can eat. Deyanira drank first and then ate.

"You know things," Doña Marina said in between bites. "You know what your mama is feeling. What she is doing and why she is doing it. It helps you move around people. You know what they are feeling and thinking. You can see in your mind. If someone's papa beat them that morning, you'll see it and you are kind to them without letting them know you know. *Amor*, you see bullies and why they are bullies and you try to avoid triggering them. You stand up for people who feel scared. You can feel their feelings even from down the street."

Deyanira sat there wide-eyed; she couldn't even blink. No one knew these things. She barely knew and understood them herself, so how did Doña Marina know these things?

Doña Marina told Deyanira, "Yes I know your secrets, *chica*. Don't worry, I won't tell anyone. The spirits tell me many secrets."

Deyanira stared intensely at Doña Marina, scooping rice into her mouth as if she hadn't eaten in days.

Doña Marina continued weaving her words. "You also will go into rooms and sometimes you're scared of the dark in that room. You feel the spirits in there. They found you. They want your energy. They want to feel it. You are a light. Your gifts flow through you like a river. You've had them so long you think they are normal and most people know or sense things also. You're not just a good observer or detective. You have strong gifts these spirits want to prey on. You need training and protection. You will come to my house every day and I will train you."

As Doña Marina added more rice and chicken to Deyanira's empty plate, she told Doña Marina she wasn't sure her mama would let her come back. Doña Marina stayed unbothered. She just smirked and said, "Finish up. I'll walk you home and talk to her. It is a great honor to work with me. She knows that."

Deyanira just laughed and said, "You don't know my mama.

She sees nothing as an honor for me."

Doña Marina looked disappointed, shaking her head, and muttered, "Always the mother wound for the powerful ones, always." Doña Marina's statement confused Deyanira. As an adult, Deyanira understood the message fully.

As Deyanira predicted, her mama came outside with a look of frustration and annoyance across her brow when she saw Deyanira walking up with Doña Marina. Her mama tried to argue with Doña Marina and explained that Deyanira needed to help care for her sisters because their papa was going to the States for a job.

Doña Marina huffed and told Deyanira's mama, "She lives at the crossroads. If she doesn't get training, spirits will haunt her, consume her, and attack those who live with her. Including you. They want to be heard. She will go crazy without help. She can bring the *niñas* with her."

Deyanira's mama's face lightened and took on a more ominous facial expression. "She will be fine without training like I was."

The thought of Deyanira possibly losing her sanity into adulthood made her mama snicker to herself. *She is just an odd kid and never showed to be extraordinary in school or to me.*

Doña Marina raised her finger to Deyanira's mother's face and said, "Watch it!"

Then Deyanira's mama changed her tone back to a quieter, fussier muttering of excuses.

After Doña Marina glared silently, Deyanira's mama reluctantly agreed that Deyanira would train with Doña Marina as long as she could bring her little sisters. Doña Marina nodded her head in agreement and it was done.

Doña Marina grabbed Deyanira's hand and said, "Come

tomorrow morning." She then turned and left to return to her home.

That night, the news spread through the neighboring houses about Doña Marina's visit. In reflection, Deyanira's mother was the culprit in spreading the *chisme* to anyone who would listen. The children of the community walking by Deyanira would tease her that the *bruja* would eat her heart. That her mama sold her to the *bruja* for eating too much. She cried secretly in the yard on the side of the house. Her Tia came by to babysit while her parents went out for a drink and heard Deyanira's whimpers through the window. Her Tia stopped scrubbing the tub to hear her cries. She stood slowly, her thighs groaning, a reminder that her youth was fleeting.

As her Tia rounded the corner of the house, she saw Deyanira crouched and crying. Her Tia sat on the ground next to her, wiping Deyanira's tears with her off-colored tank top.

Her Tia brushed away her hair from her face and hugged her tight with the other arm. "Oh, *mi amor*, why are you so upset?"

Deyanira released a flood of tears and cries from the depths of her belly. Her words were more noises, deep breaths, and moans. Her Tia hugged her with a firm embrace, petting Deyanira's hair away from her face as she continued. Once Deyanira tired out from the release, she sniffled and spoke quietly. They were not complete sentences, just pieces of the awful things the children said.

Her Tia, relieved, chuckled before responding, "Oh *mi amor*, she is not a *bruja* and she will not eat your heart. I am so sorry your mama did not explain these things to you. You must've been so confused and scared. My sweet girl, you are safe. You are very special. You are a medium and a very special strong one, I hear. Doña Marina is the most powerful seer we have had in this community and she has felt nothing like you before. She said you could provide enough electricity to light the entire island with your gift's raw energy. I do not know all the things the future holds for you, but I know she won't eat your heart and your mother didn't sell you. Doña Marina is a diviner and a healer. She does practice within Santería and Espiritismo, which can scare some people. Mostly though, Doña Marina *helps* people. Many people. Sometimes she tells people what is wrong in their lives, how to heal things, and even what their destiny is. Doña Marina speaks with their ancestors and the saints that favor them. She has many gifts and we always consult her when we need help. One day my *perrito* was very sick, and I didn't have money to take him to the vet. I thought he was going to die. I brought him to Doña Marina. She gave me some things to do and my *perrito* got better. She healed him. I always honor her. She is a trusted friend, you'll see. She said you are more powerful than her by far. If you can learn how to heal people like Doña Marina, think of all the *perritos* you will heal and save for their owners."

Tia poked Deyanira's side searching for a giggle. "You are going to do great things, my love. You don't need to be afraid of her. She will protect you and teach you to protect yourself. There are spirits, demons, and evil things that will see your light and come for you. You need protection, *amor*. I couldn't live with you getting hurt. I wouldn't be able to live with myself."

Deyanira felt relief and pride. She also felt safe. She mumbled through the hug, "I wish you were my mom."

Her Tia cried a single tear because she too often wished the same. She wished to save her nieces from her sister's torment. Her sister struggled with being a mother and often blamed being a mother for ruining her life.

Chapter 4

At dawn, Deyanira woke up with her papa. While he got ready for work, she got herself and the babies ready to go to Doña Marina's house. Her papa sat quietly drinking his *café* while her mama made his breakfast. She then gave the girls each a piece of bread with *guayaba* spread.

Once the youngest, Alma finished her bread, Deyanira scooped her up and rested the tot on her tiny eight-year-old prepubescent hip, making her way for the door. Maribel and Camilla sat on the porch awkwardly, trying to get their shoes on without help. With a deep sigh, Deyanira sat Alma down and helped the girls with their shoes.

Her mama sat on the porch smoking her cigarette and staring off in the opposite direction. "You know you get these powers from me, right? I used to tell my mother when the family was going to come over, and then they would show up. I had the gift too, but my mother told me I was scaring her and to stop it, so it went away. You get this from me. I'm a good mom because I didn't tell you to stop."

As an adult, Deyanira realized she could never have a relationship with her mother because she was always jealous of Deyanira. Something buried deep inside Deyanira's mother told her that Deyanira was the thing that held her back from doing great things. She had Deyanira young, and her energy often felt like an elder sibling jealous of the younger one. There was never nurture or love from her mother. Deyanira just wouldn't realize it until much later in life. A seed sown into her mother from a past life. Sometimes in past lives, evil takes root. It burrows into the spirit and infiltrates the spirit's other lives.

For many lifetimes, Deyanira's mother has been her tormentor. In some lifetimes, they lived on the island, and in other lifetimes, they lived in foreign lands. In some lifetimes, her mother murdered her, and in other lifetimes, she tortured her. People say you choose your parents, and that isn't true. No one chooses pain and torment. Sometimes awful things happen, and they don't make you stronger for your destiny– they are blocks to move past. Freedom of choice ripples out and affects others. When someone chooses to neglect and torment a child, there is a ripple effect. The goal of the oppressor is to keep you small. Sometimes, that goal reaches across lifetimes and ties those people to each other because their spirit is bound to their abuser. It is a deep soul-tie to that parent because maybe in another lifetime, they were an abusive lover or captor. Just as evil burrows deep into one's spirit, Deyanira's pain and fear burrowed into her own. She feared leaving her mother in some lifetimes, and that fear transferred across all lifetimes. There was an energetic, unconscious cycle of torment between Deyanira and her mother.

Walking to Doña Marina's home was so hard for Deyanira. Alma was fussy and kept dropping her bottle. It would roll off the road into the grass. Keeping Maribel and Camilla off the road and safe was too stressful for an eight-year-old. The idea of trying to learn about her gifts and juggling the girls made her choke up with tears.

She muttered, "This is impossible."

Deyanira was ready to give up on training before she even began. Once they got to the door, she had the little ones take off their shoes and enter the home. Inside the home, Deyanira smelled sausage frying. The little ones ran into the kitchen as if they had been coming to Doña Marina's home their whole lives. They hugged Doña Marina's legs from behind.

"Titi, Titi," they chanted. It was such a weird thing for Deyanira to witness. Her sisters were not trusting children.

"*Niñas* know, *mi amor*. They know when a person is safe. It's the adults in their lives that convince kids that unsafe people are safe. They teach kids to not trust their gut."

Doña Marina smiled and laughed, bending down and kissing each little one's forehead. "Ay Bendito! Are you hungry, my little babies?" They jumped up and down with excitement. Doña made everyone plates and told Deyanira, "When you are done eating, go outside to learn, and I will care for the little ones." She took Alma's bottle and filled it with milk from her small refrigerator. "Eat up *mi amor*, we will start outside soon."

After they finished eating, Doña Marina led Deyanira outside to the front yard. "Okay *mija*, get your shoes on and go down to the river like you always do."

Deyanira plopped down on the porch to put her shoes on. She asked Doña Marina what she needed to do at the river. Deyanira wanted to be an excellent student. After all, Doña Marina already had done too much for her.

She gently touched Deyanira's hair with love. "Listen *mija*, you won't use what I am about to tell you until you are older. You owe me nothing. Training you is an honor. It is a gift. Many Deities and beings gave me this opportunity as a blessing or reward for my bloodline. The divine brings people along the way in your life to you. You are the sun, people should beg to orbit you. You owe no one nothing. We all have our part to play. It will take many years and exhaustion before you return to this moment and truly understand how amazing you are. You are a flowing river of everything beautiful. There is ancient wisdom and love for humanity flowing through your spirit. I will train you to unlock the wisdom you already have hiding away in your spirit. As you grow, heal, and gain confidence, you will open the road to this wisdom. I'm just holding your hand on the journey to opening those roads. If all these roads were just opened before you were ready, it would break your mind and body."

Doña Marina hugged Deyanira and kissed the top of her head with love and protection. "Because your mind is the gateway to your spirit, we start every day with you doing as you have always done. You ground yourself in nature and the spirit of the island. Our island is alive. You won't realize it until you step on dead land. Only then will you understand you were connecting with the island in these moments of your youth. You naturally knew as a young child to go to the river. Every morning, you will go there for a couple of hours the way you always have, and not return until you feel it is time. Stay guilt-free from being there. You need lots of time for yourself, *mi amor*. A lot. As you get older, you will see that most of your time will be in solitude."

Eight-year-old Deyanira did not know what solitude meant, but Deyanira, in her late twenties, revisited this moment and cried from the revelation. Doña Marina was giving her permission to give herself space from the world she constantly could hear, feel, and heal.

When Deyanira returned to Doña Marina's, all the little ones were sleeping in Doña Marina's bed and Doña Marina was making rice and eggs for lunch. Deyanira sat down at the small table in the kitchen and watched Doña Marina cook.

Doña Marina didn't turn around; she just began the lessons. "You need to build confidence in your knowing instead of just blindly following it. One of your gifts is that you are a strong empath. You feel what is happening with people, but you are too flighty. Amor, you bounce around just being reactive to what you feel. You feel your mama is sad, so you sweep the house and keep the little ones quiet, and maybe even tell her a joke to help. Does that sound right?"

Deyanira hung her head in shame and released a mousy yes from her lips.

Doña Marina took a deep sigh of frustration. "Argh these mother wounds. *mija*, I am not yelling at you. You have done nothing wrong. *Oh, mi amor*, you are a little girl with a big heart who wants to take on everyone's pain so they feel better. You must understand that doesn't help them. You are stunting their growth and making yourself exhausted. Think of it like this: when you have school, do they give you homework?" Deyanira nodded yes. "OK, if your mama did your homework every night so you could play, it may help you at the moment, but later in life, when you need the knowledge the homework would have given you, you won't have it. You are not helping people by trying to take their pain or problems. Because what they need to feel is a block, and if they can push through it, it will open new roads for them. Each time we face something and see the emotions and truth behind it, we remove a block to a road that guides us to something we desire."

"Now onto magic," Doña Marina blurted out.

Deyanira's face shone with excitement and amazement. "Magic is real?"

Doña Marina knew that would perk up any eight-year-old. "Yes, magic is real, but not like you may think. Magic is like calling the most complex math and science "stuff." The ancients understood that everything is connected and all things have energy and require energy. Before entering the forest or taking any fruit, we give an offering to the trees and land. There are ways to explain this with magic and the mundane. These actions help you connect. Spiritually, you are honoring the spirit of the land and tree with an offering of love. The nutrients of your offering also replenish what you may take. It is an exchange of energy. Creating balance, because if you leave it to the land to balance things, it'll be unpleasant."

"We've lost the old ways. People just take and take and take. Also, too many people have done magic, performing rituals, doing spells without offerings; or giving an offering that is not equal to the ask itself. Magic is about energy and belief, but also about bloodlines and the favor of Deities, Orishas, Semis, land, and spirits. Those things have to balance, and if they don't, the magic can be poison to a bloodline."

Deyanira's eyes teared up. "I understand nothing you're saying. This is too much. What if I poison my bloodline? What does it all mean? It all sounds so scary."

Doña Marina turned from the stove to make eye contact with Deyanira, "Oh *amor*, you aren't feeling fear, you are feeling respect. I am planting a seed for a later harvest. So you don't have to worry about understanding everything or making mistakes. Everything I am saying to you now is the ancient wisdom locked inside of you. You just have to hear me, and the emotions you're feeling right now will guide you to recall this wisdom when you need it. You could never poison your bloodline, but it isn't my place to explain to you why. That knowledge will become available when it is time."

Deyanira released the expectation that she had to understand everything being taught at the time it was given. "So, are *duende* real? Sirens? Will I be friends with them?" Deyanira asked, excitement twinkling in her eyes. The spirits reminded Doña Marina just how young Deyanira still was.

"They are very much real. Most magical beings are. But they aren't to be made friends with. We give all of them the same energy. We give everything respect; I will teach you. You balance fear with respect. We don't invite the *duende* into our lives, and we avoid them out of respect. I have never encountered a vampire that sucked blood, but I have encountered one that took energy, and energy is your life source. Blood is just the river that carries it. When you are trying to connect with or receive from a Deity, Semi, or Orisha, you can't just treat them like your ancestors. You should feed them offerings of things they like. You learn things they like by communicating with them or by communicating with the people who have a relationship with them already. It is just like feeding a guest that comes to your house. However, if you wanted that guest to help you paint your house, or build you a shed, you would have to pay them, right?"

Deyanira nodded finally at a concept she understood, but she still had questions. "Doña Marina, what is an Orisha? Are they the Saints? I have heard of them, but I don't know about them."

"Oh, let me back up. The Orishas are powerful primordial beings worshiped and honored by our African ancestors. We, on the island, honor them through Santería. In other places, they are worshiped and honored through other religions." Doña Marina paused and looked into Deyanira's eyes as if she saw something new. She shook it off after a moment and continued, "You know what the Semis are right?"

Deyanira nodded yes, and Doña Marina continued. "Asking a Deity, Orisha, or Semi for blessings, guidance, protection, or curse requires you to pay them."

"So you give them money?" Deyanira asked, feeling defeated. Her understanding lasted less than thirty seconds.

"Oh, although money carries energy, they have no need for it or its energetic imprint. Depending on what you are asking for, a chicken will usually do the trick. I will teach you that lesson on the next new or full moon. Remember, blood is the river that carries energy, so spilling it for the Deity or Orisha is offering them *that* animal's energy. Certain requests, at certain times, require certain offerings of a chicken or goat. This will help bring favor to what you ask of them."

Deyanira didn't know how to feel. On one hand, she felt connected deep in her spirit to what Doña Marina was saying. The spiritual practices made perfect sense, but also it felt evil to murder a chicken.

Doña Marina's face frowned, and she glared at Deyanira. "People think offering a chicken and its blood to a Deity or Orisha is devil worshiping. They don't realize that the white man started that lie. They taught us to keep our spiritual debts large while they have a fat bank of their human sacrifices of our ancestors. They conditioned you to believe things our ancestors did were evil. While all they do is evil, they paint themselves as saviors. These are universal laws, *mija*. Checks and balances are required. If you ask for something or pray for something, and you do not give that offering of a chicken, then now you and your bloodline owe a debt. It will have to be balanced at some point. No grandchildren deserve to suffer because their *abuela* wanted a luxurious house and good health."

With a huff, she returned to the food on the stove. "Now onto spirits. This lesson is very important for you because you are a powerful medium. All spirits see you, feel you, and will seek you out. It is important to cover your head with a wrap as I do, or put this protection oil on your forehead and back of your neck in the morning and before bed." Doña Marina handed Deyanira a small bottle of an oil murky with herbs and continued. "There are many kinds and levels of spirits that I am going to teach you about. We have good ones, bad ones, and scary ones. Good spirits are elevated ancestors. They died and crossed over, returning to themselves to learn from this lifetime's lessons. I like to say mistakes, but they want you to hear *lessons*." She laughed to herself. "Your people are very strict about your training."

Deyanira interrupted Doña Marina. "What do you mean by *my* people?"

"Well *mija*, you have a team of spiritual guides. That team can be comprised of deities that favor you, elevated ancestors, animal spirits, or land spirits. They change as you evolve. There may only be a few that are there with you for your entire journey. As you grow, you will need different guidance and different favors, as well as different protections. Back to ancestors. The ancestors that return to their rightful place beyond the crossroads receive healing and learn. They are elevated for us. Many of them are ancients because a lot of our current ancestors are still on earth stuck, or learning from their lessons still, and not released to guide us."

Deyanira interrupted, trying to grasp concepts and connections beyond her years. "So they go to heaven?"

"Oh, hmm, OK *mija*, heaven is an ending and destination that was given to us. You can believe there is a place you reach once you have completed your universal understanding, but I've never heard of an ending. As a medium, you'll meet your ancestors at the crossroads to commune with them when it is time. The in-between where the energy of all meets. There is a place where your people watch you, guide you, and protect you. They meet you there and you can talk to them about life. You are too young to go there and not get lost, but when the time is right, the door will open. Most mediums call down these spirits to speak. Oracles are the only ones powerful enough to go to the crossroads and return."

Doña Marina made the plates for lunch. "Just know they manage you and your desires. An example is if you need money to buy a house. They will find a bloodline that owes you *or* your bloodline a debt. Or, they will find you someone who has a karmic debt that needs balancing. They will seek those people's ancestors out and broker a deal, but you and the other person have free will. So they guide a person to you, but they can't make you or them do what is needed. You have to know your value and they have to believe they need you. If you help them for free you create more debt for them in the long run. Another example of free will would be that you tell a person how much your services cost, and they choose not to hire you because they don't want to pay. They have free will to do that, but it'll cause them to have a period of discomfort to hopefully guide them back to you for help. You cannot give your gift or advice for free, or even accept underpayment because you are a vessel. Their offerings keep you from exhaustion. It is like paying the telephone bill, but you are the telephone. You understand?”

Deyanira didn't want to nod yes, but she heard more than she understood.

Doña Marina knew, so she bumped her hip into Deyanira's chair to lighten the mood. “It's okay if you don't understand. As long as you hear me, you can return later to figure it out.”

It always shocked Deyanira when Doña Marina knew what she was thinking or feeling. It never got old, no matter how many times it happened. “What do you mean, return later?” Deyanira asked.

“Oh, that isn't for me to tell. Just know they will eventually show you all the things you can do and all the things you cannot.”

Deyanira's mouth was a gaping hole, only slightly shutting to form the words, “I am a time traveler?”

Doña Marina cracked up laughing, “You're pretty smart trying to figure things out. No, you're not a time traveler, silly, more like a time walker. Many gifts will unfold for you as you heal and grow. Be careful not to get addicted to finding the ‘why’ behind everything. If you don't have to know, don't waste your time looking for it. Your people said enough talk about that gift. For now, they don't want it to open up too early.”

Doña Marina cleared her throat and continued. “Now bad spirits. There are a few of these. First, we have the ones that don't know they are dead. When a person cuts themselves off from their feelings and just wakes up every day doing the same thing and maybe drinking a lot, doing drugs, or working too much, their spirit is separated from their body. When the body dies, the spirit does not know it is free to return to the crossroads. Sometimes those spirits will be stuck in a loop. These are the spirits sometimes people say they see. For example, the one everyone says they see coming from the kiosks? That is a man who died when I was a child. He got hit by a car one day when I was young because he drunkenly stepped in front of it on his way home one night. I have tried to help his spirit wake up to the idea that he is dead, but without a blood relative, it is too hard for me to pull him out of his routine, so every night he walks home unaware he is dead. He is harmless in the sense that he will never take your energy because he doesn't even know he can try. However, the dense and low energy of his spirit will feel like a weight on your chest if you get near him.

"Now there are spirits that know they are dead and refuse to cross over. There are a few types of these, but there are two main ones for you to be worried about. The first type died and then realized they made the wrong choices while alive on earth. So crossing over to return would mean accountability and acknowledgment. Those spirits choose to stay on earth as a spirit wandering the earth or they choose to settle into a space or energy that feels familiar. They wander around in the dark here. Sometimes they can accidentally bind themselves to a location, but mostly they can move anywhere. They are wandering in the dark though, and usually are the spirits most low-level mediums find. Therefore, other mediums are dangerous because their gifts are minimal and can only connect with the dead, not elevated spirits. This is dangerous because these spirits can attach to people in their bloodline, draining them of their life source.

"You will see a family full of sickness, or possibly, the next generation carrying more illness than usual. The entire generation– so a group of *primos* that all struggle with school and adult life, not just one child. Those spirits will also come for you. You are like a sun in a universe without stars. They see your energy as a source to juice themselves up. Like, if you walked into a haunted house with spirits, they may move a chair or break a glass because they are stealing your energy. It is very dangerous for you. You will always be more powerful than them, though, and you have to hold on to that belief. You tell them to get out and believe in yourself when saying it, and I promise they will run from you. Energy cannot be destroyed, but it can be manipulated. You can take their spirit and bind it to an object and throw it in the ocean, or you can call on the ancient ancestors of your bloodline to separate their energy. This is something you should be very cautious of because it also has to be agreed on with the Deities, Orishas, and land spirits. They pull apart the energy of that person's spirit and essentially hide the pieces. The spirit will slowly lose consciousness of any previous human life and will just be random energy surges in an area. They can become vortexes of energy that draw in other entities, and that is why you should never do this without a direct message and permission."

Deyanira nodded in acknowledgment.

Doña Marina continued. "These next spirits are the most dangerous to you and others. They are more powerful and can heavily influence people and energy on our plane. Like the other spirits, they choose not to cross over, but they were psychic in their life, so they are powerful spirits who often come to manipulate things. They think they know what is best, and if they can just get enough power or energy, they can get people from their bloodline to do what they want. They are dangerous to you because they can either steal your energy for their agenda or use you to connect and attach to someone you are reading for. That person could get possessed or drained to death."

Deyanira's eyes got wide. "I don't want to help people get possessed. Can't I just not do this and be normal?"

Doña Marina walked over and hugged her frightened little mentee. "You can choose to not help people, *mija*, of course, but you still need the training to protect yourself and others. Just know we do readings for a few reasons. First, it is nice to have a karmic bank full from the people you help. Second, it really is about the lessons. You will gain so much wisdom and spiritual training in these readings. Oftentimes the people you read for are those who need help in an area of life you are struggling with as well. I know this is an immense responsibility, and it sounds scary. Possession normally isn't like people say it is. Possession of a bloodline ancestor looks a lot like doing things and not really understanding why you did them. Like, if your abuela was not elevated. She was a powerful psychic, but if you were married and she didn't like your husband, she could possess you to say something mean to him, and afterward, you wouldn't know why you said it. Don't tell people this though because you'll just have a lot of assholes telling their wives they are just possessed." She laughed out loud at her own joke.

Deyanira asked, "My abuela was a powerful psychic?"

"That is all you heard? You have never met this abuela, but she will be with you, always providing love and support when you feel the most alone."

Chapter 5

Deyanira repeated the routine of going to Doña Marina's house to drop off the little ones and going to the *Rio* for clarity. She felt stronger and more connected to her knowing. Deyanira learned so much in her training days with Doña Marina. She learned she could talk to animals and they would understand her. The Orisha Oya often brought gentle breezes during her peaceful times by the river and strong winds when Deyanira was upset. When the warm, powerful winds rushed against her body, it felt as though they were pulling the anger and sadness away from her. Water became a powerful connection as well for Deyanira. The Orisha Yemaya used the ocean and salt water like a sword to cut away lingering. Deyanira learned to use it to cleanse, protect her home, and to cut off the energy of others trying to attach themselves to her. The more she changed and protected herself, the more her mother treated her poorly and looked at her with disgust.

Doña Marina told Deyanira she was ready for her first *mesa blanca*. Deyanira didn't realize until she was older that Doña Marina gave Deyanira's mother one hundred dollars to let her out of the house without the little ones.

She took Deyanira's measurements and sewed her a dress and a hair wrap. Doña Marina taught Deyanira how to wrap her hair gently. When Doña Marina pulled out the simple white dress that she made for Deyanira, Deyanira burst into tears. It was so beautiful and it just felt like love. The energy of the dress was an aura of love. The energy overwhelmed Deyanira's spirit. Deyanira put the dress on and skipped around Doña Marina's house; she felt so beautiful. She twirled around in a circle, watching it umbrella out around her legs. Looking down as she spun, watching her skirt twirl, she felt like a *Bamba* dancer.

Before the *mesa blanca* started, Doña Marina instructed Deyanira to remove her shoes. Doña Marina also asked her to wash her hands and the back of her neck with salt water. "Come now, I have much to teach before they arrive," Doña Marina exclaimed.

Deyanira sat at the table and ate the cake Doña Marina had previously cut for her. Doña Marina spoke while washing the dishes. "Now, as a powerful medium, you live at the crossroads, remember?" Deyanira nodded yes, eating the delicious cake. She wished she had water to drink, but she knew Marina was busy. "Little girl, ask for what you need. You are not a burden. Take up space! Remember, you are the sun. Being in your orbit is an honor." She got Deyanira a glass of water while she fussed at her.

Deyanira laughed and said, "Maybe I just like it when you read my thoughts. It is crazy."

Doña Marina hip-bumped Deyanira's chair, laughing.

"Remember, not all mediums can talk to Deities or even elevated ancestors, only the strong mediums can. Many pretend to because they want to be special. You will soon feel why this is a hard gift and will come to hate people who wish to be you or pretend to.

Deyanira interrupted. "I don't know if I would hate them."

Doña Marina, "Trust me you will, *amor*. Your gifts are stronger than anything I have ever seen. You will talk to Deities with ease and for that, they will come to you and exhaust you. Learn to be firm and tell them you need rest. Otherwise, they will use you up. People! People will use you up. Don't tell people you can do this. They will ask you to speak to the Deities for them and when you bring the message down, they will tell you that you are lying and their God wouldn't say that. Deities are often different from how spiritual leaders have described them. There are some trickster spirits, too. They will pretend to be who you are calling on. You should always call down your elevated ancestors and guides first. They will show you if it is a trickster. They'll alert you with a sudden headache or stomach ache. You are young and powerful. Once you align with your gifts, Deities, and spirits will call on you a lot. As you get to know your guides, you can tell one to be a gatekeeper for you. Mediumship is exhausting sometimes. Tonight, you will be here for a *mesa blanca*. You will observe me and a few other workers channeling messages for a few different clients. While you are in the room, I want you to feel your body. You should feel a change in your body as spirits, Orishas, or other Deities enter the room and speak. Remember, you must never let someone try to sway you into a religion. They may mean well, but most times, they just feel your power and want to claim it for their religion. However, doing so will cut you off from hearing the Deities and nature spirits from around the world that are not of that religion."

Doña Marina taught Deyanira how to protect and cleanse herself for the *mesa blanca*. She always spoke with firm words but made sure her eyes were gentle and loving.

Doña Marina was worried about Deyanira. She had so much to teach her, and the preparation to become the Oracle would still take many more years yet Doña Marina's intuition told her Deyanira was going to pull away soon and shut off her gifts. It was an unsettling feeling of what was to come.

Doña Marina knew that the ancient knowledge locked inside Deyanira needed to be coaxed out with love, or she would be cracked open with pain. Doña Marina was plagued with concern that energies and forces would cause Deyanira to lose her mind. She was worried earthbound spirits would siphon Deyanira's power and make her ill. Doña Marina was blanketed with sadness. Doña Marina remembered how people treated her grow up with her gift. Deyanira was one hundred times more gifted than Doña Marina was. The ancestors and deities brokered Deyanira's birth many generations back. Many strong bloodlines designed and orchestrated connections that led to the making of Deyanira.

Doña Marina could feel that the girl's early life was going to be a road full of trauma. Doña Marina wished she had more time to show Deyanira that she was extraordinary. Even without gifts, her presence healed and soothed others. Her laughter filled rooms and her hugs filled voids. She was the daughter Doña Marina wished she had. Deyanira was a gift to all who encountered her. Deyanira would also birth a powerful being. The child would be more powerful than any human on Earth. Deyanira's child would be a harbinger of sorts and of what was still undetermined.

Doña Marina's mind was wandering and Deyanira could see her eyes were glassy with tears. She felt the sadness and pain Doña Marina was feeling. Deyanira hugged Doña Marina and thanked her for all her help. Doña Marina leaned over, realizing

Deyanira was taking on her fear so she could feel better. She kissed Deyanira's forehead. Cupping her cheeks, Doña Marina said, "Let me show you how to release that."

She proceeded to teach Deyanira how to brush energies off her body and use breathwork to expel the fear she absorbed. Then she hugged Deyanira again and said, "Remember, my tears are not your burden, you are the sun, *mi amor.*

They set the room for the *mesa blanca.* Deyanira helped smooth out the white tablecloth and placed the bowl of water and flowers in the center of the table.

Deyanira then sat soberly in the room's corner as the people started arriving. Only the mediums who were going to channel that night were allowed in the room. They led their clients to a bedroom where a man was setting up chairs. Deyanira retreated to her thoughts as she smelled the fragrance of the flowers and burnt herbs. Deyanira's eyes explored the painting on the wall of the ocean. Then her eyes darted to the chair at the head of the table. The wooden chair was warped and leaning on three legs. It wobbled and creaked when the medium sat down. Doña Marina walked over and touched her shoulder. "We are going to light the candles soon. You need to be present. No more daydreaming. It is dangerous."

Deyanira perked up and adjusted her body in the chair. Her bottom was already a bit numb from the lack of cushion. There was so much going on;– Deyanira understood there was an importance to the *mesa blanca*, but wasn't old enough to know why. As an adult, Deyanira was grateful for her travels to these moments. Each time a new lesson surfaced, it usually helped a current situation.

As the candles were lit, the mediums brought in the first client and began praying. One medium called down the spirits and started divining a message for the client. Deyanira felt her body shift. She felt her mind open and she felt the messages coming down. Her body tingled with goosebumps, charging with the energy of the spirit. There was a knowing entering her mind. It opened like a flower blossom in the first sunlight, then there were words and pictures connecting with her mind's eye, creating a story. Deyanira felt the big picture come together.

The message coming in was too much energy for the medium divining at the table. He began sweating and speaking with long pauses. He stuttered, "And in the next year, they say you will get pregnant."

Deyanira was full-on channeling as well, and she spoke up. "Excuse me, that is not what they said."

The medium broke his connection when his ego inflamed.

Suddenly, Deyanira felt an energy surge swell in her body and she began speaking in monotone, channeling a message. "You will begin a new life. There will be a new life this year. The old way you have lived must die. You will grieve your old life, but the new life will come and be beautiful if you nurture it. You must care for it *and* yourself like a baby. *Señora*, you are the baby. You need your nurturing. It is your time to care for you."

The medium infuriated, told Deyanira to shut up. Doña Marina slammed her fist on the table, scolding him. "*Mesa blancas* have more than one medium for this reason. I had spoken to all of you about her gifts and power, as well as the visions I received. Do not let your ego taint this session."

The client then quietly spoke. "Doña Marina, I do not have the blood anymore. I cannot have babies. I am in my fifties. I am planning to move to the States to open a bakery with my sister. Our family is angry we are leaving, and I was feeling bad like I should stay for my grandchild."

Deyanira jumped in and said, "If you live for yourself now, then your children and their children's children will have a life of wealth and good health because you have helped them elevate their lives."

At this point, the man folded his arms and mumbled, "Where is the faith that she can have a baby without the blood?"

Doña Marina, being the true feisty *boricua* woman she is said, "What are you pouting about now? Say it louder! There was a reason I don't allow male mediums in my *mesa blancas*, you are too much drama. Turning everything into a discussion about you!"

At that point, the man's ego erupted, and he forgot he was a student and guest. He stood up and slammed his chair into the table. "WHERE IS THE FAITH? If the message was pregnancy, then you prepare for pregnancy. You don't question how it is possible."

Before Doña Marina could remove him from the room, Deyanira rose from her chair. Her body felt like it was filled with hot lava and fire. The rage felt like it was going to tear her skin. Her eyes expelled tears, but they burned as they came out and ran down her cheeks. She had never felt this much rage before. It was as if she could push fire from her hands and burn him if she willed it so.

Deyanira spoke in a powerful bellowing deeper tone. "How dare you! You let your ego mislead her from her destiny. Your ego has ruined you. We had plans for you. Your bloodline is powerful and has the favor of Yemaya. She has been trying to guide you and connect with you but you are tainted with the white man's patriarchy. You are constantly praying to me, Ogun, instead of being open! Shame on you. You block yourself from the Orisha you are meant to connect with, and instead, you beg to feel me in your spirit. You spit on your connection to Yemaya every time you beg for a connection with me. You wanted my attention, so now you have it. You couldn't live the life of one of my children if you had three people helping you. You are a coward full of shame who refuses to see the life and gifts given to him. Tonight, as you sleep, I will take your life, and you will return to try again next time. Yemaya has been protecting you this whole time, trying to get you to heal your wound in your masculinity. You are a waste of her time and energy. I am taking you."

Then, Deyanira collapsed.

Disoriented blinks through blurred sight revealed a room of women chattering and the smell of cake and *café*. Deyanira wasn't sure what happened. She only had broken pieces of memory from earlier in the night. She sat up too fast and felt her head throb. Her arms and legs felt too weak to lift. They were heavy like they were wrapped in damp towels.

Doña Marina rushed over. "There you are, *mi amor*. Channeling an Orisha on your first night will knock the wind out of you." Deyanira rubbed her eyes into focus and asked what happened. Doña Marina just shushed her and said, "Don't worry, I will explain later."

A flash of memory came to Deyanira of words spoken to the male medium and she gasped, raising her hand to her mouth in shock and horror. Doña Marina knew what Deyanira was feeling. She comforted her and explained that it wasn't her fault. "You are just like a telephone. He was going to lead that woman away from where she was guided to go because he wanted to feel powerful. Anything that happens to him is not from you or because of you. You hear and channel very well. As you get older, you won't faint, I promise. You held the energy of an ancient being for a long time before fainting, and you are only ten. That has never been done before. Close your eyes and go back to the moment before you started channeling. He was struggling to hold the energy in the channel. He was sweating because the energy was too big for him. That man stayed in it because his ego told him the connection was important, and holding it made him feel powerful. You held that energy with ease while moving and standing. He has gone home to make some offerings and to plead with the Orisha. You did great tonight. You helped that woman see her fear, feel it, and then assured that woman that opening her bakery was still her path. You helped her push forward, even when it made her heartbreak. So, when she is in the States, lonely and troubled, she will remember those words spoken. She will continue living until she is reborn. You channeled the right message for her and her bloodline. As an oracle, you received much favor for speaking the words as they were given."

The women left one by one, and Doña Marina walked Deyanira back home in the dark. It was close to midnight and the coqui frogs were singing their songs. Deyanira typically loved the serenading of the coqui. Deyanira couldn't enjoy them that night, her guilt wouldn't allow it. Doña Marina and Deyanira walked in silence. Deyanira wished she could forget for a minute that she sentenced a man to death. When they arrived at her house, Deyanira looked at her feet and told Doña Marina goodnight. As she walked toward the house, she felt a gentle tug on her headscarf.

"*Mi amor*," Doña Marina said sweetly. "You are just the vessel. Remember, like a telephone. If a doctor calls and says you have terminal cancer, no one gets mad at the telephone.

You can grieve the bad news, but you cannot take responsibility for it. Sometimes life brings pains and lessons. You cannot stop giving the bad news. It will stunt a person's growth. Because yes, even he will grow in death if they take him. He will return as a little girl and learn to embrace the feminine. If the Orisha takes him, he will return to a new life to try again, and he will remember this life in his dreams. He will do well next life if they take him. Things to help him release the trauma of this life, so better choices may come."

Deyanira burst into tears and her knees buckled. Doña Marina grabbed her before Deyanira hit the ground. "I didn't ask for this. I don't want it. I don't want it. I didn't ask for this."

Doña Marina rocked her, humming softly. Eventually, Deyanira fell silent. Doña Marina looked at Deyanira and, as sympathetically as she could, said, "None of us do, *mi amor*. None of us do."

Chapter 6

Deyanira woke up late, drained from the *mesa blanca*. She did not know what a hangover felt like at that age, but as she got older, she realized that *that* morning was a spiritual hangover. She crawled out of her bed slowly and in a daze; the light hurt her eyes and head. Deyanira staggered into the kitchen, rubbing her eyes as if she could rub the haze from her mind. Her Tia was wiping the counter with a nervous face. Her mama had gone to San Juan to buy airplane tickets to Chicago for all of them to go visit her papa. The calls and money had long stopped, and she had had enough.

Her mama acted like something bad happened, but she knew in her heart that her husband had left them to start a new life. Deyanira's mama's ego was in shambles. Her daughter was thriving in her spiritual gifts while her husband had abandoned her with kids she never wanted. Deyanira's aunt came to stay with them because she was concerned Deyanira's mother would hurt the girls. Deyanira spent most of her days with Doña Marina, and she always took the little ones with her. Her age limited her from seeing the dangers of her mother's pain.

Tia's face was heavy with hidden emotions. Deyanira sat at the table watching her Tia busy around the kitchen. She asked her Tia if her mama was okay. Her Tia dropped a plate, and it shattered on the kitchen tile. She then cussed under her breath. Deyanira stood to help with the mess, but Tia stopped her from entering the kitchen, fearing she would cut her feet. As her Tia knelt on the floor, collecting the broken bits of the plate, she wept. Deyanira was more confused than ever. She panicked and blurted out, "Is she dead? Did *mi* mama die, Titi?"

Now a look of regret washed over Tia's face. "No *mija*, no. Your mom is healthy and safe. Remember, you did nothing wrong. *Tu* mama wants to take you to see your papa in the States. Doña Marina is coming to see you soon. Go wash your face and get dressed."

Deyanira did as she was told, even though deep down she wished she had demanded answers from her Tia.

Doña Marina met Deyanira on the patio in the back of the house. Deyanira was in the backyard, reading one of her books. She found comfort in books that offered supernatural situations and life lessons, even though her mama said she was too young for their content.

Deyanira finally had the courage to ask. She had been wondering something since she saw her mama's interaction with Doña Marina in front of their home that day. "Why don't you like my mama and why does she do what you want? I've never seen her do what people ask of her, even family."

Doña Marina asked her to put her book down. "If I tell you, there is no going back. You will hear things about *tu* mama. What I'm about to say could crush you."

Deyanira pondered quietly. She had grown so much and matured in these two years of training with Doña Marina. She was old enough for the information now. Deyanira asked Doña Marina to tell her.

Doña Marina took a deep breath. "I was your Tia's best friend growing up. She was the only person who loved me and made me feel safe. My parents were not kind to me. They were scared of my gifts. I have been able to channel for people since I was a child, but I had not really mastered who I did it for and when. It just spontaneously happened back then. I was in your Tia and Mama's room, lying across the bed and talking with your Tia when your mama walked in. Your mama tried to yank me off their bed, but when she touched my shoulder, I started channeling. I told her that her first child would be a powerful healer and psychic. The child would change the world and fight against evil. Her child would be a hero so powerful they would move through time, as easily as walking into rooms of a house. The child would cast magic so strong they could move objects and kill their enemies with words. This child would do great things and travel the world, leaving your mama behind, forgotten on the island. Your mama was furious. She beat the shit out of me that day. Your mama had just found out she was pregnant. Your father married her soon after."

Deyanira interrupted the story. "Wait, my mama, knew I was special? You told her when she was pregnant with me?"

Doña Marina put her hand on Deyanira's arm. "Not exactly, *mi amor.* Your mama and papa had a baby before you. You had a brother. They named him Samael. He was beautiful. The baby laughed all the time and never cried. He had such a good energy. Then, at two weeks old, he suddenly died in his crib. Samael's death devastated your papa. Your mama was disconnected and kept telling people that these things happened all the time. She wanted your papa to take her out drinking on dates, and they fought constantly. She moved back in with her parents.

"I brought your mama some rice because I knew her to be complicated with her emotions, and everyone grieves differently. She ran from her feelings and drank to dull them. I came to your *abuelo's* house, and they let me in. Your mama was lying in her parents' bed depressed and everyone assumed she was finally grieving her child. I walked in and touched her side. I told her I was so sorry about Samael. When I touched her, I saw your mama holding a pillow over the baby's face in the bed. Her face was filled with jealousy and anger. I could hear her thoughts at that moment, and they were things like, *no one cares about me, they only care about this baby. He is so perfect, they say. You got a boy first try; that is perfect.* Then her thoughts went to the time I told her the baby would be powerful, and then she was pushing the pillow down harder to drown out the muffled cries of Samael. Her last thoughts in that vision were, *you can't be great, leave me on the island.* She was smirking when he choked on his last breath. I recoiled and fell backward. I scurried towards the opposite end of the room. I just curled up crying. Your mama sat up and wiped her eyes and said, 'My husband won't take me out to have fun because he is too sad about the baby. You were wrong. The child won't be powerful, and he can't leave me because he is already gone.'

I asked her how she could do such a thing and she told me she had never wanted a baby. She had only wanted your papa to marry her and take care of her. I couldn't believe my ears, and that was the moment I hated my gift. I thought I caused your brother's death. I didn't tell anyone later because I convinced myself that your mother had the sadness and that we all missed the signs. Some women get the sadness after birth and they can hurt their babies. When I came to talk to her about your training, your people told me she did not have the sadness. I told her that day that if she didn't let me train you, I would tell everyone she killed Samael. I saw her kill the baby, and I would tell your papa to have her locked up. That is why she let me train you, and I also offered to take the babies to help her. I think your family always suspected, though, because when you and your sisters were born, your tia and abuela always took turns and stayed until all of you were older than a year. If your abuela had to leave the house and your papa wasn't there, your tia always took the babies with her, never leaving you or your sisters alone with your mama until you were all toddlers."

Deyanira's chest tightened and she could see all the dots connecting. Her mama wasn't stressed out. She just didn't want kids. All the hurtful things her mama had said to Deyanira were on purpose. Deyanira didn't want to believe it. It was too much for her young mind to comprehend. She told Doña Marina, "Maybe she had the sadness. Maybe it stayed." Doña Marina nodded silently.

Returning to this moment clawed at Deyanira's spirit. She preferred to focus on the end of her conversation with Doña Marina. It was the day her world broke— mentally and spiritually. Deyanira had to realize that day her own mother hated her and could never love her. Once the dust settled on the idea of her mother murdering her brother it was more believable to her than not. She always in her spirit felt her mother was capable of murder. The shock was more so the murder of a tiny baby than the act itself.

"I have so much to teach you. Your gifts are a lot, and without help, they can devour your mind. You are so special, *mija*. You can move through realms made for gods. *Amor*, you will walk through them with ease. Your existence was brokered hundreds of years ago. Lifetimes ago, powerful ancestors sat down with Deities and mapped out how to make you. You do not cause things to happen, but you carry the power to make things happen if you wish. You are a light in the dark to the many. Your destiny is to illuminate truth. This is a heavy cross to bear, *mija*. Especially if you shine a light on a truth that means death. Your mother is taking you to the States, and I do not think you will return for training. Your ancestors will find you someone in the States to help you. Be open. Remember, without training, you are left vulnerable."

Deyanira was confused and overwhelmed by Doña Marina's words. In one breath, she had said her mother was a murderer. That she was a baby killer. Had her mama known it was Deyanira, she would've killed her instead. Then, with the second breath, she'd told Deyanira that she was special, but couldn't help her. Deyanira felt hated and loved at the same moment and had no way to reconcile the two very different feelings. It was the hot and cold of a perfect storm to conjure a tornado within her.

The only time she ever felt love was when Tia came to her room on summer nights. Deyanira's thoughts carried her to those memories when she pretended to fall asleep while Tia spoke sweetly over her head, providing a momentary feeling of comfort and safety. However, Deyanira was thrust back into reality, and anxiety flooded her body. The information overwhelmed her. It was too much, too quick. Her child's body and mind couldn't hold the news of leaving the island without a possibility of return, her mother wishing her dead, and her mother *murdering* an older brother she never knew she had. Deyanira felt so powerless all while being told she was extraordinarily powerful.

Doña Marina's body language was anxious and unsettled. As if she knew her words were seeds being planted for a much later harvest, but would bring no fruit on this day. She sat silently, looking for words to force the harvest. What could she say to make Deyanira understand her gifts were not a curse? Doña Marina was looking to control the situation and outcome. She could hear the spirits getting angry at her attempts. Finally, Doña Marina settled with a slow and lingering breath. She placed her hand on Deyanira's leg. "Do you remember the man from last night?"

A tidal wave of emotions hit Deyanira, and she knew immediately who Doña Marina was talking about. Deyanira escalated from shame to deep despair, and then to rage. She felt as if she was in the rapids of the ocean after a tremendous storm. Deyanira couldn't breathe. She started gasping for air, and the yard began to spin. Deyanira might have been sitting in a chair in the backyard of her house, safe, but her mind and spirit felt as if she was drowning, failing to keep her head above the water. Deyanira felt dizzy from the lack of oxygen and let out a deep wail from her spirit, wilting the flowers in her backyard. Her wail pushed the life force from the plants into the atmosphere and Doña Marina's hair stood up for the static energy released into the yard.

Deyanira lost consciousness for a moment, and her lifeless body slumped in the chair. With the energy gathered, lightning struck a tree ten meters from the patio. There was peace for Deyanira in those thirty seconds of unconsciousness. No grief, no thoughts or feelings,—only blackness. A dark void of peace that, to most people, might seem terrifying, but for Deyanira, who felt everyone and everything all over time, the void was a sanctuary.

As an adult, she returned to this moment, often searching for clues on how to return to the void. Adult Deyanira had a humbled understanding of the relief that drugs offered addicts;

she understood the temptation and allure.

Reality drew young Deyanira out with the crack of lightning. She awoke to Doña Marina's cries. Doña Marina knew Deyanira would wake up terrified of herself and want to run away from her gifts. She knew the chain of events that was about to unfold. Deyanira's rage and grief mixed like a gin and tonic, a perfect drink in moderation, but for Deyanira, it was bottomless and therefore deadly.

Deyanira spoke from her belly like a volcanic eruption. "Go away. I hate it here. I will never come back. I hate you. I wish I had never met you. Wait, did I cause that lightning? This is not a gift. It is a curse. I do not want it and I will not use it. I will bind it up and lock it away." Deyanira closed her eyes and envisioned pulling a glowing ball from her chest, placing it in a clay pot, and corking it. There was glowing dust connecting her body to the clay pot on the shelf. The glowing dust resembled what she imagined fairy dust looked like. She felt lighter, but the dense heat of her gift still pressed against her from afar. Doña Marina knew that Deyanira had locked away her gifts. She had foreseen it and tried to prevent it, even knowing these were not preventable events. She loved Deyanira like a daughter. Last night, Doña Marina had begged all the Deities and spirits to stop this chain of events. Her heart couldn't take the hurt and loss. Doña Marina's eyes filled with tears and she reached for Deyanira, whispering her name, "Deyanira, *por favor.*"

It was too late. Deyanira ran into the house and locked herself in the bathroom.

Tia settled Deyanira down and left her in the cool tile of the shower. Tia poured some *café* for Doña Marina and brought it to the back porch. She approached Doña Marina from behind, realizing that she was wiping her eyes and nose. Tia's heart broke for Doña Marina. As Tia rounded the small outdoor table next to Doña Marina, regret seeped into her mind. She left her friend. She had abandoned her years ago. Her choice loomed over her like a small dark cloud. She'd chosen her sister over her friend because her sister had forced her to. Her poor friend was just Mari then. Mari's parents tortured her, and the community was afraid of her. She was all alone without Tia. Doña Marina fell in love with being a mother figure to Deyanira and now will be alone all over again. Tia placed the cup of *café* on the table and placed her hand on Doña Marina's shoulder. They sat in silence for what felt like an hour. However, only a moment or two had passed. Doña Marina slowly stood up as her body and heart ached with grief. "*Adios mi amor*," she mumbled quietly under her breath in Tia's direction.

Doña Marina climbed the winding street to the entrance of her home. She walked slowly down the path weeping as the plant on her path touched her arms to console her. As Doña Marina entered her home she was struck in the head. The blow was hard— a hammer to her skull. The force came with the intent of murder. She felt her body give way. She wasn't panicked about her release from this body. Instead, Doña Marina was worried about Deyanira and how her death would seal the child's fate further into repression and oppression. She crawled to her couch as her heart slowed and her breathing labored. Blood trickled down the nape of her neck, to her back. Her thoughts raced. *How could I tell Deyanira it wasn't her fault? She did not kill me.*

Doña Marina assumed her killers were there because they had found the energy burst Deyanira produced when she channeled Ogun. Doña Marina could feel her spirit slipping away and separating from her physical body. Her consciousness felt lighter and freer. She stood over her body temporarily as an earthbound spirit. She looked down at her own lifeless body and saw a group of hooded people in her home. They started chanting in Latin and she saw it tethering her spirit to them. She called out to Oya. "Help me. Protect me. She needs me."

Her voice carried into the air and her prayer was honored. The trees outside her house bent as if a hurricane had descended on the area. The force shook the walls and floor of her tiny green home, blowing the hooded people back and rendering them unconscious. Doña Marina expressed her gratitude to Oya and looked back over her body. She wondered when her body got so lumpy and why she hadn't worn a nicer outfit to be discovered in. Her silly thoughts made her laugh.

Doña Marina could feel Deyanira from afar as she enjoyed her own laughter. She knew it meant only one thing. She beamed with gratitude. Once Doña Marina completed her transition, she would take her seat at the table of guides for Deyanira. She would be on Deyanira's team and become one of her spiritual guides.

Her thoughts of Deyanira carried her to a bedroom she was unfamiliar with. She looked down in front of her to see an exhausted, grief-ridden Deyanira sleeping. Her tear-soaked pillow held her in comfort while she slept. Her hair stuck to her face with sweat, and her cheeks flushed red from the heat. Doña Marina tucked Deyanira's hair behind her ear gently. The cool touch of Doña Marina's spirit made Deyanira smile in her sleep. She returned the smile. Before Doña Marina left, she leaned over and whispered, "It is not your fault, *mija*, none of it. I am with you always and when you are ready to speak to me, again, you will see me. Be well, *mi amor*."

With those words, Doña Marina began her journey to the

crossroads and Deyanira slept away her troubles.

Chapter 7

"*Mi amor*, is your bag packed? We need to get to the airport."

"Si, Tia. *'stoy lista.* I'll take our bags to the car." Deyanira took her red duffle bag with dingy yellow straps to the trunk of her Tia's Honda. She struggled with its weight; her mama must've packed a lot of clothes for this visit. Deyanira loved her Tia and often wished *she* was her mother instead. She only dared to say it once, though. Deyanira got her little sisters all together and in the car. "Mami, I got all of them for you."

Deyanira climbed into the car after getting the little ones in the back seat. The baby sat on Deyanira's lap and Deyanira pulled the seat belt across for them both. Tia and Mama came to the car angrily, and they started down the street to the airport, or so Deyanira thought. They had to slow down at the bend in the street because there was a crowd of people and cars off to the side. Deyanira looked up from her book when the car stopped. Her eyes investigated the commotion on the side of the road. She visually explored the cars and the group of people. Tia rolled her window down to inquire about the scene. Deyanira realized the cars were outside the path to Doña Marina's home. Tia received whispers of information through her car window that something happened to Doña Marina. Tia knew her sister would have refused if she asked to drop by—

so she didn't. Asking for forgiveness was always easier than asking for permission, anyway. Tia pulled over even though Mama was furious. "We're going to miss our flight!"

Tia told Deyanira to stay in the car with her mama. She just needed to check on something. Deyanira sat in the car and tried to read, but her anxiety and panic forced her out of the car and down the small path to Marina's home. Her mama told her to get back in the car and, at one point, grabbed her arm to return, but the look on Deyanira's face startled her mama, and she released her arm. A few people silently gathered on the outskirts of the porch. Deyanira walked past them and opened the creaky door.

Deep down, Deyanira knew Doña Marina was gone. She could feel the emptiness of the body and the residue of life splashed throughout the home, like a baby splattering food from a highchair. When a spirit leaves its body, an energetic residue drips against the walls of the death area. Doña Marina was everywhere and nowhere when Deyanira walked into the small front room. Her physical body was covered in a white sheet.

Tia was talking to some men about notifying the police when Deyanira startled her. "*Amor*, why are you here? I told you to stay in the car."

Deyanira couldn't respond. She just released tears. They streamed down her frozen face. She felt her legs give way and accepted she was going to fall to the ground. She welcomed the fall because holding herself up felt too hard. She was falling backwards, and suddenly, Deyanira felt hands pulling her up. She didn't dare to look back because in her heart, she knew there wasn't a real person behind her. She wasn't ready to process the idea that a spirit was holding her up in the moment of her grief. After a few moments, Tia turned Deyanira's tiny frame towards the door and with gentle hands on Deyanira's shoulders, guided her back to the car. Once Deyanira returned to the backseat, they started back down the mountainous road in silence.

Deyanira broke the silence in the car. "I was so mean to her. Did I kill her too?"

Tia gasped at the idea of such a heavy burden on her poor niece's head. "Oh no! You did not kill her or that man from the *mesa blanca*. Someone attacked Doña Marina in her home and that is all we know. The medium passing away was a consequence unrelated to you. Doña Marina knew you loved her."

Deyanira's mama rolled her eyes at the idea that Deyanira loved Marina in any capacity. "Doña Marina knew you were going to distance yourself from her after that man from the *mesa blanca* died. She had a vision you would cut her off from teaching before she came over. She loved you like a daughter, even though you only knew her for a short time." The rage Deyanira's mother felt could blow up the entire island. She yelled at her sister. "You are a terrible sister and will never see the girls again."

As Tia pulled up to the terminal, Deyanira's mother started hitting her head and pulling her hair. The girls cried from the back seat, and Deyanira's mother screamed at them to shut the fuck up. Her mama swung her arm into the back seat but missed the children. Deyanira's mama jumped out of the car, pulling the girls out one by one, leaving a handprint on their arms. "Marina died because she was an evil *bruja*. I never should've allowed you to go with her. She could've gotten you killed with her." Deyanira's mother turned and with a stern tone said, "Stop crying. We are going to see Papa."

The girls quieted down and tucked away all that unprocessed grief. It was safer to tuck away grief than risk the wrath of their mama.

Chapter 8

When Mami and the girls got to Chicago, they discovered Papa was living with another woman. Deyanira realized, when she got older, her mama knew that was why the money stopped.

Papa opened the door, shocked and scared of what Mama would do. Boricua women are fiery women. It was in their blood, but Deyanira's mama said nothing. She didn't even tell her children goodbye, or that she loved them. She just handed him the girls' bags and walked down the hall. The little ones were so young they didn't understand what she was doing, but Deyanira knew. She chased her mama down that hall, to the bottom of the stairs, and out the door.

Papa took the little girls inside and crowded the window watching Deyanira. Her face soaked with tears as she yelled, "*Vuelve! Te necesitamos! Cobarde! Eres una pendeja debil! Si nos dejas, tendras una vida rota y te volveras loca. Te odio!*"

A defeated Deyanira returned to her papa's apartment complex and sat weeping at the top of the stairs. It wasn't so much about missing her mama as it was her mother definitively at that moment, sending the message that they were never to return to the island. As she sat at the top of the stairs, she solidified the idea that Mama left them with Papa because she hated Deyanira. Her little sisters lost their mother because their mama hated Deyanira. She felt like a pariah. All she did was break things. She was lost to the idea her mama didn't want any of them. Self loathing prevented her from accepting it had nothing to do with her.

His new wife didn't know about the children and she definitely didn't want to raise them. Their new stepmother was pregnant with her first child with Papa. Behind the bedroom door their stepmother screamed at their papa, "Give them back or I'll leave!" . Eventually, they settled down beyond the door. That night, the girls were on the floor of their papa's small apartment. Their stepmother didn't want them on her nice couch. All four of them huddled together—the babies laid on Deyanira and Deyanira laid on a blanket.

The next day, their papa went to work, and the beatings started. Their stepmother feared Deyanira. Deyanira was young, but she was big enough to fight a pregnant woman. Their stepmother gave Deyanira money to get rice from the store. It took Deyanira a long time because she was only ten and her stepmother gave her the vaguest of directions. She didn't know how to speak English then and the streets were busy and confusing. On the way back, Deyanira found an older woman who she described the apartment building in Spanish to and the nice older woman helped her back safely.

When Deyanira returned, Maribel was trying to bathe one of the babies because Alma had wet herself when it was her turn for a beating. It was too hard for Maribel to hold Alma up in the tub. Maribel was only seven and the belt buckle had cut her arm. She had a runny nose from crying, and she couldn't wipe her tears because she was washing Alma's chubby toddler legs. Anytime their stepmother heard them cry out from the kitchen, she yelled at them to shut up. Little Maribel never mastered holding in her emotions, even if it meant getting beat more for crying. Deyanira left the rice on the counter and made her way to the bathroom. She locked the door quietly. Deyanira examined the two little ones—red, fresh welts and cuts covered their tiny bodies from head to neck, from their backs to their legs.

Something broke in Deyanira. Everything was too much. All the hope and fight in her washed down in the bathtub's drain that day. She was terrified, but her face was devoid of emotion. She didn't know what to do or say. Deyanira asked what had happened and Maribel just let go of the toddler in the tub. Alma fell into the water and Deyanira had to lunge and grab her. Maribel laid curled up on the light blue fuzzy rug in the bathroom and cried while Deyanira quietly finished washing and drying Alma.

As she wiped Alma down with a towel, Deyanira felt a tug in her spirit. Something was cautioning her about disconnecting from her emotions. The feeling was like a faint whisper being carried by the dust between her spirit and the clay pot holding her powers. "There is no hope. You made me a murderer, killing the only person I felt safe with. You pulled me from the only home I've ever had to this awful place full of *gringos*. You put me in an apartment with a woman who wants to kill my little sisters. So, fuck you, I quit," she mumbled under her breath.

Maribel stopped her cries to ask, "What?"

Deyanira reached over and pushed her hair behind her ear. Maribel winced in pain at Deyanira grazing a knot above her ear. They tried to stay hidden in the bathroom, but their stepmother was pregnant and needed the toilet. After Deyanira cleaned up Camilla's wounds, she unlocked the door and pushed the two little ones out of the bathroom.

Later that afternoon, Deyanira was trying to keep the little ones quiet and entertained in the front room, like she often did at home when her mama napped. Suddenly, her stepmother came from the back bedroom lightning fast it was as if she was a super villain in a cartoon on Saturday morning. She was enraged, belt in hand swinging without even choosing a target. Deyanira threw her body on top of her sisters and told her stepmother to just hit her, because she could take it.

Deyanira shielded the girls from what seemed like one hundred lashes, until their stepmother lost wind and waddled in retreat toward the back of the apartment. Once they heard the bedroom door close, Deyanira collapsed from the pain. Her shirt was ripped and bloodied.

Their papa came home and their stepmother told him the girls were awful children. They were like wild animals. She told him she was going to lose their son because she was bleeding from the stress. If he would not send them back right away, then he needed to beat them too so they would at least listen to her. He took the girls into the bathroom and told them to pretend to cry as he hit the sink with the belt. Deyanira tried to explain to her papa that they were not bad, and she beat them for no reason. She tried to tell him she was worried about the babies being hit so hard. She feared their stepmother would hurt them really badly. He just brushed it off and said their stepmother would come around; they just had to be patient with her.

When their papa went to work the next morning, their stepmother didn't send away Deyanira. Deyanira was no longer a threat to her. Deyanira did not have the confidence to physically fight her stepmother. Deyanira would rather take on the pain of her loved ones than give it to their enemies.

Deyanira tried to shield the little ones again that morning, but only beating Deyanira did not satisfy their stepmother. She was so mad at their papa for lying, so she gave them the beating she wished she could give him. Deyanira wouldn't let her little sisters go, so their stepmother grabbed a broomstick and began hitting Deyanira in the head. By the third blow, Deyanira's body fell; she slumped over on the floor, unconscious. Maribel thought their stepmother killed her. Maribel ran over and buried her face in Deyanira's chest. She begged God to wake her up. Maribel moved away from the precious babies' little bodies. She left them open for their stepmother and her broomstick, and her stepmother began hitting the babies. Maribel was so scared of Deyanira dying that she didn't even hear the little ones' cries over her own cries to God to bring Deyanira back to life.

The crack. It was a deafening crack, so loud. There was no way to describe something like that other than lightning striking a large tree branch. It woke Deyanira out of her unconscious state. Three-year-old Alma screamed. Her tiny disjointed forearm dangled lifelessly. A horrifying sight to see a toddler's arm completely disconnected at the elbow. Their stepmother didn't stop. She just moved on to the four-year-old Camilla.

Deyanira, with blood pouring into one eye, stumbled to her feet. She grabbed Alma and signaled to Maribel she was running for the door. That was enough to empower the fight in Maribel. Maribel ran full speed towards their stepmother. She took her small shoulder and jabbed it hard into her stepmother's hip, causing her stepmother to fall forward into the wall covered in wood paneling. Maribel grabbed

Camilla's hand and bolted for the door that Deyanira had swung open. Deyanira, barefoot and covered in blood, led them out the door. They ventured down the hall, to the bottom of the stairs, and out to the street. Maribel didn't know where Deyanira was going or what she was doing, but Maribel followed.

They crossed the street and ignored people gasping at the sight of their bloodied and broken bodies. Alma fainted from the pain and dangled lifelessly in Deyanira's arm. Maribel didn't understand why Deyanira didn't stop walking. Suddenly, Deyanira stopped and started yelling, "Abuelita! Abuelita!"

Down the block, a small heavy-set Mexican woman turned and responded. Deyanira knew they needed help in Spanish, otherwise, their stepmother could lie. Police were called, which involved DCFS, and because of the angel abuelita translator, they were safe. The police arrested their stepmother.

The abuelita was the kind old woman who helped Deyanira find her way back to the apartment the day before. Divinely orchestrated were those chains of events. Deyanira may have tried to lock away her gifts, but they were a part of her, connected by the dust. She had a gut feeling that she needed to find the Spanish-speaking abuelita.. Their stepmother went to jail and their father's newest daughter was born there. The son their stepmother promised was a lie. Papa never had sons besides Samael.

Chapter 9

At the hospital, the sisters had separate rooms. Deyanira was told to stay in her room so she could rest. They all waited for their Papa to come and see them. The girls waited for him to tell them he was sorry and loved them. They needed him to hold and comfort them, so they knew they were safe. He never came.

A social worker came instead, with a cook from the cafeteria to translate. The social worker explained that their papa surrendered them, and he had asked her to help find them a home. The girls didn't understand what that meant, but they nodded when asked if they understood. Deyanira asked if they could just return to the island with their mama.

The social worker said they didn't know where their mother was, and they did not know how to find her on the island. So, the four children were in a foreign land without parents, love, or safety. Deyanira felt helpless. The social worker left, and she cried out to her ancestors in the room. She didn't cry out for help; she cried out in malicious anger. "Fuck you, all of you. This life is horrible. I'm the chosen one— or my kid is, whatever. I want to die. Take all of this away. Just make it stop. I don't want this anymore. You're all useless. Fuck destiny and fuck you." She cried herself to sleep that night, curled up in the freezing hospital, under her thin sheet and hospital gown.

As she drifted between wakefulness and sleep, the veil thinned, and she saw a battle in her room. She saw native warrior women with red paint around their faces fighting ghoulish spirits distorted from pain and anger. Deyanira blinked, and the battle vanished. Her exhaustion pulled her eyelids shut as she slept in that freezing hospital bed amongst the battle.

When it was time to leave the hospital, the social worker and the cafeteria worker came again. The social worker said she found a woman who would take them in as foster kids. "It is hard to find people that take four girls so make sure you behave or I will have to split you up." The social worker spouted off to the cafeteria worker. The girls nodded again, unaware of what was happening. Off they went to their foster mother's house. The drive from the hospital wasn't long. They saw the tallest buildings they had ever seen and streets filled with cars and people. Everything was so busy and loud.

Being Boricua, Deyanira thought she knew loud, but Chicago was the loudest place she had ever been. She longed for the quiet of the island, where the noisiest thing to hear was an angry wife fussing at her drunk husband through their open windows. When they pulled up to the large brick home, Deyanira thought it was a mansion. Her mouth opened in awe.

The social worker looked in the backseat and saw Deyanira's face. Laughing, she said, "I bet you are used to huts where you are from."

Deyanira just smiled because she did not know what the social worker said, but returning as an adult to this time always made her cuss. "Stupid, brown teeth, stinky *gringa* bitch," she mumbled through her teeth every visit.

The social worker took them out of the car and shuffled them up the stairs of the large red brick porch, to the front door. Deyanira ran her hand up the cement banister and she climbed the stairs. The energy of the home was kind. The cafeteria worker did not come–she was a hospital employee, so the social worker's instructions were mostly hand gestures to usher and herd the girls.

The social worker knocked on the front door and out came an average-sized, middle-aged black woman. As the door opened, the girls smelled the most amazing fragrances. Their little mouths watered and craved the unknown food in the house. There was a familiarity to the aromas that felt like home. Maribel's stomach grumbled, begging to be heard. It made Alma and Camilla giggle. The hospital food was hard on their stomachs. They were used to fresh food grown in their backyards. Their bodies missed beans and rice. They missed *bacalao*. They missed the *pan*. The bread in Chicago at its best was terrible compared to the island bread. Even as an adult, Deyanira stood by her belief that Puerto Rican bread was the best in the world.

Their foster mom's curly hair was pinned up under a white bandana; she wore denim overalls and a large pink button-up shirt. Deyanira thought to herself, *Is she cooking, cleaning, or fixing something?* Her face was round and smooth like satin except the dimple on her right cheek. Her smile was warm and radiant. She stood no taller than five and a half feet tall. The girls looked up with their mouths wide open in awe at her beauty.

Deyanira suddenly realized that Papa did not give any of their clothes to the social worker. They stood there on that porch with nothing but each other. She hung her head in shame.

Deyanira had never felt so empty. The social worker tried to introduce them to their foster mom, so Maribel blurted out, "*Hola.*"

Their foster mom laughed from her belly. She had the best laugh, and it made everyone want to join in, even if they didn't understand what she was laughing at. Then she crouched down, eye-to-eye with Maribel, and said, "Oh honey, we don't speak that around here, but we'll manage." The social worker left and their foster mom called down the older girl in her care. "Hey, go down the street and get your Messican friend for me. I need her to help me with something."

Inside the home, the girls shuffled to wash their hands and explore.

The young Mexican neighbor came down right away. The neighbor was a young *gordita* girl. Her complexion reminded Deyanira of *panas hervidas* thinking about it made her miss her home and people. The neighbor's hair was thick, but the straightest hair she had ever seen. Deyanira only saw hair like that in drawings. Deyanira thought she looked like a Taino. Doña Marina used to read them picture books about the Taino Indians.

Their foster mom was indeed cooking, cleaning, and fixing something. She was cooking an enormous pot of black-eyed peas and rice and another pot of some green vegetable and pork. She was cleaning the table and fixing a chair with a loose leg, all while talking to the girls and the neighbor.

Deyanira would come to find out that the neighbor ate at their house a lot. Her mom made their foster mom *tamales* on weekends to say thank you. The neighbor got there and the first thing their foster mom did was hug her. Deyanira thought her hugs looked so nice, and then she reminded herself to stay on guard.

"You hungry?"

The neighbor declined the meal because she was too nosy and eager to understand why she was summoned.

"Now look, I need to tell you something, and I want you to tell them for me, okay? I want you to come down here three times a week and help them with their English, and I'll pay you twenty dollars, deal?"

The little neighbor's eyes lit up at the idea of making twenty dollars for herself each week. She smiled and waved at Deyanira and the girls. "*Me llamo* Julissa." Julissa was later disappointed by how smart the girls were and how quickly they learned English, but grateful to have new friends who also spoke Spanish.

"Tell them I will protect them. Tell them they are safe here and I would die before I let anyone hurt them again. Make sure they know it is okay to be scared, but all I will do is love them and feed them. Oh, tell them they can call me Big Mama," Big Mama said.

Julissa chuckled and started to translate, and Deyanira thought her Spanish sounded funny. She said some things weird. The babies didn't understand some of her words, so Deyanira translated by piecing together the words she knew from context.

Julissa thought *their* Spanish was all one big word and a bit like a song. They spent many nights in the future teasing each other over the differences in their Spanish. Big Mama then showed the girls some hand gestures they could do until they learned the words, such as hungry and thirsty. Julissa also taught simple Spanish words to Big Mama in case she wasn't there to translate.

Big Mama told them that tomorrow, they would go shopping for new clothes. She asked the older foster girl to show Maribel and the babies to their room. She had Julissa ask Deyanira to have a seat. The older foster girl signaled for Maribel to follow her upstairs and picked up Alma with one hand then held Camilla's hand with the other.

Maribel pointed to the bathroom and stayed downstairs. Maribel didn't want to leave Deyanira alone with their foster mom. She didn't know her or trust her. She never wanted Deyanira to be beaten again. Their stepmother almost killed her, and Maribel felt like she couldn't let that happen again. Maribel tipped-toed back down the hall from the bathroom and hid around the corner of the kitchen to listen in. She wasn't sure what she would do to protect Deyanira, but she would not leave her alone.

Big Mama began for Julissa to translate. "They told me about how you protected your sisters and helped them escape." Her voice cracked with tears. "I want you to know that in this house, I do not and will not hit anyone. You do not have to take care of your sisters here. You can just be a kid. You are just a kid. You only have to be a kid in this house. You have chores, but you are only responsible for yourself. I promise to take care of them, so you can just be a kid. I will protect you as well. You are just as important as those little ones. You matter to me, and I will keep you and those babies safe. I know it will take time for you to trust me, but you'll see I will always take care of you. If you ever feel you aren't loved or protected, tell me right away and we'll talk it out."

Maribel heard a commotion suddenly. She peeked around the corner to see that Deyanira had fallen to the floor, weeping. Her face was on the kitchen tile and her cheeks flushed red with emotions. Julissa was crying herself. She tried to comfort Deyanira in Spanish, but she was just a child overwhelmed by what was happening. Julissa just sat next to Deyanira on the floor and stroked her back gently.

Big Mama did not skip a beat. She crawled right onto the floor with Deyanira, eye to eye, cheek to the tile, moving the hair back from Deyanira's wet eyes. "Big Mama is here, baby. I just want to love you." The clay pot Deyanira that locked her powers in cracked slightly, and the dust became a stream of light trickling into Deyanira.

Maribel sat silently crying in the hall with her hand over her mouth until the older foster girl came downstairs. She sternly signaled for her to go to her room. Maribel wiped her eyes and she climbed the stairs to a hallway with three doors.

The older girl opened a door and gestured for Maribel to follow. The bedroom was amazing. There were bunk beds for Maribel and the babies, and Deyanira had her own bed across the room. The sheets on the babies' bottom bunk were Care Bears, and Deyanira's and Maribel's bedding was Smurfs. They had never had their own beds before. There were toys and books in English for them. The babies were already playing with a floor full of toys, laughing contently. Maribel sat down next to them and played with the blocks.

Chapter 10

The first few years at Big Mama's flew by, and the girls settled in well. They were loved, safe, and cared for at Big Mama's house. They went to school and became close friends with Julissa. Children came in and out of Big Mama's house at that time. Some were there for a night, a weekend, or a couple of weeks until the family could be located for permanent placement.

After talking to the older girl before she left for college, Deyanira realized that Big Mama's house was more of a short-term haven for kids. She only took in full-time kids with no one. Deyanira loved it at Big Mama's. She read books and was in a choir at her school. She loved to sing on the stage. One day, Deyanira and her sisters came home from school and as they got to the porch, they could hear Big Mama on a call in the kitchen; she was upset.

Her words were quick, and she seemed flustered as she stuttered through the call. The girls came in and washed their hands as part of their after-school routine, before starting homework. Big Mama got off the phone and asked Deyanira to go down to Julissa's house and ask if her older sister could come down and watch the younger three girls. She had an errand to run and wanted Deyanira to come with. Big Mama ran the household like clockwork, and it was really weird to break from the routine. Deyanira felt nervous. There was an unsettled feeling surrounding this situation, and she was concerned it would put an end to her blissful life at Big Mama's house.

Once Julissa's sister arrived, Deyanira got into their large conversion van's passenger seat. Big Mama slammed her driver-side door, and it startled Deyanira. Big Mama asked Deyanira, "What's wrong baby? Why you so shook up?"

Deyanira looked at her feet. "Are you getting rid of me?"

Big Mama burst into tears. She put her face in her hands, elbows resting on the steering wheel. Deyanira's brain told her that Big Mama had to get rid of her but felt remorse in doing so. Deyanira reached across the console and put her hands gently on Big Mama's elbow. Big Mama wiped her face. "Oh, honey, I will never get rid of you. I am so sorry I made you feel that way. I brought you with me because I have to ask something of you, and I apologize for asking. My mama is sick. She is from the south, in Louisiana. My family called to tell me she's not going last much longer, and I should come to say goodbye. So, we are going to drive down there to say goodbye. I may need you for a small time to help with the girls so I can say goodbye and plan her funeral. I promise it won't be a lot. I just may need a little help."

The idea that Big Mama, after all she did for them, asked Deyanira to help and also felt bad for asking for help confused Deyanira. She was so happy to help. "Of course, I will help with the girls. You have done so much for us. I'm so sorry your mom is sick."

"Baby, you and your sisters don't owe me for raising you. It has been an honor. You all are a blessing in my life. You understand?"

Deyanira nodded emptily.

"Now, we have to go visit my son. I need to tell him. He was closer to my mama than me. I brought you with me to talk about the trip without your sisters around *and* to introduce you to my son."

Deyanira was shocked that she had been living with Big Mama for three years and she never knew that she had a son. There was so much turmoil inside of her. All of the leftover emotions about Big Mama possibly getting rid of her were still there boiling. Deyanira started mulling over in her head new emotions of betrayal. She told Big Mama so many private things. Things her sisters didn't know. Big Mama knew about Doña Marina being murdered and how it felt when her mother left, how she missed her Tia and the island, but how could Big Mama keep that she had a son from Deyanira?

Deyanira felt dirty and gross. She started rubbing her arms, and she shut her eyes to prevent her body from bursting. The powerful emotions grew, and as they grew, that trickling stream connected to her powers in the clay pot grew brighter and brighter. As the stream of light grew brighter, it formed a glowing rope tethered to the top of the clay pot. Once solidified by Deyanira's emotions, it yanked the pot she so carefully placed on a shelf in her head. It tilted and wobbled, then toppled down until it smashed open. Deyanira's eyes shimmered with golden light when the clay pot burst open. The radio of the van changed channels, the lights on the dashboard flickered, and the gauges bounced from one end of the gauge to the other.

"What in the world is going on with this van now?" Big Mama said out loud as she banged on the dashboard.

The van came to a stop at a light, and Big Mama felt the urge to explain why she didn't talk about her son. "Hey Suga, I need to explain. I'm so sorry I never told you about my son. I'm not allowed to or supposed to rather. That's the agreement I have with the social workers. My son has been in jail. He got involved in some stuff when he was young. I was young when I had him. Baby, foster kids usually come from poor homes or come from no family at all. If they knew about my son, my foster kids may try to find him. They would try to get work, money, and protection. So to get approved to help kids with nobody to care for them, I had to agree to never see or speak to my son. He was angry at first, but then he understood. Falah is a good person, and he does good for people. He just also does some bad. So keeping yall safe, I have to stay away from him."

Deyanira felt a deep empathy for Big Mama's son. She wasn't sure why. It wasn't the typical empathy she felt for people. This was stronger; it made her heart ache. They left the van, and the pain and ache of heartbreak got stronger, crippling her. It was as if the burden of his lived experiences and emotions were being filtered through her.

They approached a large home not well maintained, but not dilapidated either. The dead bush in the small patch of overgrown yellowed grass had glass bottles turned upside down on the branches. The wind chime hanging on the front porch was peculiar as well. The wind blew and the antique iron keys strung together by thick red string clanged slightly as they reached the top step. The door to the home was blue, and Deyanira thought it was odd and stuck out. A large, solemn man answered the door. When he opened the door, he looked bothered and angry that someone was at the door. His eyes locked with Big Mama, and his expression changed. His brow released, and his face softened.

Big Mama said, "Hey baby, take me to him."

This large man's spirit immediately transformed into a teenage boy whose head hung low. "Yes, ma'am."

He led Big Mama and Deyanira down the hallway to the backroom. In the backroom was a desk and bookshelves full of books wrapped around two of the four walls of the room. In the office chair behind the desk was a mountain of a man: beautiful dark brown skin, a bald head, and glasses. He looked as if he had stolen Big Mama's face, her dimple included, except for a goatee. The painful energy pouring out of the man behind the desk became so intense that Deyanira felt overwhelmingly nauseous from his emotions. She doubled over, grabbing her stomach. Big Mama stopped in her tracks to care for Deyanira, which only caused the man to ache more, hurting Deyanira further. Her stomach felt as if she was going to explode, and her mind was woozy. Deyanira fell over and said, "Close the door quickly, please."

Big Mama, without a thought, closed the door. Curiosity caused the man's pain to deter just enough for Deyanira to stand and stagger behind the desk next to him. She placed her hand on his shoulder and leaned on his arm, which was almost the size of her entire young torso. She leaned towards his ear and said, "I am so sorry you are hurting. You are important." Deyanira glanced over at Big Mama. In Deyanira's mind, she saw Big Mama on countless nights crying herself to sleep, holding her son's baby picture in her hand. The images ran through her mind like live pictures with different clothing in different seasons and different furniture, but always the same position, the same baby picture, and tears.

Some nights, Big Mama had a washcloth in her mouth to prevent her wails from waking the house. Deyanira leaned into his ear again and told him what she saw. She said, "Love is complicated, and choices aren't always black and white. Big Mama didn't mean to abandon you. Sometimes, when we try to break cycles, we accidentally recreate what we are trying to break. She loves you; her inner child just wanted her own abandonment acknowledged. Big Mama helps kids like us to save herself. She is in a loop, but it never fixed things. She aches and longs for her baby. She carries a lot of regret about what she missed with you. She cries every night wishing she could fix it."

Falah's spirit transformed into a young adult, maybe in his late teens. Tears flowed down his face and nose running. As he wept, Deyanira took on his emotions as they flowed out of him. He cried and felt lighter because Deyanira filtered his emotions into raw energy through her heart space. The sight of her son's pain caused Big Mama to fall to her knees and break down in tears as well. When her tears flowed, her emotions also became raw energy that flowed into Deyanira's heart space. Big Mama felt lighter than she had in twenty years, maybe even longer. Some time passed, and Big Mama made her way behind the desk and embraced her son. For years, his spirit had longed for the safety of her embrace. Deyanira could see the cracks in his spirit growing smaller; they were more like scarring.

Deyanira fell into the chair in the middle of the room with a flop of exhaustion. Big Mama and her son started conversing. They were opening up to each other with their most vulnerable moments and feelings. She told him he was her heart, and she was so ashamed she wasn't around more when he was young and she worked too much. Big Mama said, "Lottie warned me, Falah. She warned me about you getting involved in bad stuff when I was pregnant, and I didn't listen."

Falah wiped his face and laughed. "If Lottie told you I was

going to do this in the womb, then it went exactly how it was going to go, Mama. Her knowing hasn't been wrong before. I never felt important to you. I always felt like you were trying to care for everyone else. I always got what was left over, but I didn't get into this stuff because of you. It's complicated. I did this with Granddad."

Deyanira's stomach suddenly had a sharp pain, and fear and panic rushed through her body. Her eyes lit up golden and she jumped out of her chair and shouted, "We gota go, we gota get out of this room! Run!" She ran for the door, swung it open, and ran to the front of the house. Big Mama and Falah chased after Deyanira because they were worried something was wrong with her.

Just as they reached the kitchen, the back of the house was sprayed with bullets. Windows crashed, loud pops echoed from the alley behind the house, and someone in a brown Buick emptied their guns' clips. Falah grabbed Deyanira and Big Mama, tackling them to the kitchen floor and covering them with his colossal frame. When the noise stopped, everyone in the house except Falah, Deyanira, and Big Mama ran into the alley for retaliation. Falah's emotions heightened and Deyanira felt his shame and guilt.

Falah's emotions were a pot boiling over into hysteria. Big Mama, soon after the incident, started spiraling as well. Her energy was sticky with regret and shame. She spiraled deep into the thought of DCFS removing Deyanira and the girls because she had brought Deyanira there. Her breathing became labored as the panic gradually escalated. Deyanira stood tall and dusted herself off. "Both of y'all knock it off. You just released all that heavy baggage, so don't go making more. Now Miriam and Falah, y'all are working my nerves. The girls will be safe from DCFS. We love our kids no matter what their paths are in this family *and* what choices they make, y'all know that. Especially because their paths aren't always what society tells us they should be. Tell Falah what you came to tell him. Hug him, tell him you aren't disappointed in him and you love him and go on home. Miriam baby, I love you, but you always had a way of trying to be the best of what society saw as the best, but they did not build American society for us. I taught your boy that and he has made me proud, and maybe one day, you'll be able to see and know why. Falah, son, now is not the time to get too thick in it with your mama, so hug her and plan this trip down south as a time to think about your next moves."

Big Mama stood frozen with her mouth wide open, eyes locked on Deyanira. Big Mama couldn't speak. She squeezed out in a mousy tone, "Daddy?"

Deyanira winked at Big Mama and said, "Love y'all."

Then Deyanira's body collapsed onto the kitchen floor with a heavy thud. Her breathing was jagged with exhaustion as she slumped over on the floor. Falah scooped her little body into his arms like a baby doll. Once he felt her breathing, and her heartbeat he sighed with relief. Falah rocked the thirteen-year-old as if she was a baby in his arms. He made eye contact with his mother and asked, "Did you know?" Big Mama, still wide-eyed and trying to process what had just happened, could only shake her head. Falah tried to bring his mother back to reality as best he could. "Mama, what did you come to tell me about? What is Granddad talking about?"

Big Mama took her hands and brushed off her face, arms, and chest. She took a deep breath. "Ms. Henrietta is sick. Lottie said she isn't going to make it. It's time. We have to go down there, but we can't ride together, and you have to say we are cousins in front of the foster babies. I'm so sorry. Calling me cousin will make sure I can hold you and cry with you in front of the babies. I am so sorry. I know this arrangement hurts you so much. I am done taking in babies. These are my last ones, I promise. I want us to be a family again."

Falah took a deep breath and continued rocking Deyanira. "Mama, it's okay. I understand now. You were just trying to love yourself through these babies. I see that now. You have to tell Lottie about what just happened with her and Granddad, you know that, right?" His eyebrow was up, and he was nervous about what Big Mama may say. "I know you and Lottie don't get al–"

"Oh Jesus, I know," she interrupted with the biggest sigh. "I'll talk to her. You know I can't stand that woman."

Falah knew Big Mama disliked Aunt Lottie, but her reaction at the mention of Lottie's name always made him chuckle. He walked with Big Mama out to the van, still cradling Deyanira's body as if she were a twenty-pound toddler. "You want her in the backseat, Mama?"

Big Mama opened the passenger door and put the seat all the way back. "No, baby, put her here and then get back inside where it is safe. You know I love you, my sunshine." She reached up and placed her hand on his cheek. He smiled and received his mother's unconditional love.

Falah laid Deyanira down on the seat and then buckled her seatbelt. He was stalling to be in his mother's energy just a little longer, like a child asking for one more bedtime story. Falah turned around to step away from the van when Big Mama jumped into her giant son's arms and blew raspberries on his cheek in the silliest way. He toppled back towards the van and laughed. "You remember when you were in high school and I used to do this?"

He nodded and gave her one more silent squeeze before he released her and returned to the house.

Big Mama drove around for a bit. Then traveled down Lake Shore Drive to give Deyanira time to wake up. She didn't want to bring Deyanira home without discussing what had happened. Big Mama's mind wandered to her youth and Falah's laugh as a baby. She remembered how safe she felt with her father and how much she missed him.

After a while, Deyanira briefly cracked open her eyelids and realized she was in a moving van. Startled, she jumped up. The last thing she remembered was the gunshots.

Big Mama placed her right hand on Deyanira's shoulder. "It's okay, baby. You're safe. What do you remember last?"

Deyanira took a deep breath and explained she only remembered the gunshots, nothing else after that. Big Mama wanted to know how Deyanira knew her first name, and the question confused Deyanira. "I don't know your first name. Everyone calls you Big Mama, even your friends and the secretary at my school. Why?"

Big Mama filled in the missing pieces of the day for Deyanira. Immediately, Deyanira realized her gifts were back, stronger than ever, but her body was out of practice. It was the only explanation of everything that happened. How she knew they weren't safe in the backroom and how she knew how to help them feel better. It explained why she didn't know what happened after Big Mama's father entered her body, and why his spirit caused her to faint. She was out of practice.

She broke down and told Big Mama everything about her life with Doña Marina that she had left out. All her training and the *mesa blanca*. She told her how she locked her gifts away and must've unlocked them by accident recently. Deyanira was a ball of emotions. She was concerned she would or could hurt someone. Deyanira was worried Big Mama would be scared of her gifts and send her away. Big Mama reminded Deyanira that without her gifts, she would probably be shot and dead, which made Deyanira less scared and more hopeful. The thought of Big Mama's father taking over her body like that also terrified her. She sat quietly, yearning for Doña Marina. Deyanira didn't want random spirits taking over her body. She remembered Doña Marina telling her that without training, the spirits could cause her to go mad.

Big Mama was in a drive-thru getting happy meals for the girls and a burger for Deyanira. She told Deyanira not to worry. "My Aunt Lottie has gifts like you, and I'll ask her to help you when we get down there. We leave in the morning."

Chapter 11

Deyanira's attention was pulled out of her childhood timeline for a moment, and she thought Solanine had finally arrived at the crossroads. She wasn't sure why the fates pushed her to review her childhood. She had been time walking long enough to know that it was important to go with the flow when they placed her in. Her experience of time walking was usually more choppy across unique events throughout history and her lifetime. Rarely has she walked several consecutive events.

She turned out of the timeline and glanced behind her to see the door. "Argh!" she groaned. She entered the room behind the door; it revealed a large table. It was the table where her ancestors, guides, and deities that favored her sat to discuss her life's journey. Any spiritual bartering was done at these tables, especially for people with special gifts. Her ancestors bartered the coming of her birth and her child's birth as well. As the Oracle, she was called to this room occasionally for meetings and warnings.

Deyanira huffed and rolled her eyes, flopping down in the chair. "Yes, Abuela? Why am I here?" Abuela and Deyanira's council took their seats as Abuela passed Deyanira. She popped Deyanira with a scarf and winked. "Hush, we aren't bothering you, *cariña*."

Deyanira laughed. With arms folded, she stuck out her tongue at Abuela.

"You are always so silly, *mija*."

Discussions swirled around the room of different priorities and upcoming happenings. Deyanira rose from her seat and walked around the table, hugging ancestors and thanking deities. The room quieted down, and Abuela's eyebrows perked up as if she were listening in the distance to something. "*Mija*, no delays when the girl comes, okay? Grab her and get back. You can explain everything to her when you wake up."

Deyanira cut her eyes and questioned Abuela's peculiar advice. "You know I have to explain to her here, otherwise some of her spirit may fight to return with me, and she'll come back fractured and crazy."

Abuela shooed Deyanira out of the door and said, "If you have to leave her, that is okay. Pay attention to the signs *mija*, we have much to discuss here, so get back out there."

Deyanira was annoyed. "Why bring me here just to speak in mysterious riddles? I was out there and I was paying attention, and then you called me into this room just to kick me out. Is that all you wanted? The council has convened to discuss matters about me that I cannot be present for, but I was called to be present. When I am an ancestor, I will not speak in riddles, and I will actually say what needs to be said, so my descendants aren't confused and unsure."

Deyanira often fussed at her council of guides, but she always listened. As the door reappeared for her exit, she reflected on Abuela's advice of leaving Solanine, and couldn't make sense of it. Why go through all of this only for her ancestors to advise Deyanira to leave her? She shrugged and walked to the next event in time to review. "All will be revealed, I am sure."

Chapter 12

The bus down to Louisiana was full and smelled musty. Miriam was nervous and excited. She had never been away from her father before. On stormy nights she still crawled into his bed for safety. She worried her father would be mad at her for sneaking out of state so young. She just kept whispering, "A girl needs her mother."

Miriam tried to pace herself while she snacked. She knew the ride was long. She was a nervous eater, so her sandwich and apples were gone before they drove through Alabama. Luckily, the ride was almost over. Miriam tried to take a quick nap to pass the time. The elderly woman next to her nudged Miriam. "We're here, baby."

Miriam slowly woke up and thanked the elderly woman. On the ride down, the elderly woman asked Miriam why she was headed to New Orleans. Miriam, usually more reserved, told the woman her entire story. How she never met or spoke to her mother. How her father told her to stay away from her and focus on their new life in Chicago. She wanted to ask her mother why she gave her to her father. She wanted to ask her mother if she ever thought of her.

Miriam knew she was lucky. She knew she had an amazing father. He loved her very much. He always protected her and encouraged her. Charles was a heartbroken man, though. He never recovered from his wife's abandonment. The elderly woman nodded, silently taking it all in. When Miriam finished pouring out her deepest and darkest vulnerability, the elderly woman took her hand and squeezed it. "Baby, a girl needs her mother. You could have the best daddy in the world and you still want a mama. That's okay. Just remember, no mama sends their baby away because they don't love them. They usually send them away to protect them, even if it's to protect their baby from themselves. She may not be a good mama, remember that, but she was mama enough to protect you from herself."

Miriam tried to accept that her mother may not be loving and may turn her away, but she just couldn't believe her mother would do that. Miriam dreamed about this day since she was little— her mother opening the front door, overwhelmed with joy and emotions when she saw Miriam. She would open her arms and squeeze Miriam, weeping with joy and apologizing for not being able to raise her. Making up some excuse about being too sick to mother. Miriam convinced herself she wasn't romanticizing things, and it was just as likely of a storyline as one where her mother didn't want her. Her emotions got the best of her when the elderly woman tried to reason with her expectations. "So why are you going to New Orleans?" Miriam interrupted abruptly.

. "Oh well, I am going home to die." The elderly woman laughed at Miriam's facial expression. "I left for Chicago long ago and had a good life, but something about being buried with your kinfolk brings love and power to the land and your descendants. I am older now, and my kids are grown-ups who have given me beautiful grandbabies, but I feel in my bones my time is near, and I want it to happen at home in Louisiana. I have a niece I am going to stay with. She will bury me with our family when it is time."

Miriam felt so sad for the elderly woman, but the woman pulled at her chin. "Chin up. I had a good life, a beautiful life even, and no one escapes death. Knowing it's coming helps make it easier to cross over. Don't be sad for me, maybe a little sad for my kids, but not me." Miriam imagined that this was what it felt like to have a granny. On the trip down, she snuggled up to the elderly woman's shoulder, smelling her mints and perfumed scarf.

Miriam stepped off the bus and felt her stomach fall into her behind. What if she couldn't find the shop? What if she got lost? The elderly lady, like an angel, interrupted Miriam's internal spiral, "You know where you are going, baby?"

Miriam pulled out a tattered envelope sent to her father's house when she got her first period. Inside the envelope was a charm necklace and a note that said *make her wear this, signed Lottie.*

Charles had given Miriam the necklace and told her to wear it as much as possible. He said he'd gotten it from some native a while back on a road trip, but Miriam saw the envelope in the trash with the note. She fantasized about her mother, Lottie. If they looked alike, if she was funny, and if she liked the same foods. The elderly lady looked at the address and signaled for Miriam to come with her. They walked over to her niece's car and the elderly lady told her niece she'd give her gas money to drop Miriam off safely. Her niece saw the address and scuffed rolling her eyes, then waved for Miriam to get in. Miriam threw hers and the elderly woman's bag in the trunk, and climbed in. They pulled up to a dark small shop. Miriam gulped air. *There was no turning back now*, she thought.

There were all these trinkets and contraptions outside the shop's doorway. Miriam entered the shop's door, ringing the bells above the frame. "I am not doing any more love spells until after the full moon, so if that's why you came, you can leave," a voice bellowed from a doorway towards the back of the shop. Speechless, Miriam just stood in the middle of the shop, staring in the direction the voice came from. The beads in the doorway were parted by hands with red nail polish. "Girl, are you deaf?"

Miriam snapped out of it. "Are you Lottie Nolden?" The words came out of her mouth, broken into syllables and shaky.

Lottie's face dropped when she saw the charm necklace around the girl's neck. "What are you doing here? Did something happen to your daddy?"

Miriam's heart broke. No warm embrace or overwhelming love from this woman. "Why did you leave me with my father? Why don't you want to be my mother?"

Taken aback by the pain in Miriam's voice, she burst out laughing, "Whew *Cher*, you are definitely your mother's child, and that ain't me. Your mother is my sister, Henrietta. Have a seat and call your daddy, so he is not worried. Then we'll call your mama."

Chapter 13

"Dey-Dey baby, come on in here and meet my mama and auntie," Big Mama called out to Deyanira on the front porch.

Louisiana felt like Puerto Rico to Deyanira in so many ways that she asked to sit on the porch for a bit when they arrived. The heat, the smells, and the spiritual energy. This land felt alive. This was the closest she felt to her island life since she had left. The women in the house were all chatting and fussing over her little sisters. They barely noticed her on the porch.

The energy in the room felt exhausting to Deyanira, but the porch gave her the sun, heat, and peace. Being outside was like recharging a battery for her. The land of Louisiana was awake like the land in Puerto Rico. It whispered to her spirit with affection. Deyanira opened the blue wooden screen door and entered the living room full of women and her sisters. Directly across the living room from the front door was a hallway; there stood Big Mama, waving Deyanira in. As Deyanira entered the room, she felt a similar energy to Doña Marina's home after she passed away. There was life force energy scattered all over the room, but it was faint and still connected to the tiny-framed frail woman in the bed. Deyanira walked over to the bed immediately and cradled the sick woman's hand. A rush of emotions from the woman hit

Deyanira. In her mind, Deyanira saw the woman's life flip through, like moving pictures downloading into her knowing. As the emotional energy attached to these memories emerged, it entered Deyanira's heart space. To Big Mama, the exchange only lasted seconds of sweet Deyanira touching her mother's hand, but to Lottie sitting in the corner watching, the exchange was a lapsed time of witnessing an energetic exchange.

Lottie was a powerful psychic. She watched Deyanira enter and thumb through her sister's life experiences and emotions like a magazine in the checkout line. The level of power it took to connect in that way was huge. She didn't even think Deyanira understood what she was doing. After a few moments, Deyanira's left hand broke free from Ms. Henrietta's hand, and she rubbed Ms. Henrietta's cheek gently.

Deyanira's eyes filled with tears and she leaned over towards Ms. Henrietta. "You have to tell her. Before it is too late. Tell her."

Ms. Henrietta waved Big Mama over to her bedside. She told Deyanira to have a seat. Lottie could not believe this child navigated walking through time and still was grounded in the present without fainting. Ms. Henrietta squeezed Big Mama's hand and spoke her truth as Deyanira saw it.

Ms. Henrietta was a woman far past her prime when she met Charles. There were rumors going around that she couldn't have children. Others whispered she was married to Papa Legba himself and couldn't marry a mortal man. However, most people settled into the idea she was one of those women that liked women. She wore pants when she wanted, smoked cigars, and often carried a switchblade and brass knuckles. She was a tiny brown-skinned woman, short in stature, no taller than five feet tall. People from out of town often underestimated her. She confused people with her ways— a woman so small, not afraid to fight men twice her size, no matter their race. Ms. Henrietta was a midwife, herbalist, and Voodoo practitioner.

In bed, Ms. Henrietta said, "Voodoo is in our blood, you see. Our great great great granny was Marie Laveau's first daughter. The Voodoo queen herself. Nobody talks about us because Marie gave her daughter to the father. Marie fell in love with our great great great granddaddy. He was a beautiful young man. Skin dark as night. Looked like God himself pulled down a piece of the night sky and made a man out of it. My granny used to tell me all about how her mama said he had a smile that could stop time. Died with all his teeth, too. He was a young carpenter on Marie's daddy's plantation, and they met often under the full moon. He told stories of how in love they were until the day he passed on. She was only fifteen when she got pregnant. She hid it from anyone and everyone she could, but especially her white daddy. By the time she came down to the midwife for the slaves, our great granny's head was hanging out between her legs. Marie was a child and too exhausted to push, so the midwife had to pull the baby out of her. A sea of blood rushed out of Marie's young body. Marie died on the floor that night. Our great-granny came out, covered in rolls like an older baby already getting milk and food. She had a head full of curls already, too. Baby came out ready to take on the world. It was tragic, though the midwife couldn't stop the blood that flowed out of Marie, touching the four corners of that place. Granddaddy cried and cradled Marie's body, rocking her back and forth; he was covered in her blood from shoulders to toes. Then, just when he kissed her forehead and laid her down, she gasped for air. Large breaths, like she was trying to suck all the air out of the room for herself.

Her eyes lit up golden when she opened them, according to the midwife and granddaddy."

Ms Henrietta paused to wet her lips with ice. "The midwife kicked Granddaddy out. Told him she needed to tend to Marie. Handed him the baby and said scat! Marie stopped him only for a minute. Her weak tone beckoned him to bring the baby near her, so she could get a look at her child. Marie reached down with two fingers into that disaster between her legs. Brought those blood-covered fingers up and wrote on the baby's chest something Granddaddy didn't understand. She said, "Her name is Miriam; you hear me?"

Granddaddy nodded and left. Granddaddy didn't know exactly what she said in that room that night. However, when he came back, Marie was gone, and the old woman was cleaning up the blood. She told him that the African Lwa had brought Marie back from the dead. She had a job to do, and she couldn't have their daughter around to do it. The midwife told him not to worry, that Miriam was blessed and protected. The baby's sacrifice of a life without a mother would not go unfavored. Nonetheless, Granddaddy was gona have to raise her. The midwife told him she'd find someone to nurse and care for Miriam, but she was all his now."

Ms. Henrietta paused only for a second, holding back tears. "That next morning, a young white man came looking for a carpenter. His carpenter got sick and died on him. He offered a large amount for our granddad because he was young. Our granddad started crying when they came to pick him up. He told the man about our granny, baby Miriam, and how she was gona die without him because she was all alone. He told the white man that Miriam's mama died in childbirth. The white man told him to bring Miriam because he was a talented carpenter and Miriam could be his child's playmate. The white man had lost his wife in childbirth recently as well. Granddaddy and the white man became friends. As close of a friend as you could be with a white man. When the man passed, he gave Granddad and Miriam their freedom *and* a piece of land. Nobody in the family understood why Marie did what she did until Lottie was born. Lottie has the gift of sight–"

"It ain't a gift. It is a curse, and it's shitty," Big Mama said. "Makes her think she can say mean things and call it the truth. Do whatever she wants and blame it on her gift."

Ms. Henrietta placed her other hand on top of Big Mama's hand to quiet her down. "Pass me that water, baby," she said.

Deyanira saw how tired Ms. Henrietta was, and exhaustion concerned her that she might not finish. "Ms. Henrietta, tell her the rest, please," Deyanira urged.

"Yes, baby, you're right. Did your daddy ever tell you how we met?" Big Mama shook her head. Charles was a proud and strong man. He never remarried or brought women home. He never spoke about his past with Ms. Henrietta, except occasionally saying, "We had to come to Chicago, and she couldn't. Leave it at that."

After a sip of water, Ms. Henrietta continued. "Well, you know I was a midwife and healer. Your daddy, Charles, was from a small town in Texas just over the border. Their town's midwife had passed on. You know, any smart black person doesn't trust a white doctor with their baby. His sister was having a baby and someone told her about me. She sent Charles to get me. Your daddy was a gentle giant. I never saw a man seven feet tall before and as wide as he was long but quiet as a church mouse. He didn't find his voice until after I broke his heart." Ms. Henrietta startled herself, confessing out loud that she had broken his heart.

"Charles came into the local bar searching for me. I told him I'd finish my drink and would head out. The man I was talking to had a problem with me cutting loose early, and he grabbed my arm to tell me where I could and could not go. Your daddy told the man to take his hand off me, but I already took my cigar out of my mouth and was burning the top of the man's hand with it. He jumped back to hit me, and I knocked his front tooth out with my brass knuckles. He fell flat on his back and screamed like a bitch. I threw my foot on his chest and leaned all my weight onto it. I bent down real close and held my blade to his neck. I told him that I decide what I do, when I do it, and who I do it with, and if he comes looking for me, this mountain of a man was gona kill him. Your daddy and I walked out, and he was silent. I thought, oh lord I scared him. He told me later that was the moment he fell in love with me." Ms. Henrietta laughed at the notion of violence opening the road to love.

"I packed everything I needed to go with your dad and gave Lottie instructions for my clients. When we arrived at his family's land, it was a small farm with houses for everyone in the family. They were sharecroppers. His daddy, him, and his brother-in-law. There was also a cousin living on the land to help, but he isn't important. Your daddy told me that since he was the only one without a family, he would move into his parents' house and give me his place. I was still not in love with him at that point. I was forty and after all those years without love; it took a minute to warm back up. I checked on your aunt and she was about ripe. Smart woman to send for me when she did, otherwise I would've been too late.

"After a few days, the baby came. There were some complications, and she lost some blood. So I stayed to make sure she didn't catch any infections and healed properly. Her milk didn't come in right away either, so I had to fix her some tea to make the milk come down. I was missing an herb and asked your daddy to take me to the field so I could find it. We talked and laughed, then stopped for some barbecue. That's the day I fell in love with your daddy. He was patient and loving. After a while, the milk was flowing and your aunt's body was healed, but I stayed. I was in a trance. I won't tell you too much, just know after forty years, ain't much you haven't done, but your daddy proved that wrong and taught me a thing or two."

Lottie let out a chuckle to break the discomfort Big Mama was feeling. "One day I woke up, and my tits were swollen and hurt. I was forty years old. There was no way there was a baby in me, but there you were growing right in my belly after all those years. I thought your granny was gonna die. You see, your daddy's family was heavy into the church. So many rules. No cussing, no drinking, lots of praying, and definitely no sex before marriage, even if you are forty. The family made up for the rules, though. Sunday dinners were amazing. Hell, all the family dinners were. Tables full of home-cooked pies and food and stories, oh the stories. All these stories about their daddy chasing them around tables when they were bad. Their mama prayed over them so much to behave, they'd fall asleep while she prayed. We didn't have that in our family. The only rules we had were Voodoo rules, books, and running wild. Learning the spirits, workings, and rituals. Learning herbs and how to protect yourself and others from evil. Other than that, we could cuss, smoke, shit we did what we wanted. The only dinner we came together for was Christmas. Our mama always had clients and no time for family dinners. She said we were 'free women.' It was how she wanted us to live. She didn't teach us to cook, and she kept us in the company of the city's undesirables."

Deyanira felt the energy of the room divide. Lottie's corner was filled with grief. She caught Lottie wiping her eye. When Lottie realized Deyanira felt her, she whispered, "You stay out of my fucking head and feelings, little girl."

"Your daddy's mama made us get married right away. I wrote Lottie a letter. I know I should've called her, but they didn't have a phone on the farm, and I was in a trance, remember? I was in love with this quiet, simple life they offered. It was so quiet on their farm that I practically bathed in it. Like a quiet energy, not just sound. I gave birth to you, and everything went smoothly. Your daddy was so mad I insisted on caring for myself, but also, he didn't work too hard to find me a midwife, so I think he knew we'd be okay. I named you Miriam after Marie's baby. Do you know what that name means? Did your daddy ever tell you?"

Big Mama's eyebrows peeked with curiosity and she replied, "No Ma'am."

"Well it means, wished for child. The child of prayers answered, basically. That was you for me. I never knew I wanted to be a mama until I met and fell in love with you. I also thought I could heal the bloodline's mother wound by giving you her name and loving you more than air; I guess I might've cursed you in that way."

Big Mama was crying but squeezed her mother's hand with love. "It wasn't a curse. It is beautiful; thank you for telling me."

"Your dad's mama came, sat next to me on the bed, and told me I had some making up to do. I didn't understand what was happening. She reminded me I got pregnant before getting married and made her family look bad. Then I had the nerve to give him a daughter first. Just another mouth to feed on the farm that already had enough mouths. The least I could do was name the baby after her. I didn't know what to do or say. After some time, I told her your middle name could be Ida. She knocked my plate of food on the floor, mad, but then ran out and said I gave the baby her name. We're gona call her Little Ida. I think that was the first time I felt lonely on that farm. It was as if the trance wore off a little when I fell in love with you. I stuffed that lonely feeling down though because I was in love. I was in love with you and your daddy. You were my miracle. My Miriam.

"Your daddy loved to read. Unusual for a Texas farmman and unusual for his family. The only thing they read was the bible, and poorly at that. He read to you and me every night. You took turns sleeping on our chests. Your daddy would lay awake all night watching you sleep, scared to fall asleep and crush you. Your granny came over more and more, chastising me. I wasn't who she wanted your daddy to marry, and when he wasn't around she made sure I knew it.

"Then one day Lottie showed up with her bright red lipstick, cigarette in her mouth, top down, and the radio blaring Little Richard. Typical Lottie entrance, she stopped the car fast and kicked up a cloud of dust in their drive. I was consumed with loneliness and the strife of being left with your granny picking on me while your daddy was away at work. His sister avoided me because she wanted to keep her mother pleased, and she was also mad that I had a daughter. They needed boys on the farm, and at my age, it was unlikely we would have more kids. I was out of my element. I wasn't raised that way. I was raised around powerful women and men who worshiped women. Well, that loneliness must have sent out a beacon to

Lottie's ol' psychic ass. She came running, ready to fight. I was nervous, angry, and embarrassed. Your granny came out to greet her. I could see them from our house. Lottie saw me though, and I could tell she ignored his mama. I was so upset by the time Lottie got to me. I started cussing her out for coming there and embarrassing me, instead of hugging her and telling her I missed her. I had become a shell of the woman I was. It scared me that Lottie's actions were going to make my life with his mama harder. You know there is nineteen years between us? Lottie and I. Lottie slapped the shit out of me. Slapped me so hard I couldn't see straight. I was stunned. She asked me, what the fuck did I think I was doing there with you. She reminded me that I had altars and offerings overdue to the spirits. These were debts owed. She avoided you. Wouldn't look at you. Told me to leave you there for a few days with cow's milk and come tend to the altars— if I wasn't going to build them at my new house. I refused. Then she said, fine, bring the baby, but you have to leave and come back with me now. I had a vision."

Big Mama interrupted Ms. Henrietta. "I knew it. I knew you were the reason I didn't have a family and a mama. You're just selfish! You just missed your sister. You saw her happy with my daddy, and your lonely ass lied talking about you had a vision."

Deyanira knew this had to unfold the way it did, but even she gasped at the words because they were so far from the truth.

Lottie stood up from her seat and pointed her finger right in Big Mama's face. "Now you look here, you spoiled brat. You do not know what I gave up so you could keep breathing air. I don't lie, and I don't make shit up. Am I harsh with you? You're damn right. Because the truth is, your daddy's bloodline killed ours. You. You living, staying alive, killed us.

Do you want to know the vision? Let me give it to you so you understand. Your daddy's family bloodline was dead. Meant to die off. When a bloodline disconnects from their emotions to chase hard work and the white Jesus master taught them about, they cut themselves off from elevating. Elevating is like what you think heaven is. They get stuck here as a spirit wandering the earth in the dark, as a ghost. That was his family's destiny, but your mama fell in love with their quiet. Do you know what that quiet was? Dense energy. They were all simpletons except for your daddy. They sucked the life out of anything around them. Truth be told your daddy was carrying all of them on his back.

"Their crops were failing because there was no more life in that line. Your mama worked with herbs and energy, so for the first time ever, she didn't feel any energy, and it was like a vacation. She didn't stop and think about why it felt so damn quiet. People were coming. Coming to take the land by force. White folks were jealous of the town and land the black folks had. They were going to burn the whole town and take the land. Everyone was meant to die. I was told I could save your mama, and that was it. If I tried to save you or anyone else, our bloodline would die. I told your mama what they said and told her to bring you back with us, but she loved your damn daddy. So she told him she needed him to trust her and take the baby to Chicago. She would follow him once she closed up the shop. She sent you and your daddy away and that night, I miscarried my baby. I was barren after that. No more babies, just death. Over and repeatedly, until I sent my husband away, so he'd stop trying. I gave up my baby for you to live, but I gave up all my babies so your daddy could live. Your mama never joined y'all because she knew that when your daddy found out his whole family was dead and she didn't help them, he'd never be able to look at her with love again. She has been carrying the guilt of not saving his family full of dummies. So you see, our bloodline dies off. Your son won't have any biological babies. He's never laid with a woman to my knowledge. You can't have any more babies, and we are old and shriveled up. So you show me some respect. I didn't take your mama away from you. Your daddy took my babies from me, and I got your mama as the booby prize.

"I love my sister, but I'd rather you have her, and I have my babies. So you think me telling you your son was going to be a successful criminal was mean and hard for you to deal with? I had to tell your mama that it would be better for the bloodline if her man and child died. Oh, and all these new people she fell in love with and called family? They're gona die tonight, and you have to let them. Yes, even that baby she delivered that brought her there. So fuck off, you big crybaby. There are worse things than hearing your son will be a criminal. I need some air. I only ever tried to do right by you, girl, and you are dead set on making me your villain. You got one thing right though, it isn't a damn gift; it is a fucking curse to have to tell your sister that everyone she loves has to die or our bloodline dies." Lottie stormed out of the room and straight to the porch.

Deyanira said, 'I'll go check on the girls and Lottie. Big Mama don't worry, stay and talk to your mom."

Chapter 14

After getting her sisters plates of food and sweet tea, Deyanira headed for the porch. Lottie was nowhere in sight. Deyanira wandered off the porch and down the drive. She reached the end of the drive and noticed a path across the small country road, in the thick of the bushes and trees. Deyanira followed the path to see where it went.

After a while, the path opened to a clearing and pond. Deyanira couldn't decide if it was a lake or a pond. She walked closer to the pond until she heard Lottie open her metal lighter. "You have to be careful down here, little girl. This isn't Chicago and it isn't 2002 down here."

Deyanira looked at Lottie, confused, but too scared to ask for clarity. Lottie laughed to herself and took a drag of her cigarette. "In Chicago, that's just a pond and you can walk near it. Here, about fifteen gators and God knows how many snakes live in that water. If you get too close, you're dead. It may be 2002 in Chicago and you can walk around freely, but down here, you aren't light-skinned enough to be white, and you are brown enough to not matter if you come up missing. So down here, you stay on the porch and if you see white people, you go back in the house. You understand?"

Deyanira nodded. "You know, I can't walk around in Chicago

either."

"This isn't a pissing contest of who got it worse, little girl. Stop that shit, never fall into it. It's a trap. Besides, you are safer than you think; my nephew makes sure of that. Now, how do you do that?"

Deyanira, again confused but even more scared to say the wrong thing, just stared at Lottie. "Oh, girl, there is nothing to be scared of. No one knows everything. There is no shame in learning. Shame isn't even real. Now, how did you thumb through my sister's life like a magazine in a doctor's waiting room so fast, and not faint? That takes a lot of energy. I could touch you and find out, but I assume that works both ways, and I don't need you thumbing through my life."

Deyanira understood now what Lottie was asking. She just wasn't sure she could give an answer. "I don't know, really. It is hard to explain. Memories, emotions, energy, spirits, and sometimes danger... it is like if we were in a boat, and as we go down the river, I run my hand off the side of the boat. My fingertips are just barely touching the water. Barely making a ripple, but if you were to ask me how the water feels, I could tell you."

"Wow, you really have no idea what you're doing, but you do it all at the same time. You aren't telling people how the water feels when they ask, honey, you are giving them an itemized list of every animal living in that river, the current, the temperature— basically since it was created."

"It scares me. I locked it up once in my head. Locked it away, and I was normal for a while."

Lottie tossed down her cigarette bud and grabbed Deyanira by the cheeks, cupping her chin in her hand. "Now you listen to me and you listen good. Don't you ever do that again, you hear me? People like us locking it away to be normal only go crazy, and *big* crazy. You can't come back from that. You are locking up all that energy in your body, but your body can't hold it. Promise me you'll never do that again." Deyanira's cheeks hurt, but she saw Lottie's care for her, and it felt safe. Then she felt it, Lottie's energy, and they connected.

Lottie saw just a small portion of Deyanira and pushed her away. "I am sorry that man died. By the time you're an adult, you will understand though. It won't make anything easier, but you'll understand. Also, the fact that you fear having that power is exactly why you have it. People who want to murder people with their minds probably shouldn't be able to, don't you think, kid?" She gave Deyanira a booty bump and a smile. "Let's head back in before they notice we're gone. Don't tell them I was smoking. Everyone wants me to quit, but Marie gifted me and my sister a death at eighty-six like her. I don't know if it's a gift or curse, but that's how I feel about most things from spirits."

Aunt Lottie was funny, but her energy was heavy. Deyanira couldn't help but stare and admire how beautiful she was. "What are you looking at, little girl?"

"You're so beautiful," Deyanira said.

Taken aback, Aunt Lottie blushed. "Well thank you *Cheri*."

Walking back up the drive, they saw Big Mama on the porch fanning herself and squinting to see them through the bright sunlight. Deyanira hopped onto the first step of the porch as Lottie grabbed the railing to help lift her elder knees. "Leave us for a minute, baby. I need to talk to Aunt Lottie."

Deyanira entered the room where Ms. Henrietta lay. Her breath was more labored than before. Deyanira walked towards her and held her hand. A tear ran down Ms. Henrietta's face.

"You didn't kill his family and you couldn't save them. Ms. Henrietta, you can grieve their loss, but it isn't your fault. You can't carry that guilt over to the other side; it'll weigh you down."

Ms Henrietta interrupted. "You don't understand, I was happy there. We were a family. They loved me, and I let them die."

"Ms. Henrietta, you know I have gifts like Auntie Lottie, right?" Ms. Henrietta shook her head slightly. Her body was giving out. "Okay well, mine are a little different. I can see your memories, but not the rewritten version you tell yourself to feel like it was a great time." In a low and raspy voice, Ms. Henrietta said she didn't understand. Deyanira took a deep breath in preparation of the hard truth to be spoken. "Ms. Henrietta, you tell yourself you were happy there, but you weren't. You were happy with Charles and loved him, but you weren't happy there. You were numb. They didn't love you. They loved him. And they didn't love him in the way you loved him. They love through obligation. Love is free, and they couldn't ever live free. His mother was a tortured soul. She lived to torture those who loved her. She tortured you. Your love for him freed him from torturous love. He found his voice and power because you helped him escape. Trust me, if the spirits wanted him and Big Mama dead, they would've died another way. You cannot stop fate with your freedom of choice, only delay it; Doña Marina taught me that. Speak your truth. You were on a farm full of people, and you were lonely. You can love him and know it was unhealthy for you to stay. Both can be true. You can be sad his family died and know it wasn't your fault that you couldn't stop it. The love you gave him was the catalyst for him to do great things, in the name of love, in Chicago." Deyanira startled herself and shook her head as if to shake the knowledge off. "Sorry, I don't know what that was. I don't even know what catalyst means."

Chapter 15

While Deyanira was in line at the coffee shop mindlessly scrolling through her social media as a therapeutic disassociation, she suddenly felt intense energy. It was overwhelming, bubbling over, but not erupting. In her mind, she saw a pot of water on a stove bubbling and boiling. The top of the pot kept the boiling water contained, but the boiling water was severely damaging the pot. She searched the line of people for the distressed person whose energy she felt. Nothing.

Then, she saw a young man sitting in a chair scrolling on his phone. He was tall, over 6 feet tall. She could tell his height, even in a sitting position. His long legs were raised to his chest like a bird perching. His physique was lanky. His hair was lined by a barber with curls, freely laying atop his head. He reminded Deyanira of the island boys. There was a fleeting thought that her daughter would have resembled him if she was born a boy, and that made her smile. He had a light mustache. The type of mustache young men had before the hair came in fully. It made him ambiguous in age.

He occasionally broke from scrolling on his phone to take another bite out of the sandwich on his table. His eyes were laser-focused on the phone as if his life depended on not breaking his focus. The cashier drew back Deyanira's attention, asking if she wanted her usual order. Deyanira nodded and longed for the day when the coffee shop cashier in the hospital wouldn't recognize or know her order. Deyanira paid and moved to the pick-up side of the counter.

Deyanira preferred coffee from this coffee shop over the cafeteria because the energies in the cafeteria were just from exhausted parents of sick kids. The coffee shop's energies were expectant moms or elderly patients for their check-ups and, if she was lucky, the gorgeous male nurses on break or shift change.

After receiving her coffee, Deyanira felt the pull. It annoyed her. She was barely holding herself together and on the verge of a breakdown. Her daughter's heart condition had thrown Deyanira into over a hundred hospital stays and four heart surgeries. This *last* surgery was the most complicated, and she was trying to push crippling distress out of her mind and ignore it for just ten minutes of coffee time.

The urge got stronger and it was pushing her to check on the young man. She took a deep breath and doubled back to the young man in his chair. She sat in the chair next to him. It was an uncomfortable oversized lounge chair. It almost swallowed her five-foot-tall frame up. She fell backward with an "oof," frantically trying not to spill her pleasure in a cup.

Deyanira quietly waved a hand with a pleasant smile, trying to get his attention, but her efforts were ignored. He pretended not to hear her. She knew he did though, because she could feel his energy spike when she spoke. She said in a gentle, yet firm voice, "I am a psychic. I can help you."

He froze. His thumbs no longer scrolled on his phone. Still, he didn't provide any eye contact or verbal acknowledgment. She said, "You're an empath. A powerful one. I don't know that I have ever felt one so tuned in, especially so young. You avoid people. You can feel everything they feel. It has to be overwhelming, even if they are happy, but people are rarely happy. It must be so intense for you. Their emotions, coupled with the everyday sounds of people in the city. It has to be exhausting for you." He looked up, his eyes glassy with tears.

Deyanira said, "You don't have to say anything. Let me give you my phone number, and when you are ready, you can text me. People think empaths are sponges for energy and emotions. Many spiritual people teach them to block absorption, but empaths, when trained properly, are filters, not sponges. You are meant to filter dense energy to keep the energetic field of the world balanced. I can teach you how to let it flow through you like an energetic river."

She then held out her hand, signaling for him to hand her his phone. Deyanira could feel that he was too overwhelmed to put the number in himself. He handed her the phone, and she added her first name, Psychic as her last name, and showed it to him. "This is me. Just text when you are ready."

He took his phone from her, and she took a deep breath as she stood up. She closed her eyes and touched his shoulder. Deyanira pulled some of the energy out of him. He sat up straight, as if a building was lifted off his back for the first time in his life. She said nothing. When she was done, she just released his shoulder and started walking towards the elevator. Mid-stride, she paused and turned around, "Hey when you get home, take a hot shower and rub salt on your shoulders, back of neck, chest, feet, and carefully on your forehead. It'll help release the energies you absorbed from the hospital." For the first time in the interaction, he made eye contact and nodded slightly, thanking her. She walked back towards the elevators, ready for the cuddles of her broken toddler and updates from the doctors making rounds.

Deyanira's deepest and most sound sleep occurred on nights Calida was in the hospital. Friends and family were always confused when Deyanira would say that. They would bark back, but she's sick, or her surgery had her little body in ruin. How could you possibly sleep? They would ask. Deyanira felt like she could finally *and* truly rest on these nights because there was a team. A team of people kept Calida alive. They had machines to monitor everything. She didn't have to check her breathing, oxygen levels, or heart rate in the middle of the night. In those moments, Deyanira gave herself permission to care for herself. She allowed herself to rest and to give her spirit, mind, and body what it craved. While sleeping, Deyanira dreamed.

In her dream, she was on the island sometimes. It was hard to capture the essence of the island in her dreams anymore. Her childhood memories had faded. Her spirit ached for the sound of the Tanama River, the smell of the flowers, and the songs of the coqui frogs. Where she walked barefoot, feeling the grass beneath her feet down an unrecognized path, yet familiar. Lottie taught her at the age of fifteen how to meet her abuela's spirit there for guidance and support, but the scenery was always misty and faded. She couldn't conjure forgotten lands from nothing.

Chapter 16

As Deyanira's head hit the pillow in Calida's hospital room, she drifted quickly into a deep sleep, fostering an immediate dream-like state. A dark haze was in front of Deyanira. Something was materializing before her eyes. It was Doña Marina's house, with herbs and flowers growing in coffee cans around the porch. She ran her hand along the wall and it gave the sense of comfort and peace she needed. She approached the battered screen door and slowly gave it a tug. The sound of the door opening made her chuckle. The moan of the metal door begged for rest and she could relate.

Deyanira entered the small front room of faded familiar memories, and everything wove together when she smelled the *arroz con gandules*. She remembered Doña Marina teaching her to cook it with the pork fat and fresh herbs from the porch. She walked through the dim front room into the brightly lit kitchen to see Doña Marina. It had been so long since she saw her face and felt her energy. Deyanira walked toward her and in disbelief, traced Doña Marina's face with her fingers, starting at her temple and down her cheek.

Doña Marina always made Deyanira feel safe. When she was young, she didn't realize how much Doña Marina's energy was like a warm, fuzzy spiritual blanket she could wrap herself in.

Deyanira sat on the floor, laying her arm on the 1950s metal chair's tattered green cushion. Doña Marina pulled another chair and sat next to Deyanira. Her head made its way to Doña Marina's lap, and she wept. Deyanira wasn't sure what was happening. There wasn't one event or thing attached to these emotions. It was a flood of tears carrying emotions from everywhere stored in her body. "I'm just so tired. I'm so sorry."

Doña Marina placed her hand on Deyanira's head, gently stroking her hair. Deyanira grabbed Doña Marina's waist, her head still in her lap and let out a wail. The wail came from the depths of her being. All her fears, pains, obligations, transgressions, and exhaustion rode that wail like a surfer on the most gnarly wave.

Doña Marina held Deyanira in silence as she wept. Her embrace was firm and secure. The message was obvious that Deyanira was safe to break. She had felt so alone since Big Mama passed away and Lottie's disappearance. She was thrust back into caring for her sisters and using her gifts to care for others, then immediately caring for Calida. During her pregnancy with Calida, she was alone. Her first ultrasound revealed the baby's heart condition. While other moms got asked if their baby was a boy or girl, Deyanira had to sit down with the head of pediatric cardiology to discuss her options on how she wanted to proceed. All the doctor visits, so many doctor visits. Never with someone to hold her hand, tell her it was going to be okay or acknowledge how scary it was for her. No one to remind her that she needed to rest or eat. She didn't know how to tell herself. Deyanira's maternal experience warped how she viewed motherhood. Full self-sacrifice was her life vow to her tiny human. This vow could've been exhausting in a normal circumstance, but a baby with a rare heart condition broke her. It was funny how ancestors forced people to break generational curses or go mad avoiding those curses.

Doña Marina held Deyanira for as long as Deyanira's spirit needed. As Deyanira felt lighter, she lifted her head and told Doña Marina how much she missed her. She tried to apologize for being so cruel as a child, but Doña Marina stopped her. She held Deyanira's face in her hands. "Oh *mija*, I have always been with you. I am here on your team of guides. When I died, they pulled me to you. Now, if we could work on getting you to listen to us when you feel us guiding you, that would be great." Doña Marina booped Deyanira's nose gently. "If you listen to your body more, you wouldn't feel so tired and stuck. *Mija*, life is like the ocean waves. We have to move with the tides, otherwise we can get buried and stuck in the sand or drown. Do you remember when you were a child and you went to the beach? Remember when the waves came in? If you stood in one place, letting the waves just come in around you after a minute or so, your feet were buried, right? You have to feel the waves, not just let them happen to you. Feelings help guide you. Where to move and how to move. There should be no guilt in caring for yourself also. You are detaching from your feelings so you can be of service to Calida. Feel, so you can grow and protect yourself. By feeling, you can sense what dangers are near and protect Calida as well. Do you understand you are important?"

Deyanira wiped her eyes. "You said I would birth the strongest being the world would ever come to know. She'd save us all."

Doña Marina was grateful she could correct her earthly mishap. "Oracle, oh *mi amor*, she is important because you are important. Do you not see? You are the Oracle, not an oracle. You are going to change the world. I am so sorry that as a young medium I didn't get that message right. You will eventually wage a spiritual war, and Calida will inherit that from you. You matter. You are the foundation of everything and unfortunately, as you get older and come into your gifts, it will feel like a burden sometimes. Calida is only here because of you. You are the most powerful spiritual being the world has ever seen. You are birthing yourself free of the limitations this world puts on you. You will right centuries of wrongs in your lifetime."

A spiritual road opened for Deyanira. Energetically, she felt lighter and more powerful. Her eyes lit up golden. Doña Marina rejoiced by clapping her hands, "Oh, there it is! You're ready for the next chapter of your journey. This is about you. You figuring out how to love and live. You can love Calida, but not to where you stop living. Come now, stand up. It is time for you to meet your ancestors and guides."

A door appeared that didn't belong in Doña Marina's house. Deyanira looked confused and asked, "What's that? When did that get here?"

Doña Marina opened the door leading down to what resembled a dimly lit basement. "For this part of your journey, we must go deeper into your mind where your spirit connects to the mind. Never go into basements with any spirit or deity you don't know and trust. Tricksters can take you down and try to lock you in, and you'll never wake up."

They walked down the stairs and were greeted by a heavy-set Puerto Rican woman. She wore a cream-colored headscarf fastened to her head. Her curls peeked from under her headscarf, tight and damp with sweat. The woman touched Deyanira's face and shifted it like putty in her hands, while she inspected her face closely.

Deyanira felt the woman's breath on her neck while the woman examined her. At one point, she was worried the woman was going to sniff her for body odor. The spiritual realm felt very real to her. She forgot her body was in the hospital and hadn't bathed in three days. The woman then loudly proclaimed, "It is you! Come, we have so much to prepare." The woman grabbed Deyanira's hand, pulling her away.

She saw Doña Marina fading into the dark room to the left, and the woman pulled her to the right. The basement was humid, and there were so many people there. All of them did different things. There was a man with a large *pilón*. He was sweating and grinding different herbs and flowers. There was another man with a large pot that resembled an iron *caldero*. The water was murky with herbs, and the *caldero* bubbled as he stirred it with a large paddle. She pulled Deyanira down the hall where the women were.

Before they arrived at the room, Deyanira could hear the women laughing and talking. In the hall, right before the room, a clock appeared. It looked like a broken grandfather clock. The arms of the clock were spinning slowly in different directions. It alarmed Deyanira, and she stopped in her tracks to watch it. The woman placed her arm around Deyanira's shoulder and whispered, "You are not confined by time. You are here, there, and everywhere all at once. As the Oracle, you get to see it and feel everything. You are also a time walker. Think back to times you dreamt about watching people you didn't know, doing something. You were walking through time. Time walking was revealing things you need to know. It will happen more often now. Especially after this bath."

And with that, the woman gave Deyanira a yank in the arm, and they were in the room full of women. Deyanira's presence silenced the room for seven whole seconds. A few audible gasps even were heard as she entered. Then the room erupted with excitement and once again, Deyanira was whisked away by the women. They pulled her into the back of the room where there was a simple white nightgown laid out. The women were all different complexions and dressed differently. Some were Native with face paint, others Latin, some were West African in beautiful bright colors dress wraps, and some seemed to be North African with head wraps, dressed with what looked like coins and beads strung together.

Another heavy-set joyous woman waved at Deyanira and explained, "*Oko mi*, now we dress you for your spiritual bath. When in the bath, we will wash you. The bath will open you up, protect you, and wash away the things that do not belong. Then we will anoint you with oils for this next part of your journey. Your gifts will grow, and you will be more powerful than ever, so you have to listen to your guides, okay?" Deyanira nodded but felt anxious about her gifts increasing.

She already was uncomfortable with what she could do, feel, and see. Her anxiety subsided as each woman came by to hug her. Each hug felt as if they took a piece of the heaviness,. She felt so loved in their embrace. She started crying again, overwhelmed by her potent emotions. Her inner child cried out for the love she had never received and finally was receiving. The women already knew the aches in her heart. They whispered things like, "We have always been with you, and we are always here to hold you whenever you need us." And, "Give it all to us. We can carry it for you."

She cried because she felt safe. She cried out with joy because she was so happy and felt loved and supported. Once the women had all hugged her, they started to dance and sing with joy. Some of them had small instruments, others sat in front of *barriles* drumming away. The room was filled with celebration. Deyanira spun around, losing herself in the rhythm and music. Her body, drenched with sweat and breath, was labored; she fell back on a chair, laughing. The room of women settled and returned to preparations.

Deyanira dressed in the nightgown; one of the men from the room with the *pilón* came to the door and said the bath was ready. All the women led her to another room, each holding an unlit candle, and fawning over her like a newborn brought home from the hospital. The women entered the room before Deyanira. Each woman, as they entered, spoke over their candle, carved what they spoke into the candle, and lit it. They wrote things like *protection* and *strength* and *love* and *abundance* and *trust*. Once the women filled up the room around the large basin, they ushered her into the bath.

Deyanira stepped into the steaming water, murky with herbs, oils, and flowers. The temperature was perfect for her. She wanted to dip her head, but wasn't sure if that was allowed. Just then, the first woman came and tilted her head back and began washing her hair with something that looked like homemade soap in texture and shape, but was dark as licorice. The other women gathered around and began washing her body, as a mother would wash an infant in their first bath. That was the moment she realized all these women were her ancestors, her lineage. She felt a little foolish for not connecting Doña Marina's mention of ancestors sooner to these women. Her body completely relaxed, and she laid back and enjoyed being cared for. She closed her eyes for a bit, and when she peeked them open, she saw the women winking and nudging each other happily because Deyanira was relaxed. Once they were done bathing her, they brought her out to a shower room. They wiped her down while they showered off her body. She felt new energy surging and tingling through her body. The women sweetly patted her dry, then sat Deyanira down on a bench and anointed her body with oils and butters.

They dressed Deyanira in a beautiful yellow dress that reminded her of the bomba dancers in Louiza, and they wrapped her hair in a yellow hair wrap. The women all clapped in celebration as Deyanira twirled around in her dress. They opened the door and told her she was ready. Deyanira walked with a little skip down the hall to the well-lit room past the men cleaning the caldero, who bowed their heads as she walked past them. The door to the brightly lit room was cracked, and Deyanira pushed it open with the confidence that she belonged there. In the pit of her stomach, she was terrified they would chastise her for entering. At the table, and around the room, there were many attendants. Some more human than others. At the head of the table was a woman, but she was very tall and had a cat head. Deyanira stopped in her tracks and not because the sight was startling but because the energy felt so familiar. The woman laughed and waved her hand over her face turning it to a human appearance. Her features were dark and her accent thick. "Is that better?" she questioned. Deyanira still stood silent with her eyes squinting. She was trying to place where she felt this energy before. The woman realized what had Deyanira in her trance.

She walked around the table, never breaking eye contact with Deyanira. When the woman touched hands with her, Deyanira was thrust back in time to every hardship she ever had and every tear she had ever cried. She was never alone. The time she laid on the floor in Big Mama's house, this woman was there, in spirit, on the floor rubbing her back. When her stepmother was beating her, this woman was there in spirit, with her body draped over her and the girls, trying to absorb their pain. When Deyanira was alone at her ultrasound, getting the news that Calida had a rare heart condition, this woman was there with her hand on Deyanira's shoulder, crying with her. She couldn't believe it. Deyanira's whole life felt alone, and this woman was there for all of it, crying with her. "Who are you?" Deyanira said.

The woman held back tears and grabbed Deyanira bringing her closer. "I am Sekhmet. I am an African goddess from ancient northern Africa. I am very picky who gains my favor and you have had me every step of the way." Deyanira understood having this deity as a guide was a true honor, but somehow it felt like there was more to their connection. Abuela pulled Deyanira out of her curiosity with a poke to her side.

The meeting of her guides began when Abuela placed her machete on the table. It called for order in the room, and everyone took their seats. Deyanira went around the table, listening and meeting her guides. "Can you tell me about these new gifts and how they work?" Deyanira asked the room.

Abuela explained that as Deyanira healed and connected with her *Ori*, that healing gave her a direct channel of raw energy from the crossroads. She could use the energy at will for her protection and protection of others. She cautioned Deyanira that releasing large amounts of energy without wearing or using protection wards would draw the Brotherhood to her location.

Deyanira was still confused about what and how she could use this energy. Abuela looked around the table because she knew Deyanira was often terrified of having greater power, and she wasn't sure how to tell Deyanira. Abuela cleared her throat and said, "What you say, so shall it be. The intentions you set, the words spoken, become reality."

Deyanira was so confused. "Wait, I thought I couldn't do things without the permission of deities."

Abuela nodded. "Yes *mija*, a few things have shifted and changed. First, your discernment has grown and you've heard clearly what can be done and cannot. So you won't touch a lottery ticket and pass it to a homeless person because you understand the energetic debt it will create. But you also have to understand that today is the day the official war has begun. You are a general to this warfare. As a general, if the Brotherhood attacks you, then you must call them to their death. They will fall dead in that instant. As you align with your *Ori*, things shift. You begin your spiritual journey receiving guidance and advice from ancestors, your *Ori*, and the deities. Once you remove blocks and align with your destiny, they shift and become more of a support system for you."

Deyanira still begged for clarity. "You're telling me I can speak death onto people without consequences? I do not want to rack up karmic debt for Calida."

"Oh, amor you won't. As a general in the war to come, you are pulling from a different bank of energy, trust me. It is like a general in the war for their country, they pull resources from the banks and budget of the government they serve to support their actions in the war. You pull from the banks of Orishas and other deities in alliance and not our lineage's bank. You were only given this power because you are trusted to never use it unless absolutely necessary. I know it is a lot for you, but you will grow into embracing it. It is time for you to get going. We have much to discuss, and you can't be here when we do."

Deyanira walked out of that room and up the stairs to Doña Marina, and told Doña Marina she felt so different. "You unlocked many of your gifts tonight by releasing the shame and guilt blocking you. Tonight, you didn't fight us or your gifts. You could've left my house when you saw me and didn't. You wanted to be there, and you were open to why. You can call on us and return anytime, whether in sleep or meditation. In your deepest sleep, I will train you in these new gifts of time walking, dream walking, rituals; and minding your words because from now on they are powerful spells."

Deyanira sat in the chair once they returned to the kitchen. "We need to talk about the Brotherhood. How will I fight them? What do they want? Can I keep Calida safe from them?"

Doña Marina sat next to Deyanira. "All will be revealed to you when it is needed. Too much too soon can alter everything. I will say: you are ahead of the curve. Most psychics do not know the Brotherhood exists, but you were guided to the one group of women on earth who know how to protect themselves against the Brotherhood. You and Calida are safe. War is always a slow boil. You have time. Now get back to the real world and start taking care of yourself as much as you do others." They stood up and hugged.

"Ms. Diaz, the doctors are rounding. Do you want to speak to them?" The nurse gently nudged Deyanira, and she opened her eyes.

"Oh, yes, thank you. I have questions." Deyanira stretched and walked over to the hospital-grade crib that confined her smiling toddler, who had IVs and chest tubes. She sang to that beautiful smiling face, "Good morning, *buenos dias*, good morning *buenos dias*."

Chapter 17

Atabey, Juracan, Maquetaurie Guayaba, and all the Taino Semis, as well as the Taino ancestors, started connecting with Deyanira slowly when she returned to the island with Calida. Their plane touched down at the height of the full moon, and Deyanira immediately felt their rage. The Semis and ancestors saw the island being ravaged by foreigners, leaving the island Boricuas homeless or in poverty. They were furious. Out of anger, they sent Hurricanes and earthquakes to clear them out, but it just gave the foreigners another avenue to exploit the land and people. The Semis and ancestors were chasing their own people away from the island and causing them to disconnect from their roots. After settling into her new home and clearing her home of the nun's spirit Deyanira became her work with the Semis and ancestors. Deyanira built her connections with the Semis and ancestors by listening. While listening to them, she was also feeling the energy of the people of the island. Their woes and pains of the exploitation and gentrification of the island. She needed to explain to the Semis that acting out in a rage wouldn't hurt the people with money, only the Boricuas.

Deyanira called the Semis, Orishas, ancestors, and her guides to her table during meditation, and told them her plans. The semis were not convinced and would rather wipe out the entire island than lose it to the *gringos*. The rage of a deity could be disconnected from humanity, and it was up to Deyanira and the ancestors to bridge that connection and convince the Semis that Deyanira's plan was the right course of action.

With the support of the ancestors on the island, the Semis, and the Orishas, Deyanira woke up early and went to a beach on the southern end of the island. At dawn, she stepped into the water and the waves calmed around her. The ocean welcomed her with loving gentle touches. In the distance, she saw turtles poking their head above the water to bear witness as she gave an offering to honor the Semis. The offering was a sacrificed chicken, yuca, coconut, coffee beans, and *guayaba*. The next morning, she repeated this on the western beach of the island. She repeated the ritual each day, on another side, until the east, west, north, and south beaches were covered with the offering for the protection of the Boricuas on the island.

Deyanira then made a video on YouTube, blurring out her face. Deyanira began the video by explaining that the ancestors and Semis were angry. She explained who the Semis were. Deyanira talked about how the island was now protected, and storms or earthquakes would no longer affect the island or its people. She began the curse at that point. "Now, about the people of the island. You are loved, you are not alone. You are protected. Anyone who is not of Puerto Rican descent on this island and using, exploiting, and hurting the island and its people will get sick. If you do not leave the island and surrender the land you purchased, you will die. If you leave, you will feel better, but if you are still buying up land from afar, your illness will return, and you will die. You cannot make amends without surrendering and returning the land to the Boricuas. If you pass the land onto your children, they will get also sick and suffer the same fate, over and over, until your bloodline is wiped out. If you are Boricua and you're tricking your people into working with these gentrifiers for your own gain, you will die quickly if you don't stop. The Semis, ancestors, and Orishas would rather see you drop dead than live amongst their children, poisoning them with your self-hate. Survival is not an excuse they accept. Beware, I am kinder than those I serve."

As she spoke, the room chilled, and the air crystallized when words left her lips. It was a cold Chicago day in November in that room, despite being on the island in September. The room was full of spirits. Her brother-in-law beat the drum in the corner. Deyanira stood in the dark and began to dance, calling down the spirits and telling them she honored them. She reached into the cup half filled with the blood of the goat she had given to them earlier as an offering. Deyanira dipped her index and middle finger in the blood. She took those fingers and drew a sigil on a banana leaf.

She slammed her hand on the leaf. "*Que comience la guerra.*" She ended the video and posted it. She then left to bury the leaf six feet under in the center of the island. Her brother-in-law later said that the room's energy frightened him when she slammed her hand down; it felt like a room full of people dispersing out the door. Like she gave assignments, and people left.

"Soldiers in a battle," she responded.

It wasn't long before the video went viral. There were attempts by the Brotherhood to suppress the video. However, Deyanira's workings were too strong. The video went viral and popped up everywhere. Deyanira worked it that way to avoid deaths. She wanted to give people an opportunity to get sick, leave, or change. She also knew she needed to put protection around her home now that the Brotherhood would spiritually search for the energy of the person from the video.

Before the full moon, the sickness started setting in. People were sick and fleeing the island for the States to better hospitals. Those doctors were puzzled and couldn't figure out how to heal those people. People started passing away, and once properties were exchanged to their heirs rather than sold back to the island, their heirs became sick. If those people didn't return the property, their whole bloodline would be exterminated. Deyanira was sure a team from the Brotherhood would arrive on the island, and the search for her would begin.

Chapter 18

Ms.   Henrietta's funeral was the most interesting thing Deyanira and her siblings had ever seen. There was music, a parade, and people from everywhere laughing and telling stories about how Ms. Henrietta helped them. Big Mama said they would be down there for at least a month to "tie up loose ends," but really, she wanted Deyanira to be trained by Lottie. Ms. Henrietta already gave Lottie what was hers before she passed away. Ms. Henrietta's will and testament included the farm outside of New Orleans. Forty-three acres of the land would go to Big Mama, along with all the money Ms. Henrietta had saved in her account.

Falah was sad after the reading of the will because Ms. Henrietta only left him a chest in the basement and the unaccounted-for contents were to be opened in private. It was Ms. Henrietta's only stipulation in the will. Falah had no need for money. He wasn't sure what he was expecting, but between Ms. Henrietta and his mother, he had spent more time with his grandmother. He thought their bond meant more than a random chest full of junk. From the age of twelve through eighteen, he spent his summers with her so that he could be kept out of trouble. The idea of him going to his granny's to stay out of trouble made him chuckle because he, in fact, stayed knee-deep in trouble most of his life, according to his mother. Big Mama receiving the house and all its contents just broke his heart, and he didn't know how to express it. His grandmother wasn't a loving, nurturing, cooking granny. She was a feisty, tell-it-like-it-is, and protect-you-with-a-pistol kind of granny.

When they returned to Ms. Henrietta's home after the reading of the will, Big Mama told Falah to sit down in the kitchen for a chat before he went to search for his inherited chest. Big Mama then told Deyanira to get her bag because Lottie was picking her up. Deyanira was going to stay with Lottie in New Orleans for a bit. "It's no fair you get to go to Aunt Lottie's. She's funny and I want to go too!", Maribel exclaimed with folded arms and pouting lips. "Me too! Me too!" Alma and Camilla sang in chorus. Big Mama told Deyanira's sisters to simmer down and go feed the chickens and stay together, then she'll take them into town to get ice cream.

Big Mama sat down across from Falah and said, "Your granny loved you very much." Falah tried to interrupt because he didn't want a lecture about his disappointment. She hushed him and continued. "Your granny loved you very much. She left me the house on paper only. This house and land are yours when you are ready to move in. She wanted you to retire from the life and business, you know. Come down here to the land and animals, and finish your life with fulfillment and peace. The reason why she left the house to me was to protect you. If you get arrested, this house is an asset for the government to take. She knew enough about the law to know that. You have to get your life in order. Quit doing that illegal stuff. Come get the house when you're ready. Also, she said she wanted you to bring your friend." Falah froze mid-air with a cup of water in between the table and his mouth.

Big Mama laughed, "Now baby, I may have worked a lot, but I know my kid. I knew you and him weren't just best friends looking out for each other. I know he fights for you and supports you with the type of love only a lover can provide. I am grateful you have someone to give you that. I don't mind he's a man. It surprised me that my mama knew, though. She just said she could smell love on you, and you know how she is." Falah couldn't speak and decided it was okay to just take a sip of water and stay silent.

Big Mama continued. "I'd love for you to pack up, and come down here next week, but it ain't up to me, and I cannot tell you how to live your life. I gave that up long ago. I know I wasn't a perfect mama. I know I hurt you. How you deal with that and work through is yours. I don't get to tell you what's what and how to do it. Just know I love you no matter what, baby, and just as you are." She hugged Falah, awkwardly smothering him with her bosoms.

He laughed and called out, "Okay mama, I can't breathe, I can't breathe!"

They laughed, and she hushed him again. "I'm going to help Dey-Dey get ready for Lottie. Go have your private time with your chest. She didn't tell me what was in it, and she told me if I looked, she'd come back and haunt my ass."

Falah went to the spare room where the chest was in. He ran his hand over the top of the wooden chest trying to connect to his grandmother's energy. With a deep breath he opened the chest and atop one of the items was an envelope addressed to him, labeled *Read first*.

My Dearest Falah,

By now, I am sure your mother explained the situation with the house. I hope you take me up on this offer soon. You and your friend deserve a peaceful life. I didn't tell your mama or anyone else. Well, I told Lottie, but you know her. She's got the knowing, so she knew already. Nobody will bother y'all on the farm. The farm is away from people and y'all can be "cousins" when you're in town. In this chest, you will find some of the finest dresses made with only the best fabrics. I had them tailored for your size as best I could. If they don't fit, the last page of this letter is the name of a discreet seamstress who works with fellas like you.

I remember the first time I came home and saw you had fallen asleep in one of my dresses, with my makeup on. I wanted to swoop you up and tell you that it was okay, you can like what you like. You were so young. I was scared if I did that you would stop visiting. So instead, I had dresses made that were slightly bigger than my size and placed them in my closet. I bought foundation that matched your skin tone, and eyeshadow that brought out your eyes. I would say something in passing about some dresses I recently received from a woman tucked in the closet and then I'd run off to town saying I'd be at least three hours. As you got older, it got harder to find dresses in your size because you take after your granddaddy. At the end of the summer, I started sneaking into your room and measuring you while you slept, guessing how much you would grow in the winter months. In this room, there should be a total of twenty hat boxes. They all contain wigs sized out to fit your big head. All different colors and textures. At the bottom of this case is makeup that matches your complexion. There is nothing wrong with you. You are who you are. Live your truth, even if it is only in this house. You know I ain't a mushy person, but I love you just the way you are. Next to the makeup is a photo album. In that album, you'll see me with a few of my lovers all dolled up for parties and whatnot. I only ever loved one man, your granddaddy, but women, I have loved many. Don't ever feel alone. I'll be with you, always ready to kick anyone's ass that fucks with you. Now get your ass out of Chicago.

Your Granny,
  Ms. Henrietta

Time walking sometimes made Deyanira uncomfortable. She tried to leave when she entered this private moment of Falah's. She felt nosy and uncomfortable. However, she needed to know. Her destiny and Falah's were interconnected. Falah's bloodline and Deyanira's bloodline would wage the war on the Brotherhood when the time came.

Chapter 19

Deyanira hopped into Lottie's old Buick with an excited energy. Lottie asked Deyanira, "Why you so happy? What did my niece tell you we were doing?"

Deyanira, without a thought, blurted out, "You are going to train me on my gifts because I am powerful."

Lottie stopped the car at the end of the driveway and put the car in park. "Now let's get one thing straight here, little girl. I am not some damn sidekick here to help you become great. I am great. A significant force. I am showing you things I know to be true and have mastered. Things I've learned from my ancestors and things I've learned myself. But I am not training you like some lackey, so you can shine on my dime, you understand? We are partners."

Deyanira nodded, but not understanding what she said wrong. As an adult, whenever Deyanira returned to this moment, she understood Lottie's message. Lottie was not a tool or a thing to be used to enhance Deyanira's journey. She was a human being with a journey and her own gifts, and she was important. It was important for Deyanira to understand that humanity was the key. Using people made her no better than the Brotherhood. Lottie's role in the war against the Brotherhood was just as important as Deyanira's role, just a different capacity.

When they reached Lottie's place, the different herbs and candles around Lottie's home mesmerized Deyanira. She ran her hand across the counter, connecting with the energy. Lottie huffed at Deyanira. "You have to stop all that. *Cher*, you lean too hard on your gift, and you are skipping being human. You can get lost in always connecting with the energy of things and searching for the unknown. It'll have you out here exhausted. You aren't supposed to know everything, baby, even the Lwa don't know everything."

Deyanira knew what Lottie was saying to be true when she returned to this moment. She spent many of her early years going down rabbit holes of obsession, figuring out and connecting the dots of an energetic puzzle in the spirit realm. If someone mistreated her, Deyanira would skip down their timeline to figure out the reason behind their actions. Deyanira just shook her head and apologized. Lottie chuckled and said, "You aren't sorry, but when you're old and tired, you will be."

Lottie spent the first few days explaining that many gods, Orisha, Lwas, and Semis were often manifestations of belief branched off from original beings. She explained that some were actually all-powerful beings while others were people turned into all-powerful beings by belief.

Deyanira asked, "So which God is the first God that made us?"

Lottie chuckled at her naïve innocence. "Oh, honey, the beginning of humans is more complex than that, and it is only to be revealed to you when you are ready. That isn't for me to say. Now, what I will tell you is that everyone has their thing. Their connection to beings are either by lineage or favor. Most white folks who tell you they have the favor of an African deity or primordial being are lying. They tell lies told to them by the beings themselves. There are many white folks who practice Voodoo and Vudu, but they are part of something bigger that is coming."

Lottie kept this lesson simple for Deyanira's thirteen-year-old mind. "*Cheri*, take Marie, my ancestor, and her mission. The mission that Papa Legba gave her is a prime example. White folks beat our beliefs and practices out of us. Right? Because they saw how powerful our deities and their followers were. How many of those Indians on your island were killed because of their beliefs and the powers of those they worshiped? The God the white folks worship is a void. They train people to obey and pour all their beliefs and energy into Him; lying to the people that He would provide them with a good life, or at the very least, a good afterlife. The belief that breathed life into Him made Him a void; He consumed followers in exchange for false promises of paradise. No God requires blind obedience and a sacrifice of yourself. That defeats the point of coming to earth. Maybe at some point, he was good, but he has become exactly what their good book says the devil is. Anyway, they killed off our people who refused to convert because they figured out the power behind our beliefs. They figured out that is how Gods and primordial being get their power– through people's beliefs and their offerings. That is how they gain obedience, by stealing hope and belief. The white folks stole it by killing off the most devoted first. Then they started talking about how much better their God was compared to who we worshiped. Our beings give consequences for your actions, but according to them, when you repent, their God forgives everything. Which parent would you pick? The one trying to teach you or the one who promises no rules? They used the roots of our teaching against us though. They knew we all came from belief systems built on lessons, so even though their God is all forgiving they used him to make us feel bad all of the time. If something bad happened it was because we didn't pray hard enough or someone must be committing sins. Those white folks brought disease, death, and famine. Then they said that if our people converted to their God, He would take disaster away, and our people would be okay again. Do you see how fucked up that is? I abuse you, then say if you say I'm the greatest ever, I'll stop abusing you. So you agree to say they're the greatest to survive, and then teach your children they're the greatest so you can keep them safe. Are you getting all this, baby girl? Are you understanding? They create the very thing that hurts us and then convince us it is our fault we are hurting but if we just give all of ourselves the hurting will stop. It never really stops though does it?"

Thirteen-year-old Deyanira tried to pull back all the things her parents taught her as a Christian and connect them to what Lottie said. She replied, "How has no one realized this before?"

Returning as an adult time walker helped her chip away at something in her belief systems rooted in her ancestors' oppression.

Lottie replied simply, "Lots of people have, *Cher*, they just kill them when they get too loud. The African and Native deities and beings have been working hard to get their people back to their original beliefs, and they will always protect them. Papa Legba devised a plan with Marie. He chose her because she was so fair-skinned– she could gain the confidence of the white people. She taught the white folks how to do workings for themselves knowing they wouldn't continue the maintenance and then they would owe the Lwa of Voodoo. Papa used the white people's beliefs to fuel his power, giving them whatever they asked for, using the small offerings made. When they did these rituals they created a debt for their bloodlines. He will come and collect the debt once the balance is restored and belief returned to his bloodline followers."

Deyanira asked, "Bloodline followers?"

"We will come to a time when black and brown folks will leave Yahweh and return to the old ways of their ancestors. Then Papa Legba will come for his pound of flesh. You are ushering in a war, child. You will, when you are grown, usher in a spiritual war against the powers of the Brotherhood and restore balance to black and brown people everywhere. Your war will save humanity and the earth if we are lucky and crumble everything the Brotherhood built and is building now. You will start it but not finish it. Papa Legba saw you were coming all the way back then and planted his seeds with Marie in Louisiana to reap the harvest when the war begins. Voodoo bloodline followers are people with African blood. No matter the skin tone, there are many people, whether they like it or not, connected to him and other beings by blood. He and the others will call to them, and as the balance shifts, the call will get louder and louder. People will rebuild entire communities of proper worship of our ancestors' beliefs, and at the peak, you will be pushed to action." Lottie set a teacup with sweet-smelling tea in front of Deyanira, and Lottie sat down next to her with her own cup.

"Remember when I told you I was not your sidekick? You are special and have a great destiny. All of that is true. But thinking you are the most important part is dangerous. You are no messiah, and even their messiah wasn't a messiah. Never let your ego take over. You have to know the difference between *I am important* and *I am the only thing that is important*. You hear me?"

Deyanira understood little of what Lottie was teaching because the concept was miles beyond her young mind's understanding, and even as an adult, she struggled to understand how to know she was important but also not important. "Auntie Lottie, what is the Brotherhood?"

"Oh *Cheri*, they hunt down people like us. They kill us and then spiritually enslave us. Whenever you use your gifts for something big, it is a big surge of energy. If you are drawing from the spirits or beings, then it's a surge of energy. If you are pulling from yourself or the surrounding life, there will be a dip in energy. There are powerful, gifted people who can feel energy shifts, and some of them have been brainwashed to think they are helping the world by hunting witches. They started spreading misinformation a long time ago in Europe. They started killing gifted people, well, mostly women, a long time ago."

Deyanira was now terrified. "Are we witches? If you train me and I change the energy, will they come to kill us?"

Lottie felt awful. She forgot Deyanira was just a child. "Oh, *Cher*, New Orleans has protection around it. They can't come here. If they do, they will fall dead where they stand. I will teach you what to do when you have a place of your own. It's funny because it is their ritual we used. And we aren't witches. That is the name the Brotherhood gave us to scare people away. We are gifted healers. They created this ritual a long time ago with a European woman. She turned away from her ancestors' ways to work for the Brotherhood. The ritual makes sure when a person is killed, their spirit is bound to be in service to the bloodline that performed the ritual. So they can harness the deceased's energy and prevent them from crossing over to be ancestors to their bloodline. My ancestors met with some exceptional women who escaped the Brotherhood and came here to warn the women of New Orleans. The women and my ancestors put up a barrier to keep the city and all the gifted ones here safe. That is why this place is full of healers and psychics. Also, why the land is supercharged with energy. Are you getting all this? This is all part of your training too."

Deyanira nodded as her thoughts trailed off to Doña Marina. Under her breath, she muttered, "So I killed her."

"What's that now?" Lottie said, squinting through her glasses in Deyanira's direction.

"My godmother on the island, the one who taught me everything I knew about my gifts. She was a powerful medium. Doña Marina held these things on the island called *mesa blanca*. She was training me with them. There was one I attended where one of the other mediums got the message wrong. I told him I heard something else. I blacked out, but I didn't. A being took over and yelled at him. Told him he was going to die and some other stuff, then I fainted. That all happened at her house. The next day, he was dead. Died in his sleep. Then soon after, someone murdered Doña Marina in her house. I killed her because I channeled that Orisha and it brought the Brotherhood to her house. It should've been me."

"Oh, *Cheri*! That was not your fault. They are evil. Now the more pressing questions. Very important details. Did you go to her house after they took her?" Deyanira nodded yes. "What did you feel when you were there? Did you feel her essence? Her energy? Only a medium can know what I mean. Like, when my sissy was sick and then passed, you felt her energy around, right? Like that. Or did it feel empty of her?"

Deyanira was choking on her grief. "She was everywhere. I

felt her all over the room. It was awful. Her energy was alive and splattered on the walls. I felt her energy overwhelming me everywhere I turned, and I couldn't take it." Deyanira put her head down in her arms on the table and wept.

Lottie wrapped one arm around Deyanira and said, "I know it was a lot, but that is good. If you felt her all around the room, that means she left her body before they could capture her spirit. They do this ritual that locks a person's spirit away for their use. The Brotherhood uses their spirit's energy to supercharge the low-grade psychics they have working for them. Without the connection to supernatural things other than their version of Yahweh, their little psychic helpers would be useless. I am willing to bet that when the time is right, you'll see Ms. Marina again. I mean, you are a powerful ass medium, baby. As you get older, you'll be able to call spirits down. What concerns me is that these spirits think they can just come in and take over your body. I don't care if they are powerful beings or spirits. Your body is yours. You are not some meat-suit for spirits to try on whenever they want to. The first thing we are going do is fix it so they can't do that." They sat at the table for a little longer, sipping tea. Deyanira talked about Doña Marina and how she missed her.

For over a month, Big Mama and the girls stayed down in Louisiana while Deyanira stayed with Lottie. Deyanira learned rituals for protection, she learned rituals for healing, and she learned she was the boss. Deyanira found her voice with Auntie Lottie. She found her confidence. Things felt less scary now. Lottie taught Deyanira the ritual the group of women used to seal and protect New Orleans. She couldn't cover more than a few acres with her gifts alone, but that was enough. It took over a hundred women to protect New Orleans.

The day Big Mama and the children packed up to return to Chicago, Lottie brought Deyanira back to Ms. Henrietta's house. It had been over a month since Deyanira had seen her sisters. They had never been apart for that long. The longest she had been separated from them was in the hospital before they came to Big Mama's house. Her sisters' energy felt different like they had forgotten her, or even worse, they had gotten on with their lives without her. It hurt Deyanira's feelings when she walked up the drive and her sisters acted as if they didn't miss her.

"Did you miss me?" She said to the group of unbothered girls playing on the porch.

Maribel, in a huff, said, "Who are you again?"

Deyanira knew they were all mad she had been gone and left them. She did the only thing she knew that could fix it. Deyanira dropped her bag and ran full throttle towards them with dramatic proclamations. "I was so lost without you all. Oh, I wept for days and barely ate please, *hermanas*. I need to be loved by you. How could you forget me?" They tried to run from her but Alma and Camila were already giggling. Deyanira grabbed them both, kissing their faces. Maribel ran off the porch toward the chicken coop in the backyard, avoiding the swift forgiveness of her sister. Not long after, Deyanira joined Maribel, keeping her distance. "I'm sorry I left you. Scary things were happening to me and Aunt Lottie was helping me with them, but I should've told you."

Maribel responded with her typical rage and rebellion, launching an egg at Deyanira. It splattered all over her shoulder. Deyanira stood there with her mouth open in shock, and Maribel fell down, laughing, clutching her stomach.

"You little brat," Deyanira said as she fell atop her sister, wiping egg goo on Maribel, laughing together.

They soon all piled into the van, Deyanira, with a clean tank top. Big Mama grabbed Deyanira's elbow, yanking her backward with more force than she had ever used. It startled Deyanira and triggered all her sisters' history of abuse. They watched, terrified of what would happen next. "Young lady, what is that on the back of your neck?"

Deyanira couldn't speak. She thought Big Mama knew. Auntie Lottie came around from the back end of the van. "Now, Sug, let's talk over here. You told me to help her, and I did."

Big Mama released Deyanira's arm, realizing the small tattoo had happened recently in Louisiana. "Oh, honey, I am so sorry. I didn't mean to grab you. I thought it was a gang thing from back home." Big Mama then directed her attention to Lottie. "Are you nuts? I said help her, not tattoo her. She is a foster kid. They can take her away from me if they see it. She's only thirteen."

Lottie reached out for her niece's hand and held it. She squeezed gently but tight. "The tattoo stops spirits from entering her body without her consent. She needed that sigil at the base of her neck. She needed to take charge of her body, and if she wasn't a foster kid, you wouldn't be so scared all the time. You know it's time to make some things official." Big Mama took a deep breath and looked towards the front porch where Falah sat rocking in the chair. "They won't give them to me and you know it."

Lottie pushed back, "You let me deal with that. Because I say they will, and I got a couple of spirits that owe me a favor or two. Those are your babies. Make them yours and then you and Falah can be together more. Deyanira and Falah are connected. They won't show me how, but they have shown me their connection."

Big Mama reached for Lottie's other hand and gave both hands a squeeze. "I'm going to trust you and listen, old lady, don't steer me wrong."

Lottie gave a wink, "About time you listened."

Chapter 20

"Mami, why are you putting salt around the room?" Calida didn't like the idea of salt under her feet in her new room.

"Oh, *amor*, we are only in this apartment for a few months while I look for a house on the island. I cannot do my normal workings to keep you safe here. You are a young medium, and you are strong. All the traumatized earthbound spirits on this island will seek your light out, and I need you safe." Deyanira was lying. She could definitely do protection work on the apartment. She was exhausted and didn't feel like it. The move back to the island knocked the wind out of her. The planning, prepping, coordinating, and adjusting was too much. Deyanira just needed to be normal for a minute and not think about supernatural things.

The apartment in Caguas, the heart of the island, was impressive. She chose Caguas because it was away from the tourists' energy, also in the island's heart, away from the immense, dense energy dripping from tragedy. Not that it was not without pain and suffering, just lighter than other places she searched.

A month of settling into a routine and visiting Deyanira's *hermanas* passed before Calida asked to sleep with Deyanira. She always welcomed Calida into her bed with cuddles and love.

Deyanira asked if everything was okay in her room. Calida said she just didn't like it right now. Deyanira noticed Calida was also avoiding one of the bathrooms in the apartment. Calida's psychic gifts differed greatly from Deyanira's and her gifts were also still evolving.

Calida, as a baby, could see earthbound spirits. They scared her, and she called them monsters. Once, when Deyanira was window shopping, pushing two-year-old Calida in a stroller, Calida said, "Mami it's a monster! It's coming, run." Deyanira later realized they had been near a corner where a young man had been shot in the head six months prior. Deyanira often had to listen to cues and hints when earthbound spirits found Calida, because at her young age, she wasn't always vocal. Sometimes, the only thing she said was, Mami there's a monster. Sometimes, spirits lingered and hid in the shadows. Calida could only feel their energy or the ancestors would pressure Calida to leave the room and find Deyanira.

Abuela came to Deyanira in her dreams and cautioned her to monitor Calida, as Calida might be developing the gift of dream walking. A gift that Deyanira and many of her bloodline also had. Dream walking could be a dangerous gift for the young, and in babies, can present as SIDs. The spirit liked to drift and walk while the body rested. So the spirit could accidentally tip-toe into the minds of the people asleep in the area surrounding them.

Abuela told Deyanira what to watch out for when Calida was sleeping. Things like shallow breathing, appearing to stop breathing or holding her breath. Sometimes it was hard to tell if Calida was dream walking or if a spirit was hiding in the shadows, messing with Calida. Deyanira had seen the signs this time, but she was just so damn exhausted. She knew she should have anchored Calida in her body with a ritual the first time Calida had dream walked. She also knew a spirit was probably in her baby's bedroom, and she needed to cleanse the room, but she was just so damn tired.

For the next few days, Deyanira just slept, trying to recover from all the energy and moving. She didn't have anyone who understood what she felt or how to help. Years had passed since Big Mama's passing and Aunt Lottie's disappearance. She felt alone most of her young adult life. It limited her capacity and shrunk her confidence in her gifts.

As she slept, Abuela called her to the table. The door appeared in her dream and Deyanira rolled her eyes and sighed. "What now? I'm trying to rest." She opened the door and groaned; she plopped down at the table, slumping down in the chair. "I do not have the energy for much right now, so please let it be something simple to discuss. Being here will already make me wake up more tired than when I went to sleep."

Abuela huffed at Deyanira with disappointment, "Well, find some energy; you haven't spoken to us in almost a month."

Deyanira got up and, in a rage, flipped the table over. "I am exhausted, God dammit, and I am sick of you all calling me. I'm fucking tired. Normal moms who move across the country to an island with their child are exhausted. Normal moms with healthy kids without powers are exhausted. I have a heart-patient kid that is a fucking beacon for asshole spirits that won't cross over. I am carrying everything, and everyone is pretending I am not. There are these fucking psychics on the internet saying things like, "I just turn my gifts off when I don't want to have them." I want to stab those stupid bitches in the throat out of jealousy. I hate them. I am always fucking connected, like a network of fucking mushrooms. If I'm around people, I don't just feel them and their current feelings and situations, I feel their ancestors and about at least eighty fucking timelines they exist on. In the past month, I went through two airports full of fucking people, on top of my own shit. I know there is something hanging around the house, but dammit, I'm tired."

Deyanira had tears flowing down her cheeks. "I don't just have regular parenting things, I also have her health, her own spiritual gifts, the Brotherhood, and crazy random spirits. I can't be this fucking warrior for everything and everyone and no one... I mean, no one is there for me. Anyone who helped me or at least understood me died. Doña Marina, dead, Big Mama, dead, and Aunt Lottie, also dead. I am doing all this on my own. My sisters don't understand. They want me to run around the island with them now that I am here, and they do not know all the things I am feeling and doing. I'm supposed to train Calida, and half the time, I barely know what the fuck I'm doing. I'm terrified ninety percent of the time and unsure of everything. And if you say some whack Spiderman bullshit like, with great power comes great responsibility, I swear to God I will bind these gifts in my body, and if I die, I die. FUUUCCCKKKK."

Deyanira cried silently for another thirty seconds and wiped her face and, with a wave of her hand, the table returned to its rightful position. "Argh, fine, what is it? I'm done being dramatic."

Abuela got up from her chair and hugged her. "I know having us in spirit isn't enough. I wish there was someone on the earthly plain who understood your journey and could mentor you. The Brotherhood has done a great job of wiping out strong bloodlines. You will have another mentor in the next five years, but not now. There are so many practitioners of *Espiritismo*,

Santería, and Sanse on the island, but unfortunately, many of them have been indoctrinated with Catholicism. So their spiritual practices are rigid and full of rules. They're very limited. Their rituals work for them for what they need. You are just different, *mija*. Your gifts' foundation is *connection*. If you tried to petition the other side with strict rules and rituals, the time it took for those workings to bear fruit would put you in danger. Regular people have to practice that way for a reason. The Brotherhood severed most connections between the believers so that the practices would die when the ancient ones died. If the practices die, the deities being worshiped die too. The Brotherhood's God would only get stronger by killing and converting people. The ancestors devised a plan so that our deities were still fed, but just through Yahweh's saints and angels so they could go undetected. Our beings and ancestors were eating table scraps and crumbs from the feast that the Brotherhood prepared for Yahweh, but our beings survived and have been preparing for the war.

"I called you here because I am worried about this spirit bothering Calida. The spirit is coming to her in her dreams. I know you are tired, but I promise, on the new moon, just give us our food, liquor, and tea, and we'll find you a house. Your mundane life is meant to be a life of ease because the spiritual burden you bear is so large. Calida's health will stabilize, and you will never be without money. So rest, eat, and find out more about this spirit that is hiding from you. You may be tired, but you still have to be safe. One more thing— tell your sisters. Tell them everything. They have been on their own spiritual journey with their own gifts; their roles are unlocking. You can trust them to care for you."

Deyanira woke up to Calida tossing and turning in the bed.

Deyanira scooped her in her arms and kissed her forehead. "Mami is here, baby. You're safe with me; find my energy." Calida settled down, and when Deyanira drifted back to sleep, Calida was in Deyanira's dream, cuddling Deyanira while watching TV.

The next morning, Deyanira casually asked Calida questions while making breakfast. "You slept really rough last night, *mi amor*. Did you have bad dreams?"

Calida shifted in her chair while eating her fruit and nonchalantly said, "It was weird Mami, there were children around me, like a school, but they were dressed funny, like all the same clothes, and they spoke only Spanish, no English. There was a lady who wore black, and she had a black scarf that was around her hair and down her back. She grabbed my hand and told me she had to keep me safe. The lady said you were bad, and she would protect me. She took me to a door and when she opened it, there were stairs leading down to a dark room I couldn't see. She pulled my arm and told me to go down there with her. I ran from her though because it didn't feel good. It was scary, and I knew you weren't bad. Then I was on a couch watching TV with you, eating popcorn."

Deyanira dropped her coffee cup, and it shattered on the floor.

"Mami, are you okay?"

Deyanira's thoughts were racing. She realized that the spirit was trying to bury Calida in her own subconscious. If she succeeded, Calida might have never woken up again. Deyanira first felt guilt, then rage, and then she turned that rage turned toward the spirit.

"Yes, baby, I am okay. Come into the living room and hold my hands. Let's get rid of this spirit." Deyanira stepped over the broken coffee cup on the kitchen floor and walked towards Calida. She grabbed her hand and tugged her toward the center of the living room. Deyanira looked down at Calida, "Hey, remember now, you're the boss." Calida shook her head with the fakest confidence she could muster for her mother.

"Hey bitch!" Deyanira roared, "I know you're here. Get out of here! You tried to take my child. Face me." A gust of wind entered the room, and it blew the papers on the coffee table onto the floor. All the hair on the back of Deyanira's neck stood up, and her body lit up with energy. Her chest felt heavy, and her breath started feeling restricted with a tightness in her chest. Deyanira's eyes lit up golden, and her tone shifted to an authoritative tone. "Enough!"

With a swipe of her arm from shoulder to feet and across her chest, she cut off the spirit's attempts to harm her. "Here are your options. You will get the fuck out of my apartment and stay away from my child, or I will bind your spirit to a rock and bury it in the middle of the rainforest, away from people. You will be alone forever. You will not be able to siphon energy from the living you will slowly devolve into a vortex or be forced to cross over. You know my power and you can feel it. You know I will do it."

The spirit began pleading her case to Deyanira, but the moment the nun's spirit connected with Deyanira, Deyanira could see the abuse the spirit had inflicted on the orphanage's children she was assigned to govern. A white nun sent by the church had hurt brown boys and girls on the island. The spirit tried to explain Calida would be safe with her and that Deyanira should give her to the nun. Deyanira let go of Calida's hand because she no longer needed Calida to connect to the spirit.

Deyanira took her hands, moving them in a circular motion,

chanting, "This space is filled with your energy. Here you will be." Deyanira felt the energy and power surging between her hands, and she offered the spirit one last chance. "You hurt families and children and convinced yourself you were doing your God's work. When you died, you saw you were wrong for abusing those children and turned away from elevating and learning the lessons of this lifetime. You wander the land as an earthbound spirit, lonely and devolving. You think I am a danger to my child and you, a person who took children from their families and beat them, is safer for my daughter? You can crossover and learn your lessons or leave our house and her alone. If you don't, I will bind you and bury you."

Deyanira felt the violent charge of the energy of the spirit shift. The nun wasn't ready to crossover, but she had no interest in being bound to a rock and banished. Deyanira slowed her hands, which confined the nun's energy, and then released the energy, carrying it through the apartment and out the door. Deyanira walked over to her purse, pulled out a small glass case, removed a needle, and pricked her fingertip. She took that finger and drew her sigil of protection on the entrance of the apartment. It sealed the home from allowing spirits to enter or, in the nun's case, returning.

Calida was in awe of her mother's power but also equally scared. The reality finally sunk in for Calida that the nun had tried to take her away forever. Supernatural dangers were far worse than the stranger danger of the mundane world, and Calida was having a hard time not feeling powerless and scared.

Chapter 21

"Okay, *mija*, here's your bag. Have fun with Titi Alma," Deyanira spoke softly and kissed Calida goodbye for the weekend. On her way back to the apartment, Deyanira's mind wandered to all the chores and errands she could get done before they moved to the new house. Her emotions grew inside of her while on the road, and she pulled over into a shopping center. "Fuck that. I need some time for me," Deyanira said out loud to herself.

She went home, packed a bag, and booked an Airbnb for the weekend. She chose Rio Peidras, and she wasn't sure why. The first night she slept a lot. The next day she woke up refreshed and enjoyed her café in the silence of the small Airbnb. She sat quietly listening to the hustle and bustle of the neighborhood. She got to know the room intimately as she sipped. The painting of San Juan's sunset needed to be dusted. The TV hummed from across the room. The creaky futon groaned when she shifted positions. It was nice to be somewhere and none of those problems were her problems. She didn't have to dust or fix anything and it was peaceful.

That night, she received a surge of energy. She jumped into the shower and catered to her body. Once out of the shower and lathered with oils and perfumes, Deyanira put on the little black dress with the swoop neckline that hugged her hips and headed for El Boricua. The small dance club was just the right spot for Deyanira to dapple in the energies she was feeling. She assumed there would be young people from the *universidad* there, and the judgment of the students would keep her from letting loose too much.

When Deyanira arrived, she felt the music awaken her body. She ordered her drink and found a place to enjoy the music. There were a few people dancing in front of the band, and watching them made her smile over her drink. Once that drink was finished, she stood closer to the dance floor, smiling and swaying her hips to the music. She caught the eye of a young woman who clearly had been drinking more than Deyanira. Eye contact was all it took. The young woman grabbed Deyanira's hand and dragged her to the dance floor; they danced salsa together, laughing and smiling. Deyanira was also dancing by herself, embodying the joy she had tapped into, and she coerced others to the dance floor. With an occasional spin, she stopped in front of someone and waved for them to dance with her. On that dance floor, that night she was Deyanira. She wasn't a mother, a sister, the Oracle, a daughter, a friend, or any other title she collected over the years. She was just Deyanira, a beautiful, sexual, and joyous woman.

Deyanira caught the eye of a young man. He was younger than her, but not by much from what she could tell. His hair was muddy blonde, and his complexion begged for shade even in the dark of night on the island. It was not built for Caribbean sun. His shoulders, forehead, and nose glowed in a pink hue. His lanky frame was tucked in a corner; a scotch glass in hand, watching silently. He smirked at Deyanira, and she pounced. She sashayed towards him in the silliest, least seductive way possible that made him laugh uncontrollably. Once Deyanira reached his table, she held out her hand and gave him a wink.

"How can I refuse that?" He said. Off to the dance floor, they went. He kept up well; his moves matched hers. Their hips were in tune and their steps aligned. Deyanira flashed her smile as she touched his chest, flirting on the dance floor.

The band took a break, and Deyanira walked away from her dance partner without a second look. As she walked towards her table, he gently grasped her hand. She paused, looking back in his direction, and allowed his hand to linger in hers before slipping away. Once at the bar, she waved done the waitress. "*Cuéntame del gringo flaco.*"

The waitress linked arms with Deyanira elbow to elbow with excitement. "Oh! He comes in every weekend. Never talks to anyone. Drinks his one drink and leaves. Tips good. He has been coming for a few years now. You are the first person I have seen him interact with, and he smiled! *Que bueno, amor!*"

Deyanira glanced in the *gringo's* direction to see him staring at her with soft, curious eyes. She grabbed her drink and made her way to his table. Deyanira plopped down in the chair across from him and told him he was an impressive dancer. Their conversation was light and flirty. Deyanira made a decision that she would not have deep conversations with anyone that night. She instructed her ancestors to keep all spirits at bay. The man started to introduce himself, and she stopped him. "I'll call you *Flaco.*"

He hung his head low and laughed to himself. He went on to explain that his friends also called him the same nickname because of his height and weight, so it worked.

"You can just call me *Hermosa,*" Deyanira said as she flipped her hair and blew him a kiss. Then they laughed together.

The band started to pack up, and Deyanira's Cinderella night was coming to a close. She stood up, adjusted her dress, leaned forward, and kissed Flaco, bidding him farewell. Back to the real world she must go. Stuttering and clumsily chasing Deyanira, Flaco asked to walk her to her car. "For safety," he added.

Deyanira smirked and nodded her consent. Their small talk to the car was full of jokes, banter, and tender touches. Once at her car, Deyanira leaned her back onto the driver's door, casually wrapping her arms around Flaco's neck. He moved closer to Deyanira, gripping her hips. The grasp of his large hand wrapped around her, squeezing her butt. It had been so long since Deyanira had been touched by a man, that she forgot how good intimacy felt. She let out a soft moan as he leaned in for a kiss. Something about that moan ignited something in both Deyanira and Flaco. The once soft kiss had grown into a fiery passionate kiss where Deyanira was biting Flaco's lip, and his breath was shuttering in response. Gently gripping escalated to extensive groping.

Flaco broke free from the passion, panting, placing his forehead on Deyanira's. He stood silently, trying to compose himself when Deyanira said, "Can you make me cum?"

Flaco's facial expression was frozen for less than a second, then he took a deep breath and leaned in towards Deyanira's left ear. His right hand moved from the stationary grip on her butt, down the back of her thigh, and up the back of her skirt. He caressed her thigh and moved his hand around the front of her leg. Deyanira opened her legs slightly, signaling for him to continue. As his two fingers pushed her soaked panties to the side, he whispered in her ear, "Give it to me."

His fingers thrust deep inside of her, and she let out a gasp, resting her head back onto the car. Flaco's left hand wrapped around Deyanira's back, offering her the support her body needed to receive the pleasure Flaco was offering. Her back arched, and her hands squeezed his shoulders.

Flaco whispered into her ear, "Breathe for me." His fingers, deep inside of her, rubbed her g-spot, like a sledgehammer of pleasure against a dam. Deyanira took a low deep breath and felt a rush energy across her entire body. First hot, then cold, and finally tingly. Her legs started shaking, only alerting Flaco to keep the same rhythm with his fingers. Suddenly, the dam broke, and a tidal wave of ecstasy released between Deyanira's legs. Her juices ran down her legs, into her stilettos, and down Flaco's wrist. His arm had her juices dripping from his elbow, onto the street, as he remained in position, fingers motionless, awaiting instruction.

Flaco broke away only to offer more. "My apartment is down the street." Deyanira couldn't speak. If she spoke or thought, she would run away and ask herself what the fuck she was thinking. Instead, she nodded, and they walked silently hand-in-hand to his apartment. The walk was hard for Deyanira. Her legs were still shaking, and she was awkwardly walking in shoes filled with her own juices. Flaco could feel her discomfort rising, and he turned to scoop her up into his arms. Immediately, Deyanira felt self-conscious and begged him to put her down; she was too big. He reassured her that in the gym, he benched twice her weight, and she was light.

Once they entered the apartment, he went into the bathroom and told Deyanria to make herself at home. The first thing she did was take her nasty cum-filled shoes off. The memory of that moment caused her to shiver. She looked around the apartment, and it was very plain. Devoid of any semblance of life. It didn't feel like death per se but it definitely didn't show a desire to live. Once he returned, she excused herself to the restroom. She sat down on the toilet and took a deep breath, calling out to Abuela. "Why does his energy feel so familiar? What is it about this apartment?"

Abuela chuckled and obliged her grandchild. "You can't just enjoy yourself, you nosy thing. He hasn't given up on life, but he hasn't been living. He has been existing. His apartment is in between living and dying. Thriving and giving up. He is at a crossroads in life. Now enough Oracle stuff, go be human."

Deyanira thought to herself that it was too late and she should go because she had enough fun. She gathered herself and walked out of the bathroom, only to be swept into Flaco's arms, with his hands resting gently on her hips. His soft kisses on her neck pushed the idea of leaving further and further into the back of her mind until it no longer existed. Flaco's body moved like water over hers. His hand gracefully glided up her back, unhooking the zipper of her dress and gliding it back down, smoothly leading her arms out of the dress with mild fingertip touches.

Deyanira's dress fell to the floor as her body and spirit committed to her own pleasure. Flaco led her backward to the bed and whispered to her, "Lay down."

She pulled herself onto the bed and laid down. Deyanira reminded herself over and over that his pleasure was not the point of tonight. Flaco's exploration ventured down her stomach. He looked up at her. "Tonight is about you. The more you cum, the more I feel."

His face then traveled down and made the space between her legs his home. Deyanira's back arched as he sucked her clit and buried his fingers inside of her. She let out a loud gasp from the sensations she was feeling. Pleasure woke up every nerve in her body pulsing through waves. Each wave was bigger than the next. As the sensations swelled to eruption, Deyanira started taking deep, intentional breaths. The breathwork only heightened and woke up more of her body.

Flaco was relentless in his pursuit, diligently committed to her pleasure. Deyanira licked the palms of her hands and unconsciously started gently rubbing her nipples. It was the missing piece. The dynamite to the dam. It wasn't just her body having an experience. Her spirit itself was orgasming. Her eyes were released tears while her body shook uncontrollably. She covered Flaco's entire head with the tidal wave he begged for. Deyanira's moans were aligned with her breath. Flaco didn't stop his quest, speaking into her clit, "More give me more."

Chapter 22

"Maribel, I just don't understand. Why do you have to go back to the island now? You are so young. Stay here with me. Let me take care of you. Go to school here. After graduation, you can go back to the island if you still want to. The babies will be grown, and you'll be older."

Maribel threw her coffee cup across the kitchen to the bare wall, splattering coffee, but not breaking the cup. "You will never understand. I applied for *Universidad* on the island. I am going there. Our home needs me, and I need it. You're so self-absorbed. You would like me to stay here and be small so you can run around. The all-powerful *bruja* with a botanica. Oh, Deyanira, she is a saint, taking care of her sisters and giving up her life for them. Blah blah. I didn't ask you to give up your life for us, so stop asking me to give up mine. Everyone's calling you and coming to you to help them fix their lives. They're patting you on the back with praise. I am more than Dey–Dey's little sister. Did it ever occur to you that I am great, and I can do great things too?" Maribel cried at that point. She bit her bottom lip, praying that Deyanira would understand and embrace her.

"Wait, all this time you had gifts too? I didn't know! Tell me all about it. Have you been doing tarot readings?"

Maribel yelled loudly, "ARRGGHHHH I hate you, I wish Big Mama was still alive." She stormed out of the house in tears.

"Yea, well, me too," Deyanira mumbled to herself as she picked up the coffee cup Maribel left on the floor.

Deyanira was so confused by everything. Since Big Mama passed away, Deyanira had been doing the best she could to take care of her sisters and protect them, but she just was so lost. She didn't know why Maribel couldn't understand where Deyanira was coming from. How could Deyanira possibly keep Maribel safe all the way on the island, raise the two little sisters, and also run the botanica in Chicago? She needed Maribel here until the girls were adults, so she could keep them all safe and her sanity intact. Deyanira had already lost too many people she loved.

She plopped down on the couch and turned on the TV. Slowly, she drifted off to sleep. Deyanira found herself on the shores of Rio de Tanama. It was a dark, clear night. The sky was blanketed with stars and a full moon peaked just above the trees. The coqui sang their songs that always brought peace to Deyanira's spirit. Deyanira nestled herself on the ground near the river. As she tilted her head backward to admire the sky, she heard someone approaching. She often met Abuela in this spot. She cried, laughed, and shared her burdens with Abuela in this spot. "*Buena*, Abuela."

Deyanira realized there were two figures approaching. She turned around to see Abuela and a woman she didn't know standing behind her. Confused, Deyanira stood up to greet them.

"Mija, we need to talk." Abuela's facial expression looked like she was worried.

"Oh no, what's wrong? I have enough going on with Maribel,

I can't take on anything else."

Abuela hugged Deyanira and silently nodded her head. "This is Lolita. She is here to talk about Maribel. *Mi Amor*, with your gifts, we block you from seeing the destinies of your loved ones. You will feel when they are veering from the best and safest path, but that is all we allow you to know. Now, it is important that we discuss your sister's destiny and how she, too, was a brokerage made long ago."

Deyanira's confusion only deepened. "I am her big sister. I have to protect her. I can't protect her on the island, Abuela. Eighteen is too young."

A door appeared, and they left the island for the table.

"Sit Mija. You left the island so young; I don't think anyone told you about Lolita Lebron, did they? Lolita fought for Boricuas to be free of the US. When she went to their Congress to fight, they called her a terrorist and locked her away. Once she was old and gray, they let her return to the island. The torture and abuse they inflicted on her in prison fractured her mind. She was a rebel fighter for us. She demanded we were heard and not silenced. When she was young, she got pregnant before she became a freedom fighter. Lolita went to a *mesa blanca* for guidance. She always felt like she was meant to do great things, and she just didn't know what they were. The spirits told her she was meant to be a great revolutionary for the people. They told her that fighting her people would cause her pain and heartbreak, though. She would have to leave both babies on the island, but only one with her mother. Lolita didn't know they were twins. She told no one. Months later, the medium that held the *mesa* was also her midwife for the birth of the twins. That night, Lolita kissed her son's forehead goodbye and never saw him again. The medium found a family in Utuado to take him. That son's life was molded and shaped, and he found a wife, who gave birth to a beautiful baby boy.

"One night, your mother left you with your father for a drink at a bar. One of this son's descendants told your mother she was beautiful that night, and you know your mother's ego. They had sex that night in your Titi's car. Months later, Maribel was born. Do you understand what I am saying? Lolita died recently, and the torched spiritually passed to Maribel. That is why it feels like there is a fire lit in her, and she will burn anything that stands between her and returning to the island. Because her ancestors are pushing her to walk her path. She needs your love and support, not protection. Your destinies may intertwine later, but it is for you to release her with love, *and* spiritually protect her from afar."

Deyanira's head was spinning. "So we don't have the same father and because of that, I am supposed to just let her go back by herself because some random lady died and passed her a torch? What if she doesn't want the torch? Can you promise me she'll be safe?"

Lolita reached across the table and placed her hand on top of Deyanira's hand. "I cannot imagine what it feels like to let her go after spending so much of your life caring for her safety. I can tell you I released my son. I let him leave me. I did what I was told. I accepted my destiny despite the damage it may have done to my children. And it did damage my children. I became a vessel of hope and empowerment, like a tool, for the Semis to connect with the people. I wasn't a human revolutionary. I was a tool in the revolution, and I was prepared for death. My daughter lived a traumatic life, and my younger son was lost early. I cannot promise you she will be any safer on the island than she is in Chicago. There will be days she will hate the torch passed to her and the burdens it brings. Then will come the days when the torch will burn like the sun and warm her. Her spirit is restless with the energy of rebellion. I know you feel like you have to protect her, but your gifts sometimes leave her feeling lonely and small next to you. Let her find her way, and love her through it. She needs this."

Deyanira understood. Maribel being angry at Deyanria for training with Lottie made sense. "*Mija*, you cannot tell her. Ever. You cannot tell her that she is not your father's daughter. She will find out when the time is right, but never from you."

A door slammed with a loud bang, waking Deyanira from the couch. She jumped, searching for the source. She walked towards the stairs to investigate. Once Deyanira reached the top of the stairs, she figured out the source of the loud noise.

She shook her head and spoke to the spirits sarcastically, "This is your rebellion leader immaturely slamming doors to wake me up because she is still mad at me."

. Deyanira walked towards Maribel's closed bedroom door. She swung it open without knocking. Maribel was on her bed with her back turned to the door. She jumped when the door hit the wall behind it. Maribel looked at the doorway with her pouty tear-soaked face, and Deyanira ran towards her and jumped on her. She started obnoxiously kissing Maribel all over her face, the way a mom would kiss their teen who outgrew daily physical affection.

"Arrgh STTTOOPPPP. Your breath stinks," Maribel groaned through a smile.

Deyanira flopped down next to Maribel on her bed and wrapped her arm around her, giving her sister a slight squeeze as she laid her head on Maribel's shoulder. "You promise me to be safe? No going out partying alone and late, promise? No getting drunk around boys? Also, to be clear, I never want you to dim your light for me. I am so sorry. I didn't handle this the right way. You are amazing and meant to do great things. Your gifts are different from mine, but just as important. I am just going to miss you. Keeping you here has nothing to do with the babies. I am not a mom, and it seems when I try to be one, I mess up pretty badly. I am your older sister. You are my heart. The idea of you leaving feels like a piece of my heart is leaving me. Your absence hurts. So do you promise to call me and write to me? I'm going to cry myself to sleep when you leave. I want you to know that you door-slamming bully." Deyanira placed her lips on Maribel's cheek and blew a raspberry.

Maribel laughed and pulled away. "I'm going to miss you too, big head. Can you try not to be a bossy bitch to the babies when I'm gone?"

They spent the rest of the night talking, crying, and cuddling.

Chapter 23

Calida sat on the edge of the bed giggling and telling Deyanira about the picture she just drew. "See her? She is going to the beach with her kitty, Mami."

Deyanira listened intently, "Oh wow that is so good, sounds like a fun day *Mija*. Does her kitty need sunscreen?"

Calida looked away, and her giggling stopped abruptly. When she turned towards Deyanira again, her face was deadpan and her breath shallow. "My stepmother wants me dead." She spoke the words in a monotone.

It startled Deyanira. "Wait what? What do you mean, *Mija*?"

Calida shook her head and giggled. "She doesn't need sunscreen, Mami. She has fur, silly."

Deyanira was overwhelmed with emotions. Calida had never met her father, nor had Deyanira discussed him. "Mami has to go on the patio and meditate, *mi amor*; I'll be right back."

The patio of the apartment was on the roof. It had a beautiful view of the lush green hilltops of Caguas. Deyanira avoided being on the patio after dusk because she didn't want her energy to tempt an encounter with the *duende*. She wasn't trying to invite an encounter with a million mosquitoes, either.

She lit a candle on the small table upstairs and closed her eyes. Deyanira called out to Abuela in her spirit while she took deep breaths. Soon, she was swallowed into the depth of her own mind— the place where her mind ended and her spirit began, and vice versa. She met Abuela. Deyanira told Abuela about the confusing thing Calida said.

"I've never told her she has a dad. She doesn't even know what a stepmom is. Whenever she asks me why she doesn't have a dad, I always explain that everyone's family is different. You know, some two mommies, two daddies, no mommies or daddies, just *Tias* and *Tios*. Where did it come from, Abuela?" Deyanira's thoughts raced, and her tone became panicky. After finding out she was pregnant, she also found out that Calida's father had another lover. He'd told Deyanira to go to the clinic and that he would have nothing to do with the baby if she kept it. Deyanira didn't understand but kept the baby anyway. It was a very confusing time for her. It was as if he was two different people. When they were together, she felt so safe and loved. When he was away from her, he was disconnected and distant. She accepted that she would never understand why he pretended to love and care for her and just focused on loving the baby. She saw on the internet, around Calida's first birthday, that he was engaged to marry his other lover. They married and through the grapevine, Deyanira found out they were expecting their first child together.

Abuela said, "If his wife wished her dead, Calida could see it. Her gifts are strong and still forming. She may have just picked up on a conversation." Abuela urged Deyanira to connect with his wife's energy and investigate.

Deyanira took a deep breath and ventured through time and space until she came to the wife. Deyanira stepped into a room and saw the wife with another woman. She tuned into the conversation.

"I saw some texts in his phone, and I know he hid this baby to protect me. I can't have the baby growing up and seeking him out. She'll ruin our family," the wife pleaded with the woman.

Deyanira believed the wife was just venting her fears and felt a deep relief.

"Okay. From the texts it seems like the kid has health problems?"

The wife nodded.

"Good. One foot into the grave makes attaching the curse to her easier. I need a name, and if you have a picture from those texts, that will be helpful. On the new moon, I will set the curse, and the child will be dead soon after. This will cost five hundred dollars to get it done."

Deyanira gasped and stumbled back out of the room, falling on her butt in the darkness of the Tanama River. A hand on her shoulder pulled Deyanira towards the light.

Abuela was there, crouching down next to Deyanira. "Are you okay?"

Deyanira asked. "How could she, Abuela? What kind of person wants to kill a child? A helpless child? Calida has been through so much already. There are two. Two women that are so quick to murder a child for their own self-interest. Is that *bruja* powerful enough to cast this curse?"

Abuela's facial expression did not soothe Deyanira's concern and fear. "*Mi amor*, the bruja is from a strong bloodline in Mexico. She is misguided. Her family left the old ways for the corruption of colonialism and Christianity. When she felt the call, there was no one to guide her with principles, only wounds."

Deyanira's eyes lit up golden. "So I am supposed to feel bad for the woman strong enough to kill my daughter?"

Abuela cleared her throat. "Absolutely not. I am telling you what makes her the most dangerous. She has no principles, only greed and power. You will have to stop them, and send it back to them."

Deyanira's eyes were no longer golden, and she was vexed by what Abuela said. "You mean to save Calida, I have to send the curse back and kill them?"

Abuela shook her head. "You can just send it back to the wife, but remember, the wife is killing based on emotions. The *bruja* is killing based on greed, for five hundred dollars. The *bruja* will kill more children and more children with defenseless parents."

"That isn't my war. I am angry and terrified, but you are asking me to take a hurting woman's life to save Calida's life. There has to be another way." Deyanira shut down Abuela's notion that an eye for an eye was the only way. She broke out of meditation. When she opened her eyes and returned to the patio, she saw that the candle was blown out, and she heard rustling in the far corner of the patio. It startled Deyanira.

"Please leave me and mine be. We honor you and your ancient presence, but we do not wish to know you." She made her proclamation as she walked back to the door, never looking away from the corner. Once inside, she recited her protection over the door.

Deyanira kept protections up on the apartment. Calida's protection from the curse was provided through baths filled with herbs. The curse was strong though and kept its attack on. Deyanira kept a *romero* plant by the door and when it wilted, she knew she needed to strengthen the protections. Deyanira finally found the perfect home for Calida and herself. It was a three-bedroom light yellow brick home in the hills of Guayama.

There was a large amount of land, and a fence surrounded the property as security. The land sprawled downhill and was abundant in foliage. There were many cocoa, chinas, mangos, aguacate, and guayaba trees.

Deyanira spent the first two weeks protecting Calida and the property. She performed the ritual Lottie taught her. She had a sign placed on the gate that read in Spanish: *Those who enter to cause us harm will die, and their spirits will serve our family for ten years in spirit.*

Deyanira really had a hard time accepting the idea of taking life. The last box was unpacked, and the house was feeling like a home. Deyanira set up the altar room last, on purpose. She wanted to focus on protection for Calida and the new home. She was avoiding her ancestors and guides because she knew they were pressuring her to do something to keep Calida safe.

The glasses were full of water, and meals were placed with their cigars and liquor. Abuela loved her shot of rum and teacup of *flor de maga té.*

Once the room was set, Deyanira turned on her drum music and sat, prepping for her meditation. She met Abuela at Rio de Tanama. The sound of the birds' song greeted her before the view was clear from blur.

"Mija, you cut us off," Abuela said with a huff.

"I just think the theory of an eye for an eye is easier than the act, Abuela," Deyanira said, splashing some water in Abuela's direction with her bare foot.

"Pfft, little girl. No one said an eye for an eye. Where did you get that? She sent a curse to your four-year-old, to take her life. I never said to curse her to death for what she did. I said to send it back to her. It is hers, so return what is hers to her. If the curse isn't powerful enough to take a life, it won't affect her. If the *bruja* didn't send the curse, then there is nothing to return to her, so she will still be safe. Now what you decide to do to the *bruja* is your business. Where did this idea of not harming someone who harms you come from?"

"If I do what they do, I am no better than them," Deyanira replied with all the self-righteousness in her body.

"That is exactly how the Brotherhood uses Christianity to bind and limit us. They didn't hide that they were bad. They flaunted it and dared our ancestors to be better. When you are at war, you do not say, how can I be better, morally, than the person shooting at me? You have to dive deep into what your actual morals are, and what conditioning is. When this *bruja* cursed your child, she went to war with you. How will you ever be truly protected if you do not also defend with force if necessary? Calida is your daughter. You worked so hard to keep her alive. Aren't you tired of *still* working hard to keep her alive? It was not the way of the ancients to allow people to cause us harm and offer them grace. That was strategic brainwashing. It only serves the people causing harm."

Abuela's words pushed through a mental block Deyanira didn't realize she had. It was conditioning. She saw flashes of her stepmother's abuse and then her mother's abuse. Deyanira realized she offered care to people who would hurt her. She saw their humanity when they didn't see her as human. She was surviving them. They conditioned Deyanira to be complacent in their abuse by striving to be morally superior. It gave her so much to think about that she sat down on a rock in the river to process it all.

Abuela said, "I'll leave you to dissect and reflect. Just remember, no one is saying to leave your empathetic, sweet, loving, and compassionate parts. We are saying you can have them and not offer them to people who would see you dead before they wished you good health and help." She walked into the river and kissed the top of Deyanira's head before fading away. Deyanira spent hours in mediation, pulling apart and dissecting the conditioning.

Deyanira spent the next few weeks sifting through her conditioning and the decision she needed to make before the day came. The moral high ground she took made her feel superior and above those who caused her harm. It made her feel good to know that she wasn't like them. She was different. All the while, they were abusing and using her. Deyanira reflected on how it was all rooted in manipulation and conditioning. As long as you felt like you were superior to someone, you stayed complacent.

She remembered the first day her stepmother beat her little sisters. She had sent Deyanira away, out of fear Deyanira would fight her. Once she realized Deyanira wouldn't, she beat them in front of her. Deyanira really embraced the ideology that no sacrifice was noble. She recalled being bullied at school and never fighting back, always accepting the cruel words thrown at her. She realized it also came from American media in the era she grew up in. The way the media celebrated Dr. King and depicted him as someone that allowed himself and his followers beaten to show the world the abuse black people of America endured. How the same media demonized Malcolm X or the black panthers as terrorists and all they did was fight back against people hurting them. Deyanira had to decide did she want to embrace this fictitious moral superiority or fight against those who attacked her without her conditioning of shame or guilt. The conditioning made her feel dirty, and she spent many nights in the tub scrubbing her body and crying.

She fed her spirit poison all those years.

One of those nights, she drifted to sleep in the tub, and Abuela comforted her. "You didn't know. Part of this realization is also giving yourself empathy. None of us know what seeds are planted in us. You are realizing before you crossover, and that is an amazing feat. You have to stop holding yourself to an unreasonable, superior standard. At your core, you are a human. A traumatized and conditioned human. You deserve all the empathy you would give others. You will have good days and bad days. Days where you stand in your power and days where the conditioning wins. Both days you are a whole person. You are beautiful and shine like the sun on all days. Remember that."

Just then, Deyanira was jolted out of meditation. She sat up, she wept. "Dammit Abuela, you're always loving on me in ways I haven't learned to love myself yet. *Gracias.*"

There was a moth on the wall in the front room. Then the next morning, there were five of them in the hallway. The morning after that, Calida slept in and took extra naps. Deyanira realized the curse was trying to take root. She needed to send it back. She gathered the items needed to send it back. Deyanira got a jar and a small mirror. She broke the mirror into pieces and placed them in the jar facing inward. She wrote Samena, Calida's stepmother's name, on the piece of paper and tied it to a stick.

Deyanira repeated, "I bind Samena's energy to this stick. Samena, I draw you and your energy into this stick."

She then placed the paper and the stick in the middle of the mirror pieces. Deyanira closed the jar tight. She took out a medium-sized black candle and inscribed it with the spell. Deyanira pricked her finger and dragged her blood across the words on the candle.

She lit the candle, saying, "With my blood, I redirect any and all energy you sent to Calida or me back to you and yours. All of it will return to you tenfold."

Deyanira then lit the candle, placed it atop the jar lid, and left it to burn. When the candle burned out, she went to the porch to retrieve it. The candle burned down into the shape of a grim reaper with his sickle, and she knew it had been done. She took it to a crossroads and buried it.

Driving home from burying, she heard spirits say, "Her womb will now and always be a tomb."

Chapter 24

"Deyanira, come home quick. Big Mama isn't waking up. ANSWER YOUR PHONE!" The text sunk into Deyanira's chest like hot lava, burning a hole straight through. Then nausea hit. Her head spun her coffee and bagel right out of her stomach and into her throat.

She stumbled out of her chair in the middle of her literature class, rushing and scrambling to the front of the class where the garbage pail sat. As she hugged the tiny pail, she spewed the physical manifestation of her pain into it. Tears rolled down her cheeks until she was empty, and reality set in. She raised her head from the pail to see her entire class silently watching her in horror. Deyanira wiped her face and mumbled an apology through her weeping. She crawled to her desk, making more of a spectacle than the pail of vomit in the front of the class. Deyanira grabbed her book bag and phone, shamefully sprinting for the door.

Once in her dorm room, she called Maribel. There was a commotion in the background. She could hear Camila and Alma in the background crying loudly and people talking. Deyanira couldn't speak. She froze. Her little sisters' aching cries in the background both confirmed the worst and triggered their past.

"Deyanira, are you there? You have to hurry. They are trying to put us in foster care. Deyanira, can you hear me?" Maribel was frantic. Her tone was serious and focused.

"I'm here. I'm coming. Tell them I am coming. Where is Big Mama? Is she okay?" Deyanira stuttered through her words, unable to tuck away her emotions for her sister. Deyanira had been safe for too long, and now she was vulnerable to feeling her emotions as they came up.

"She's gone. Big Mama didn't wake up. I tried to wake her up. I tried Dey, I really tried, but she was cold already." There she was, Maribel the human, the sixteen-year-old who was terrified, traumatized, and grief-strickened. Her voice quivered through her reply. And just like that, Deyanira's emotions were tucked away. Maribel and her little sisters needed her.

"Listen, who is there? Is it the police or a social worker? Put them on the phone."

Maribel whispered, "The police."

Deyanira was glad. She could talk her way into a delay with the police. "Officer, hello? Can you hear me?" The officer responded and immediately went into the semantics of protocol for foster children. Deyanira interrupted, "Officer, please, we are not foster kids. Miriam adopted us and discontinued her foster care placements to raise us. We are legally her children. I am over the age of eighteen and next of kin. I can be there in six hours, eight tops. I am asking you to treat this like you would a normal family that lost their mother. Allow next of kin to make it there and receive the minor children." Deyanira knew that because her sisters were not black, the assumption of foster care would be immediate.

"Is there proof in this house that you are legally her children?" The officer said, willing to bend, but blanketed in reluctance.

"Yes, of course, I would never ask you to risk your job like that. If you walk into her room, there is a file cabinet. The bottom drawer has all the important papers. There is a blue folder, and it should have our adoption order and all the records you'll need. She adopted us a long time ago. It was finalized when I was fourteen."

The officer walked back into the room, rummaged through the drawer, and confirmed they were indeed no longer foster children.

"I promise I will be there soon. Please let my sisters grieve their mother."

The officer gave Deyanira until that evening, and then he would call social services. She thanked him and said she owed him a pizza. He chuckled, "I am sorry for your loss, kid."

Off the phone, she rushed to zip her suitcase and shoot out of her dorm room. She ran into a group of girls in the hallway, knocking them down like bowling pins. Deyanira apologized and started walking down the hall, when one girl from her previous literature class yelled at her, "He broke up with you and you fall to pieces. Throwing up in class and leaving campus in the middle of the week. You're an embarrassment."

Deyanira spun around on her heels. "My mom died, you stupid bitch, and I have to get to Chicago in a few hours or my little sisters are going to be sent to foster care. And for the record, I broke up with him. So fuck you and him!" Deyanira turned around and sped walk for the doors.

She jumped in her two-door Saturn and threw her bag in the passenger seat. Her hands gripped the steering wheel, and she took a deep breath, attempting to relieve the pressure. She then ran through the checklist of everything. "Wallet? Check, clothes, check, toothbrush? Shit. Oh well." She hit reverse and drove out of her dorm parking lot. As she reached the edge of campus, she paused longer than usual and looked at the welcome sign to SIU. In her heart, she knew she would not be returning to classes again. A horn beeped behind her, and she was off to the highway.

Halfway through Illinois, Deyanira stopped to get gas and to call Falah. He answered like he always answered her calls. "Hey little sis, what's good?"

There were so many nuances of unresolved feelings between Falah and Big Mama that Deyanira paused as if someone had stolen her words because they were too hurtful to speak. He knew. Somehow Falah knew. She could hear his tears and grief. He wept with heavy breaths, tears, and snot. After space and time, Falah's cries settled down and he said, "I saw her. I saw her little sis. I was asleep, and she came to me in my dream. Is that crazy? I just thought it was a dream when I woke up. A sweet dream."

Deyanira had been silently crying, pulling Falah's grief out of him, through her, and out with her tears. "Falah, can you tell me about the dream? Is that okay? It is okay if it is too private."

Falah wiped his face and took a deep breath. "No Dey, it is okay. I'll tell you. You have to understand though, me and Big Mama, we have a complicated relationship."

Deyanira interrupted him. "You are allowed to be mad at Big Mama and feel hurt. You don't have to hide that from me. One person's villain can be another person's savior. Both sides make a whole person."

The depth of his nineteen-year-old sister's wisdom startled him. "Oh nah, sis, she's never been my villain, just someone out of my reach. You know, like that one thing you've always wanted but never quite got. She was in my dream. She showed up, and it started like all my dreams with her. I had my head in her lap, and she was caressing my head and shoulder like a mama does when their baby needs to feel safe. She whispered she loved me.

But then she said things she had never said before. She started off by saying things like, you were the most important thing to me. She said, 'I'm so sorry I didn't show you that. My inner child wanted to love foster children because, for some reason, I saw loving them as different than loving my own son and not because you weren't a phenomenal son. I never had a mother and when I finally met my mother, I became a mom myself. I think I wanted to mother motherless children because it felt like mothering myself as a child. I thought you could never relate to the pain I had because you had a mother. Your pain was so much different from mine. You had a mother in your life, day in and day out, but I was distracting and busying myself with anything, anyone, but you. I made you a motherless child with a mother. Falah, you sought to be seen by others and then spent so much time thinking you were my shame for your time in prison. You were never. When they told me to pick you or the foster kids, I should've picked you. I am so sorry. I know that had to hurt so bad. In my closet is a box of letters. I wrote to you every day you were in prison. Every single day, I told you all the things I wanted you to hear, but I was too broken to say. I feared it was too late. I was terrified I had already lost you. I just knew you didn't want me. I can see now. You always wanted a mama, and I am so grateful you were able to find that in your granny and auntie. I made a promise to you when you were born. I held you in my arms and told you I would die for you. You were my source of life. It has always been you. I love you more than air, and I am so sorry I didn't show you. The cries of my inner child drowned out the cries of the child I birthed. Sometimes when we think we are breaking a generational curse, we are really just turning it into a different pain from the same root issue. I did that for you. Instead of loving you outright, I gave you a different kind of pain with the same root problem of being motherless. You do not have to forgive me. I pray the cries of your inner child are healed before the end of your time. I will always be with you and watching over you in ways my pain never allowed me to in my life.' Then we sat in silence as we both cried, and she held me tightly until I woke up."

Deyanira and Falah talked through his grief, and Deyanira spared him hers. The call ended with him telling Deyanira he'd tell Lottie, and they'd make their way up there from Louisiana by the day after the next. He told Deyanirato not to worry about anything, there was money to take care of everything. Deyanira felt so guilty. It was as if he read her thoughts. She was silently spiraling. *Will Falah sell the house? Where will I live with the girls? How will I take care of them? I don't have any money.* Deyanira did her best to be present on the call. "You hear me, Dey? You and the girls are taken care of." She thanked him and said her battery was about to die.

Deyanira insisted on an autopsy because Big Mama was too young to die. It delayed the funeral arrangements. The autopsy showed she died of a ruptured aneurysm. Maribel recalled she went to bed early because she had a headache. There was comfort in the notion that brain aneurysms were hard to catch and quick to take people before their time.

The funeral was to be held at Gatling's Funeral Home. Falah

and Lottie took care of the arrangements. They only asked the girls for any words or pictures they wished to share in the funeral program. It was a beautiful service; the room was so full of people who loved Big Mama that there weren't any seats left. Previous foster children wept over her casket and so did the random lady from down the block who braided Big Mama's hair. Deyanira had to nudge Alma and Camilla for laughing at the theatrics of the hair braider leaping onto the casket, wailing in grief.

Then Falah leaned over and whispered, "Damn, Mama must've been one hell of a tipper." Deyanira laughed and cut her eyes at him in the same breath. She loved Falah. He was a great big brother, and she was so grateful she got to spend time with him. He wasn't as close with the younger sisters because, after the adoption had been finalized, it was mostly Deyanira who spent her summers in Louisiana with him and Lottie.

Once the surrounding people broke off into their own cliques at the repass and the conversation shifted towards gossip, Deyanira saw her little sisters' loneliness. Deynira realized she had to grieve a disconnection from Big Mama when she went away to school. It was awful. She was so lonely– depression almost swallowed her whole.

Alma and Camilla blocked out their mother or their stepmother's abuse. They only knew and remembered Big Mama. Big Mama was their entire world, and yet in this room full of people, they didn't quite feel like they were a part of Big Mama's world. So many people connected to Big Mama, but not to them. They were lost, scared, and just wanted to leave. Their grief was personal and intimate; they couldn't share it with strangers. Just as Deyanira walked towards them to ask if they wanted to leave, Aunt Lottie appeared.

"Hey, Auntie's babies. Come on over here and get you some love." She swooped Alma and Camilla into her arms and squeezed them until Deyanira thought their eyeballs would pop out. Then, she kissed them all over their heads and faces. "Let's get out of here. I'm ready for some food and cuddles in front of the TV. These people don't know your Big Mama anyway, not like you do. She was *your* mama." The babies nodded their heads in agreement and turned to Deyanira for permission to leave.

"You are so grown up," Deyanira said. "Thirteen and twelve, you don't need my permission if you're ready to go."

Lottie told them to go grab their jackets and then pinched Deyanira. "Don't do that. I know at thirteen, your childhood and youth had already been robbed from you, but you let them be young. You don't want to be their new mama, but you are. They need your love, guidance, and reassurance. Do you hear me? You're not alone. I'll be that for you so you can be that for them."

Deyanira stuck her tongue out at Aunt Lottie, and Aunt Lottie patted Deyanira's butt as she walked away.

Off into a room, Deyanira found Maribel sitting on a couch, hugging her legs to her chest, crying silently; alone.

"Hey, Aunt Lottie's taking the babies to the house if you want to go with her. I can hold down the fort here with Falah."

Maribel wiped her eyes and sniffled. "Why aren't we allowed to have people who love us, Dey? Why can't we have peace and love?"

Deyanira sat next to her sixteen-year-old sister and threw an arm around her. "What do you mean? We have people that love us still." She laid her head on Maribel's shoulder lovingly.

"I remember Dey. I am not like the babies. I remember. I

remember Mama and how horrible she was. I remember Doña Marina and how great she was. I remember Tia and how fun she was. I remember Papa, his horrible wife, and the things she did to us. All the people who were supposed to love us didn't, and all the people who did love us died. Why do all the people that love us die?"

Deyanira realized Maribel, like herself, carried the burdens of their trauma. She wasn't sure how Maribel remembered those things because she was so young, but she believed Maribel when she said she remembered. Because the pain behind her voice was there.

In that moment she wanted to be awe-inspiring and strong for her little sister. She wanted to impart words of wisdom that would stay with her until the end of her days, like in the movies. She couldn't because this wasn't a movie. This was real life and a hard question she asked herself often in the darkest of nights.

She took a deep breath and gave it all she had. "I think shitty things happen. They aren't punishments. They aren't things that we wanted. I think other people's shit pours into ours, and it hurts. Sometimes our shit pours into other people, and it hurts them. Shitty things happen, and they hurt, and they are unfair. Sometimes we have to accept that and just cry until it feels a little better. I don't think everyone who loves us dies, though. I just think shitty things have happened to us, and it has been unfair."

Maribel nodded in agreement while Deyanira cried through her monologue. "Well, first thing I'm doing when I get to heaven is kicking God in the shins because what the fuck."

The girls laughed together at the idea.

After the funeral, the people stopped coming by the house to check on Falah and the girls; Falah had Big Mama's attorney come to the house for the reading of her will. He told Lottie to take the three younger girls for ice cream and a movie. When the attorney arrived, Deyanira was flustered and asked Falah if he wanted her to leave. He laughed and said, "You think I call you little sis because you ain't family? Sit down, he's here for you."

The attorney introduced himself and began the reading. "I, Miriam Ida Greene, of 6351 May Street, Chicago IL 60621, and a resident of Cook County in the state of Illinois, declare this to be my will."

He went on to break down that if all the children were minors, they would go to Lottie, but if Deyanira was over eighteen, they would go to her. The will then went on to state that there was a trust set up for the girls. It covered monthly living expenses, and when Alma turned eighteen, it would be divided evenly four ways, transferred to them as individuals. She left Deyanira $150,000 and the house, which was paid off, as an acknowledgment for raising the girls. The attorney started breaking down the bills on how they would be forwarded to his office until the youngest was eighteen and how the girls would be paid out of the trust. His firm would wire money monthly to Deyanira's account for food, clothes, and other things the girls need. Deyanira felt awful and uncomfortable. She was sitting in this room, and Big Mama's biological child received nothing– she left everything to Deyanira and her sisters. She shifted in her seat and fiddled with her shirt while controlling her breathing.

Suddenly she heard Falah, "Little sis, take a deep breath and cry. It's okay. Big Mama took care of me when I retired. I received my inheritance earlier."

Deyanira, while relieved, had questions. "How did she have all this money? Did she win the lottery?"

Falah was amused by what Deyanira was implying. "Oh, little sis. You really grew up poor on the island, I keep forgetting. When my granddad came to Chicago, my granny sent him money to buy a house for him and Big Mama. He took that money and bought a commercial building with a restaurant and a couple of shops. He opened a BBQ place and a laundry shop, then rented out the other spaces. Big Mama and him lived in the back of the BBQ spot in the beginning. He took the rent from the other places and bought a three flat then rented them out. By the time Big Mama was ten, he owned over forty properties and twenty-three businesses. When the Black Panthers organized here, my granddad became a huge backer of the movement. When he passed on, he left me half and Big Mama half, but she kept my half in a trust because I was a knucklehead, doing knucklehead things. Big Mama sold some of the commercial properties when I got locked up, but kept everything else. She lived so modestly that most of the rent money sat and gained interest. Big Mama never spent the money she got for taking care of you girls, either. She just put it up for you to have later. My granddad was a businessman, and so was Big Mama." He ended with a hefty laugh.

Chapter 25

The kitchen was filled with fragrant spices and laughter. The sun was setting while the *coqui* sang. Deyanira's little sisters were such good Titis to Calida. Deyanira got quiet and watched them love on Calida and she scolded herself for not returning to the island sooner. Deyanira knew deep down that Calida needed the doctors at Lurie's Children's Hospital but she missed her sisters so much. They were no longer the young girls she remembered them to be. They were young women now. There were experiences of overwhelming triumphs, joys, and pleasures that Deyanira was not a part of. She looked around the room full of pride and grief at the same time. *Can they see themselves like how I see them right now? So grown up, beautiful, and brimming with excitement for life, ready to experience it to its fullest*, she thought.

Maribel walked around the kitchen island and laid her head on Deyanira's shoulder. "We did it. We made it. They are happy and loved."

A tear escaped Deyanira's eye and down her cheek, and she leaned her head on Maribel's head. She reached her left hand across her chest to Maribel's hand on her shoulder.

"*Ay, dios mio!* Look at these two, all sappy and crying quietly in the corner. Come here," Camila shouted as she sprung out of her chair and rushed towards her two older sisters.

Alma followed with a gentle and slower embrace. They left Calida alone at the table, who peered over the kitchen island at all the women in her family. Alma, with all her warmth, said, "*Mi amor*, don't be sad, get in here. We have all our love for you. It's all for you."

Calida sprang from her chair and ran toward the group of women, awkwardly hugging and knocking them over onto the counter and causing an eruption of laughter.

The brothers-in-law peeked into the kitchen to assess the commotion. "I started the fire, *chicas*," Maribel's husband exclaimed, and then swiftly retreated to the yard.

The women chuckled at his caution and started grabbing their cups and walking out to the yard. They told stories and laughed late into the night as the *pitorro* flowed into their cups. Calida fell asleep in Deyanira's lap. Deyanira brushed Calida's curls from her face.

Deyanira nonchalantly said, "How could anyone want to hurt this sweet girl?"

The ancestors were sneaky like that, and although they might not be able to possess Deyanira at will anymore, they could plant powerful suggestions when Deyanira drank alcohol or was sleepy.

"Fuck you mean? Who wants to hurt her?" Maribel's flame of passion and deep familial love was ignited, and there was no turning back the conversation.

Deyanira told her sisters and two brothers-in-law about the stepmother going to a *bruja*. She also told them about the working she did on the stepmother who lost her baby in childbirth and could not carry a child to term since. Maribel jumped from her seat and began making her inquiries. "And what of this *bruja*? What did you do to her?"

Deyanira laughed, which enraged tipsy Maribel further. "Wait, I am not laughing at you. It is the ancestors. They want their pound of flesh. Abuela ain't shit with her slick ass. She orchestrated this. I couldn't just have one night of fun with my *hermanas*."

Maribel relaxed her body and returned to her seat. Deyanira was grateful Camila and Maribel married spiritual men. Camila's husband was initiated in Santería, and Camila's husband worshiped the ways of the Tainos and Semi. Deyanira knew anyone else would think they were nuts. Instead, her brothers-in-law nodded their heads in agreement with Maribel.

Camila reached over and touched Deyanira's hand. "This isn't about revenge. It is about protection and balance. This is about consequences. We are not without consequences and lessons. Why should a person who sought to kill your child be absolved?"

Deyanira realized she had suppressed her malice towards the *bruja* because she was still working on her recovery from the move and the working she did against the stepmother. Deyanira was genuinely enraged all over again. "Let me meditate and speak with the ancestors about what we should do. I want to make sure what I am feeling is my own."

The sisters agreed but let Deyanira know they would not forget.

Deyanira, the next morning, met with her ancestors. Abuela stood in front of them with her arms folded. Deyanira laughed. "Well, I guess this is your answer. I have to do something."

Abuela softened up and explained that if the *bruja* was alive, she could always do more, and if it was in a period of time when

Deyanira was distracted or worn out, the *bruja's* curse could end in tragedy.

Deyanira called Maribel and Camila to tell them to prepare for their pound of flesh on the full moon. Alma offered to watch Calida, so she had to be excluded. Three nights before the full moon, Camila came to Deyanira's home and prepared her for the journey. She prepared a bath for Deyanira and gathered oils for after the bath was over. Camila entered the goat's pen and chose the sacrifice. She separated the goat from the group and prepared her for sacrifice. It was a great honor for the goat, and its spirit would be elevated for the part it would play.

The night of the full moon, the sisters and their spouses arrived with their heads wrapped and necks laced with beaded Elekes and cowry shells. Her sisters' skirts were long and full, swaying like palms in the wind as they walked. Deyanira sent Calida to Alma for the night to have a fun sleepover with her titi. Her brothers-in-law dragged their *barriles* out of the back of their cars. Her brothers-in-law were men of smaller stature, so carrying the barrel-like drums to the fire pit was a two-man job. Camila cleansed everyone before forming the circle, and she brought out the goat to the circle. As the brothers-in-law started drumming, the women started dancing to the beat of the *barriles*. Once the drums and chants sent the goat into a trance, Deyanira took a deep breath and stood next to the goat. She closed her eyes and asked her ancestors and Elegua to grant her safe passage. The dark became light.

Deyanira was in a bedroom cluttered with clothes and bowls of water. Brunt-down black candles crumbled on the dresser. On the lumpy queen-sized bed, the *bruja* sat slumped over. She had fallen asleep on her phone. She was heavyset, wearing a tight blue and white striped shirt. With each breath, Deyanira could hear a slight snore. Her complexion seemed pale and sickly, and her once-wavy hair seemed to be balding in patches. Undoubtedly, the powerful curses that the *bruja* released without permission had backlashed, eating away at her physically. In the corner, there was an *ofrenda*, dusty and dirty, without water, flowers, or offerings. The *bruja's* ancestors were in the corner, their pleas muted. Deyanira knew that the *bruja's* indigenous Mexican ancestors tried to stop the *bruja* from performing the curses. The ancestors knew the *bruja* was not listening because she was cursing people for things as small as spreading *chisme* at their jobs or looking at another woman's *novio*. They wished Deyanira wasn't there and wept for their descendant. However, they understood she had to be stopped. Deyanira walked slowly through the room, examining it and taking it all in. Once satisfied, she smacked the *bruja's* foot. "Wake up, dummy."

Deyanira startled the *bruja*, and she jumped in her place. Deyanira paced at the foot of the *bruja's* bed while her physical body paced behind the goat. "Do you remember a woman coming to you and asking you to curse a little girl? A child her husband had from cheating on another woman? A sickly child?"

The *bruja's* face went paler than before. She tried to stutter through excuses. "Listen, I didn't think it would work. I was just messing around."

Deyanira's eyes lit up golden. "You didn't take five hundred dollars to curse the child?"

The *bruja*, at this point, assumed her best bet was to play dumb. "Honest, I took the money, but I didn't know it would work. I just bought a book a year ago and have been doing stuff. Some people pay me, and I take it and do some stuff, but it's just dress up for me."

Deyanira now was infuriated. The *bruja* was lying. She might be self-trained, but she understood she was from a powerful bloodline.

"You think I'm dumb," Deyanira growled.

The *bruja* was trying to distract Deyanira so she could run out of the room. She soon realized she was paralyzed– only her head functioned. She locked eyes with Deyanira, petrified. Deyanira laughed and touched the *bruja's* toe.

"You really thought you were powerful. HA! You thought you were the most powerful *bruja* out there. *Brujas* cast spells, *pendaja*. They are limited. It is a pity no one taught you. You were just casting things without balance. It is going to take your bloodline generations to pay off the debts you made in the spirit realm. You should be ashamed of yourself. Growing up, you felt powerless in school, and now you have allowed that pain to seek power. Did you feel powerful cursing a child? An innocent child. You didn't even consult your ancestors. If you did, you would be alive in the morning. They would have told you how powerful I was and how powerful the child was."

Deyanira broke her monologue with a chuckle. "Did you know that the minute you cast the curse, my child knew? That is how powerful she is as a five-year-old, a thousand miles away from you. Imagine how great she will be. The magic in your blood doesn't equal to a hangnail on my baby. You will see, though. I am taking you tonight. Your spirit will serve my bloodline for ten years. Your energy will protect us and snuff out danger. You will not have free will during these ten years. Once these ten years are over, you will only be released if you choose to crossover and begin your healing. As far as your bloodline goes, I bind them for five generations to have access to their gifts and magic."

The *bruja* blurted out, "Wait, please don't do that. You know, if a gift is blocked, it can cause health issues and insanity."

Deyanira scoffed at the nerve of her begging for mercy. "You still do not understand how powerful I am! I hear your intentions as they hide behind your teeth, while you speak your false pleas. You don't even care for your descendants. You think they can break you free from my working? Oh, what a fool you are. You will learn, though, or you will remain in service until the end of my bloodline. If you are smart, you will learn a great deal from my bloodline. You will come to take accountability and learn the balance of magic. Once you are released to crossover, you get to keep that wisdom, and you will be a powerful ancestor for your descendants. If you're smart, that is."

At the end of the *bruja's* bed, Deyanira lifted her leg as if she was straddling something. It was confusing and peculiar to the *bruja*. From her waist, Deyanira pulled out her knife. The *bruja* felt a tingle in her left hand. Excitement filled her body and mind. *The spell is clearly weakening, and I get away,* she thought. She could turn her head towards her left hand, so she could focus on movement. She saw it. A kitchen knife. *How did it get there? When?*

Deyanira's eyes lit up golden again and as she slit the goat's throat, the *bruja* raised her hand and slit her own throat. Deyanira left the *bruja's* room and returned to her own body, still straddling the lifeless body of the goat. She held the goat up with her thighs and knees. Her hands and skirt were covered in the goat's warm blood. Beside her appeared the *bruja's* spirit. She was walking Deyanira's property in service. Camila and Maribel were not mediums, but due to the full moon, they saw the *bruja's* spirit briefly. They spat in the bruja's general direction. They placed the goat in the fire and prepared to give the ashes a proper burial. Camila walked Deyanira to the side door, and she undressed Deyanira beyond the gaze of the family. They entered the home to an already drawn bath, prepared with herbs. The bath would ground Deyanira back into her body and protect her. A large meal with *pitorro* was set in the altar room. A feast of thanks to her ancestors and Elegua. Once cleansed, Camila anointed Deyanira with oils and helped her to bed. Camila then returned to the family to complete the ritual and burial.

As Deyanira slept, she returned to the *bruja's* room to witness the wails and cries of the *bruja's* mother discovering her eldest daughter's lifeless body. Deyanira stayed in the room and cried. She cried with the mother and for the mother. She spent most of her night in that room, in spirit, weeping for the family and their loss. Once the room was emptied and the lights were shut off, Deyanira retreated to her ancestors, where they held her. She understood the balance. She could never allow her ego to shield her with justification. Deyanira would go to war soon. She acknowledged that in war it was either kill or be killed. She also understood that death didn't just affect the enemy. It was everyone who loved them; and their grief. Abuela held Deyanira and told her she was proud of her. Deyanira knew that when the great spiritual war came, she would not be afforded the luxury of a big-picture vision, only survival.

Chapter 26

Everything happened so fast. Miriam's father was furious, but also grateful she was safe. He got on the phone with Lottie, and she told him to let her stay for the summer and help in the shop. He agreed reluctantly. He told Lottie he would be down there at the end of the summer to retrieve Miriam. Lottie spoke safety over him and his journey down. He scoffed and hung up without a word.

Before Miriam knew it, she was in a car with Lottie driving to see her mother. She faced the window, not sure why she was angry with this woman, but her father didn't seem too keen on her either, so Lottie must be bad news.

"What did your daddy tell you about us, *Cher*?"

Miriam whipped her head around in a huff. "My name is Miriam, not *Cher*."

Lottie laughed a belly laugh so hard it caused the car to wander onto the shoulder. "You are full of venom, just like your mama. I know your name, you little brat. *Cher* is short for *Cheri*; it is what we say down here, out of love. You are a viper, ready to strike. I gota watch you."

Miriam was humbled, but only briefly. "Daddy told me she couldn't be my mother and she couldn't come to Chicago. After his family was killed, he left her where she came from.

Sometimes when I laugh, he looks sour. I think it's because I laugh like her. I don't even know her name. I don't know anything about her. He doesn't talk about her, ever."

Lottie took a deep breath. "Okay listen. Your daddy loved your mama. I'll give him that. I suppose he hasn't quite gotten over her. She isn't the kind of woman people just forget. You are looking for answers in a story that isn't mine to tell, but you have to remember, *Cher*, you just showed up here. You can't get those answers all today and all at once. That's why I asked your dad to let you stay for the summer. You have to get to know us and our complexities. We are tough women and we are fighters. Wild and untameable. Our mama raised us that way. We have layers, and you can peel back those layers this summer. Your mama feels terrible guilt about facing you. She won't know what to do or how to do it. You have to get to know each other." Lottie's car pulled down the driveway to the country house. "Your daddy ruined your mama with his country living, though. She never thought about living in New Orleans again, she only visits for work. She bought this house with chickens and shit."

Miriam had given up on her dream of a warm welcome. Their feet hit the front steps of the home, and the screeching door creaked open. There she was. Miriam studied her features, squinting from the sun. There Miriam saw her own eye shape and complexion, her chin and cheeks, her hair, and body shape in her mother. Miriam always thought she looked like her father. Miriam felt like if she got too close, their bodies would mold together and make one body as if she was just a piece of Henrietta's body that had just been missing for sixteen years.

They both stared at each other in silence for a moment, then Lottie broke it. "It's hot. I need tea with a splash of goodness if all you two are going to do is stare at each other all night."

Henrietta, with a nervous laugh, finally spoke. "Let me show you your room."

Lottie interrupted, "Oh, I didn't bring her bag. She can stay with me above the shop for a bit and help me out. You can get her on the slow days and spend time with her at the shop."

Miriam's heart sank, but she remembered Lottie's words. Then her anger stewed to a boil, *who is she to keep me from my mother?*

They sat at the table, and Henrietta served them some iced tea. "You can call me Ms. Henrietta. Everyone does." The boil rose higher. Why couldn't she call her mother or mom? The boil started swirling around her head, then dug sharply into her chest, causing her breathing to change and her heart to ache. Ms. Henrietta tried to ask basic questions about school and her grades. Miriam's answers were brief and laced with venom.

Lottie walked over to the sink and placed her cup down. "Okay, Sug, you know I don't like driving in the dark coming from here, so we are going head back; we'll see you in the morning at the shop."

She leaned in and kissed her sister's cheek. Lottie signaled with a wave of her hand to Miriam that it was time to go. Awkwardly, Ms. Henrietta leaned in and kissed Miriam's cheek, but the anger caused Miriam's entire body to recoil.

The drive back to the shop was silent, but Miriam's breathing was heavy and her fists were balled so tight her nails cut into her hand and made it bleed. They walked into Lottie's apartment above the shop, and Lottie asked Miriam if she was hungry. There was no answer, but Miriam followed Lottie to the kitchen. Once there, Lottie pulled out some pans to fry up something quick for Miriam, and Lottie turned her back.

The eruption of all of Miriam's anger came. Miriam grabbed a drinking glass from the table and smashed it on the floor. Lottie continued cooking with her back to Miriam. The eruption of anger continued and gained momentum, and she scrambled and searched for more glasses to break. One by one the glasses smashed, then the plates. All the while, Lottie turned the bacon. She briefly left her station in front of the stove and ventured to the bread box to cut two slices. Lottie spread a little grease on the bread slices and toasted them in a separate pan. Once all the dishes and glasses were broken, Miriam huffed, searching the room for more things to break, but her pause allowed her adrenaline to bottom out. She collapsed on the kitchen chair instead.

Lottie silently wrapped the sandwich in a kitchen towel and placed it in front of Miriam. Walking over to the sink, her house shoes crunched on the glass. Lottie reached under the sink to reveal a tin cup with a handle. She rinsed it out and filled it with cool water to place in front of the sandwich. Lottie then left to return with a broom and dustpan, then once again, with a mop and bucket. She leaned them against the table. "Your room is the second door on the right when you're finished."

Lottie squeezed Miriam's shoulder lingeringly, with just enough empathy to soothe, and went to bed.

Over the course of weeks, Miriam settled into her space and learned her family practiced Voodoo. She learned that they didn't think Voodoo was evil. Her father didn't raise her religious. He always said he didn't trust any God that would let his family burn like that so white men could steal their land. Miriam wasn't against voodoo, but she was uncertain and unfamiliar with the practice. Ms. Henrietta did spells for people and taught them how to do certain things on their own. Lottie didn't do that. She mostly looked at bones and cards or their hands, then told people things about themselves. Miriam wasn't sure if it was fake or not, but she knew people were always shocked—but most of them were *mad*. Women would come in and ask if their man was cheating, and Lottie would say some name and the woman would shout, "I knew it" and storm out. Lottie would joke she was the reason for all the stabbings that happened within a hundred miles of New Orleans.

Lottie paid Miriam for her time. On the days the shop was closed, or slow, Lottie would let Miriam explore. As long as she had her charm necklace on that is. Miriam loved to get ice cream on those days. She was not used to that kind of sticky heat. The boy who served the ice cream started giving her extra cherries. Then, he started telling her jokes. One day, he told her she had a beautiful smile and beautiful eyes. No one had ever told her she was beautiful like that before. Back home, everyone knew her father, and he was too terrifying for boys to risk a compliment.

Miriam smiled more and said, "Thank you."

He would find excuses to wipe tables and sweep when she was there. "You sure do like ice cream. My name is Abbee."

Miriam laughed, "I just don't like being hot. This ice cream is tearing my stomach up. My name is Miriam."

She couldn't believe she blurted that out. She was so embarrassed. Her thoughts raced from *I can't believe I told him that about ice cream* to *now he thinks I don't come to see him.*

He bursted out laughing, "Why do you think you never see me eating it? There wouldn't be anyone at the counter. I'd be in the bathroom."

They laughed together, and Miriam calmed down. The next

time she came in, he said, "I got something for you."

He ran to the back and came out with a cup of shaved ice. He poured some fruit topping on. Abbee handed it to her, and when she reached for her wallet, he stopped her. They chatted until the sun went down. He locked up the shop and offered to walk her home. They walked and talked about the books they loved and chatted about Chicago. When they reached the door, his eyes widened. "Oh, so you related to the voodoo priestess."

Miriam was embarrassed, just shrugged, and with a disappointed turn, she walked away. He grabbed her hand to stop her. "I am not scared. She knows my granny and helped my uncle when he started seeing things. I would only be scared if I planned to hurt you."

Miriam's heart fluttered, and she smiled. "Goodnight," she said as she dragged her hand from his grasp, slowly.

She sat at the kitchen table while Lottie fixed her food. "What did you get into today, *Cher*?"

Miriam was always surprised by the freedom Lottie gave her to roam. Her father would never allow it, but Lottie explained she had been running those streets since she was as young as eight years old and Henrietta even younger.

"What's this thing do?" Miriam asked, fiddling with her charm necklace.

"Well, it is spelled so that anyone who wants to cause you harm will struggle with their breathing if they get near you. It'll start off slow, maybe make them cough a little, but if they stay near you, the harm will go from struggling to feeling like someone is choking them. If they touch you to harm you, their skin will catch fire and melt it clear off their face." She grabbed Miriam's cheek and gave it a pinch, jokingly. Lottie placed dinner in front of Miriam and asked, "Why?"

"I told someone you were my aunt and they said, oh the voodoo priestess, and looked at my necklace."

Miriam's half-truths were always how she avoided telling Lottie about Abbee at the ice cream parlor. This half-truth hadn't satisfied Lottie. Her forehead furrowed as she lit her cigarette. "Hmmm, they must not be from around here then."

"Why you say that?" Miriam asked.

"Oh *Cher*, your mama is the priestess. I am the psychic. Your mama is big shit around these parts. Nobody does anything voodoo without clearing it with her. She teaches people and brings them to Papa Legba, and the Lao. Not me. Now eat your food before I melt your face off. I'm going out tonight."

Lottie gave Miriam's side a poke and headed to the door.

Miriam started meeting up with Abbee on his off days. They went to the picture show and strolled in parks. They spent a lot of time together. Then one day, when Miriam was sweeping the shop, Lottie came running from the backroom. She knocked into Ms. Henrietta, spilling the bowl of herbs she was preparing. "You stupid girl. You stupid, stupid girl."

She walked towards Miriam and kneeled in front of her. She wrapped her hands around her waist and pulled her close. Lottie placed her ear on Miriam's stomach, to be certain. Lottie rose from the floor with a deep sigh. She cupped Miriam's breast, only to show more disappointment across her face. She dusted her hands off and turned to Ms. Henrietta. "You need to make her a tea, Sug. We can't send her home like this."

Miriam finally realized what was happening. What Lottie was talking about all made sense. Her breasts were tender and her monthly was not monthly this month. Miriam grabbed at her stomach and cradled it. "Tea for what?"

"Girl, don't play stupid. Now you know you got something

growing in that belly. You're too young and got too much to do. The tea will send it back until later when you're ready."

Miriam shouted and stomped her foot. "You will not take my baby!" She threw the broom to the ground as she stomped.

Lottie barked back, "Right because mamas stomp their feet like children when they talk."

Miriam ran upstairs crying.

"You know I'm going to have to call him. You two are going to have to convince her to take the tea." Lottie scolded Ms. Henrietta.

Ms. Henrietta was overwhelmed. Miriam was just as lost to Ms. Henrietta this summer as she was in Chicago. The awkward silence tortured the two of them. Ms. Henrietta said, "Call him. He'll know what to do."

Lottie called Charles, and he yelled and screamed over the phone. "You've had her eight weeks. How do you mess up this bad in eight weeks? I thought she'd be around women and they would teach her about being a woman. Instead, you ignored her, and she went out and got herself pregnant."

Lottie interrupted him. "Now you listen here, fool. She has a lifetime of anger and hurt bottled up in that little body of hers, and it all is directed at us. If you think she would trust us with her safety and guidance after eight weeks, you are more of a simpleton than I thought. If you thought she was going to bond with us just because we got tits, then you don't know anything about people or women. We were doing our best to give her space and waited for her to come around when she was ready."

He sighed and placed his head in his hand. "Put my baby on the phone."

Miriam came to the phone and cried out, "Daddy, I'm scared. I don't want to get rid of my baby. I will be a great mom, I promise."

Charles knew this was all happening because Miriam didn't want to be like Ms. Henrietta. He knew there was no way to get his baby to drink that tea without her hating herself and everyone else for the rest of her life. He knew he would have to commit to raising this baby alongside raising her in order to help her heal. This would be his commitment to her. He regretted letting his feelings and pain prevent her from having some relationship with her mother. "Baby, listen to Daddy. You do not have to get rid of your baby. You tell your auntie I am going to come down there. I am on my way and when I get there, we will figure it all out."

A week after his call with Miriam, Charles pulled up and got out of his car. Ms. Henrietta stayed out of sight and watched him from an upstairs window, behind the curtain. Miriam ran out of the shop's door towards her father and leapt onto him. Her arms wrapped around his neck, and he lifted her body off the ground. There she was, feet dangling, crying, and blubbering over her daddy. Miriam was still just a little girl. A scared little girl who needed her daddy. Ms. Henrietta was so grateful Miriam had him as a daddy. He did such a good job of loving her and showing her love. He was her safe place. Miriam didn't leave him because she was an angry teen who hated her father. Miriam loved him. She left him to find her mother. Ms. Henrietta felt like all she did was disappoint Miriam more.

Chapter 27

When Calida answered the door, Halima asked where Deyanira was. The question confused Calida. Her eyes squinted, and her eyebrows furrowed when she replied, "She is at the crossroads retrieving your daughter. Is that my stew?"

Halima couldn't possibly leave the girl at home without an adult awake. She asked Calida who was caring for her. Calida, being the age of ten and imagining herself as very mature for her age, stood tall with her shoulders back and chin up. "Well, myself and the ancestors, of course."

Halima, in an attempt to avoid her grief and concern for her own unconscious child and dying chicken, pushed past Calida and through the doorway. She demanded to see where Deyanira was asleep. Calida walked down the hall and turned on the light in Deyanira's bedroom.

"Ya, see. She's deep in the crossroads by now, waiting for the chicken to arrive with the piece of your daughter's spirit. How is the chicken? It shouldn't be too long now." Calida's surety and matter-of-fact attitude made Halima uncomfortable. She was avoiding her emotions and wavered in her belief that Deyanira was saving her daughter. She bit her lip and crossed her arms to comfort herself. "I think you should stay with us until your mami wakes up."

She grabbed Calida's arm. When Halima touched Calida, she didn't burn. Calida's protection charm burned people who meant her harm.

She wanted to tell Halima no, but Calida felt her age and was intimidated by Halima's insistence. All the adult confidence Calida had previously in the doorway had drained from her body. It dissipated like mist clearing in the morning sunrise. All Calida could manage to say was a mousy, "I can't leave my mami here alone."

The woman nodded. "I'll have my husband come back and carry her to our house, too. Then I can look after you, and your mami can look after my baby."

Calida wished she had called her Titi Camila as her mami told her to. She wouldn't have been home alone when Halima came to the house. She tried to reaffirm. "That is against the rules. Mami says never wake her or move her. She always says to stay in the house, except for when it's time to feed the animals."

Halima had already decided this was just what she needed to distract herself from her battle with disbelief and grief. She needed to busy herself so her emotions didn't swallow her whole. Halima reassured Calida and said, "I'm sure your mami just says that because she is used to not having help. She is used to not being able to lean on people for help. If she knew how to trust others, she would have left you with me because she would know I would care for you like my little girl, and you'd be extra safe. Come now, we'll send my husband back for your mother."

Hamila walked back into the hallway, leading Calida by the arm. Calida's intuition was saying don't go, but Calida's ten-year-old mind and body didn't know how to speak up. Bassat hissed at Halima in the hallway, and Halima shooed her away.

At the crossroads, time faded, and Deyanira returned to the point where everything met nothing. There, Elegua greeted her. He whispered his presence around her body before physically manifesting. She rolled her eyes at his entrance. "You're always so dramatic."

They laughed together. He told her to leave the girl. Deyanira squinted her eyes and furrowed her brows at the idea. "Why would you all sanction my working and have me come here, all so I can leave her here? What do you want with this girl? Why her? What is special about her?"

He grew irritated by Deyanira's line of questions. She felt the irritation grow into anger and, in her experience, anger in a primordial being was not far off from rage. Deyanira had no interest in being the focal point of his rage. She blurted out, "Okay, I'm leaving, argh."

She turned around to find the thread of rope weaving to her body for her return.

Elegua whispered all around her. "Do you feel it? You got disconnected from your body. You got distracted in your journey through time. Can you even feel your body?" Deyanira grew annoyed by his riddles. He wasn't speaking of any lessons clearly.

"I was exploring while I waited. You know I always do this. I don't understand what this attempt to scold me is about."

Deyanira was also stalling, weaving the rope to her body with minimal effort, hoping to find Solanine upon her exit. Before he could reply, she waved him off and began slowly reentering her body. Just as she suspected, she saw Solanine holding the chicken, standing confused and frightened. Deyanira walked away from the road to her body and towards the girl. "Psst, put the chicken down and come with me, *amor*."

Solanine had no memories of Deyanira because of her illness, so the idea of going with a stranger in an unfamiliar place only petrified her more. Deyanira tried not to veer too far off the road. She wanted to avoid alerting and angering Elegue. At that point, she whispered, sensing the girl's reluctance, "Your mother sent me. I gave her the chicken to guide you to me. I have been waiting for you here. Now, I am returning. If you come with me now, you will wake up with your mother at your side. Otherwise, you will continue to walk that way and cross over as the dead. Only seeing your parents in the spirit."

Deyanira saw the wheels in the girl's mind turning. Deyanira knew Solanine was pretending that the thought of death didn't sound worse than anything else. Just then, Deyanira felt the energy shift. All the hair on her body was electrified with energy. "Shit! Come on, kid, it is now or never."

Elegua's energy rushed at Deyanira with the force of hurricane winds, and his voice spoke at a volume that crumbled mountains. "I TOLD YOU TO LEAVE!"

It was just the motivation Solanine needed because the voice came from the direction of "death." She dropped the chicken and grabbed Deyanira's hand, and together, they ran towards Deyanira's road. Deyanira's road became a crossroads, and Deyanira knew it was the road for Solanine's return. Something felt off and very different. Deyanira wasn't sure what it was, but it felt awful. She bent down, hugged Solanine, and instructed her to walk down that road to the light. She told Solanine that when she opened her eyes, she'd see her mother again. Solanine hugged Deyanira with a soft "*gracias*," before jetting down the road to the light.

Once Solanine was out of sight, Deyanira began walking down her road again. Suddenly, a supersonic scream came from Solanine's road. There was a burst of wind from the light, and Solanine's spirit hurled back to the crossroads. Solanine's spirit reached for Deyanira and her spirit contorted. Her spirit twisted with pain and turned putrid green with evil energy. Just then, Solanine's spirit was sucked back towards the earthly plane. As Solanine's spirit rushed past Deyanira, Solanine reached for her, scratching Deyanira's arm. Deyanira's arm felt like it was on fire. She had never been wounded in the crossroads before. Deyanira didn't understand what was happening. She became dizzy. Should she try to go back and get Solanine? How did she scratch her in the spirit realm? Deyanira turned around back towards the crossroads, but when she did, she was nose to nose with Abuela. A bright light shined from Abuela's chest, blinding Deyanira. Abuela then shouted, "WAKE UP!"

The force of Abuela's light pushed Deyanira down the road, back into her body.

Deyanira opened her eyes to a fuzzy figure standing above her. She connected the sounds of the surrounding room to screams of pain and anguish from the far-left corner of the room. Her daughter's voice from the right side of the room was yelling, "Wake up Mami, wake up!"

Deyanira's eyes adjusted to the light, and the fuzzy figure was a man speaking in Latin. He held a large dagger ready to plunge into her chest. "*Precipio tibi et obligo te ut servias nobis et domino Deo tuo in penitentia pro peccatis tuis usque in sempiternum.*"

As the sentence was completed, Deyanira saw the dagger rise up and plunge towards her in slow motion. She hadn't spoken in three days. Her vocal cords were dry. She coughed out one word. The only word she needed. "*Muerte.*"

The man's body fell lifeless and dropped to the floor. His head hit the nightstand next to the bed Deyanira lay in. The clang of the dagger hitting the floor sounded more like a thump. It must've been forged out of iron, Deyanira thought, as she waved her hands toward the woman restraining her daughter. "Death to you and all here with you."

The sound of bodies hitting the floor echoed all over the room and through the hallway. To the right, Halima was released from the bondage of her captor, and she ran to the foot of the bed, screaming and crying. Calida ran to Deyanira, jumping over the dead bodies and knocking Deyanira over backward on the bed. "*Mija*, what is going on? Where are we? Wait one minute."

Deyanira pulled on the chain around her neck, exposing a charm from within her nightshirt. The charm, at first sight, resembled a locket. Once opened, the inside revealed an iron-forged sigil with a pointy edge. Deyanira pushed her thumb against the sharp edge until it punctured her skin, and blood formed a bubble on her thumb. She smeared her blood on the sigil and said, "All of you who wished me harm and those who fell today will serve my family as protection for the next ten years, as a debt owed and paid."

Halima paused her grief long enough to recall the words on the sign outside Deyanira's gate. She read the sign as they entered her gate that night, which felt like a month ago. The sign read: *Beware, enter my property with ill intention and death to you once you enter. Your spirit will serve my family for ten years as payment.* She grabbed her husband's arm with second thoughts of entering the gate, and her husband looked confused. "Do we bring her harm?"

He shook his head, and he stepped out to open the gate.

Halima's mind and body filled with regret. She laid there on Solanine's body, "If only we'd turned around," she whispered.

Calida explained that Halima took them from their home and brought them to hers in order to protect them. Deyanira's furious face made Calida's eyes tear up. Deyanira told Calida, "We will discuss this at home where it is safe. We have to get out of here."

Deyanira wobbled in her attempt to stand and slowly shuffled to the end of the bed, where she could see Halima hugging her daughter's dead body. Solanine's chest was bloody, and lying next to her was another iron dagger with sigils across the base. Everything that happened in the spirit realm was starting to connect to the scene of the home. Elegua wanted her to leave Solanine. He wanted Deyanira to feel her connection to her body, so Deyanira would know her body was moved and unprotected. Freedom of choice could make a mapped-out ritual go array. Halima moving Deyanira's body had shifted everything on the timeline.

Deyanira sat at the edge of the bed and placed her hand on Halima's shoulder. "You have to come with us. There will be more of them."

Halima refused. "Leave me here to die. They killed my daughter and husband. I have nothing to live for."

Deyanira spoke with the fury of the Gods. "Get your ass up now! You have nothing to live for! Nothing? Your life isn't the sum of the people you love. Get the fuck up now. You risked all of us. You get up now because there are things worse than death, and those things are coming for you if you stay."

Halima's chest felt as if someone was squeezing the air out of her lungs, and someone else was preventing new air from entering. Panic caused her to scramble to her feet and as she stood up, the air flooded her lungs. Deyanira told her to grab her car keys and get to the car. As Halima drove, she tried to tell herself it was a panic attack that took her breath. Then the thoughts shifted to Deyanira. She did just kill a house full of people with words. She did just tell Halima there were worse things than death.

Deyanira let out a deep sigh. "That wasn't me taking your breath away. You angered some pretty powerful deities, though. They were just motivating you. You staying there alive after I left made you a liability, and the deities needed to be clear they couldn't allow you to stay. I will explain once we get to the house. I need to shower in salt water, drink some water, and eat. I have empathy for your loss tonight, and one day I will extend my empathy, but I don't know when that will be. Tonight, I am furious, and I cannot focus on anything other than the lessons and instructions behind tonight's events. We have too much to prepare. Calida and I have to leave in a few days, and there is training and teaching I have to give to you. Maybe after tonight, I will have space for your grief. Tonight, though, you carry it alone."

Halima was confused and hurt by the words Deyanira spoke. They pulled up to Deyanira's gate, and Halima slowed the car down on the approach. Deyanira grabbed her arm. "Do not stop the car. They are following us. Use that anger growing in your belly to speed up and ram the gate!"

Halima's anger quickly transformed into fear. "If the gate is broken, won't they get in?"

Deyanira laughed. "They die if they enter my property. They know that. Just go."

Halima drove through the gate as she was told. In her rearview mirror, she saw outlines of several people unloading out of vans, at the gate. She parked outside the house, still concerned about safety. "What if their magic is powerful too and they figure out how to get in here?"

Deyanira laughed again. "They don't have magic or strength. A mutation of a God backs them. A void. He can't give, only take. Therefore, they can only take as well. So they are only as strong as the bloodlines they kill, and none of them are stronger than me. Come inside, I'll explain after my shower."

Deyanira turned on the shower and stripped down. The three claw-like scratches down her arm burned. She touched around it, testing the pain and her arm's limits. She could feel her ancestors trying to come through and speak to her. Deyanira's Chicago attitude stopped them. "I do not want to speak until after my shower."

The steam from the scalding hot water filled the bathroom. Deyanira felt her body ache as she lifted her leg into the shower. She was more sore than normal from her time at the crossroads. No time to focus on sore muscles, she thought as she opened her canister of salt scrub. Her salt scrub recipe in this canister was for clearing lingering energy and drawing back her energy from the crossroads. Balance was key for Deyanira, and three days at the crossroads tilted the scales out of balance for her.

She rubbed the salt scrub over her body, starting with her shoulders and neck, down her torso and legs, and finally to her feet. Deyanira saved her scratched arm for last. She debated with her intuition about avoiding the wound with salt. Her intuition pushed towards salting the wound. With a groan and an eye roll, Deyanira rubbed the salt-filled hand over the scratches. It felt as if acid poured on her skin. Smoke came from the wounds, and the pain was unbearable. She moaned a death moan and rushed her arm under the showerhead, raining hot water. The pain was so intense her knees buckled, and her head became woozy. She felt Abuela behind her, holding her up and preventing her body from giving way. Deyanira smirked, and in a drunken slur, thanked her.

Deyanira took her recovery in the shower as the smoke broke up and fanned out from her arm. She knew she had to consult her ancestors about what was happening to her body. There was a pull she felt on her spirit. It felt like someone was pulling her spirit away from her body. Deyanira felt its tug, gentle and weak for now, but firm and buried. Deyanira turned the water off and stepped out of the shower slowly. She was weak in the spirit. She rested her hand on the sink and sat on the toilet. With hands on her thighs, Deyanira took a deep breath to draw in some energy to dress herself. She pushed her intuition away and gripped tightly to the mundane explanation that she just needed some food. Her beaten body slipped into her dress and sandals.

Deyanira entered the kitchen, making eye contact with Calida. Deyanira had spent most of Calida's life trying to balance her normal mundane life with spiritual lessons and preparations. Their eye contact revealed a torment deep as the ocean, locked in the prison of a young chubby body. She knew her baby needed safety in order to release the complicated emotions swirling behind those eyes— the murder of a child and her father, along with the near death of her only parent at the hands of others. The guilt, and the complexities of it all, were stealing her child's innocence with each minute of time that passed. She walked towards Calida to embrace her and care for her. Just then, Deyanira's body failed her. Dizzy from hunger, she reached out for the kitchen counter to her left to prevent herself from fainting. Her body screamed that she needed nourishment first. She slowly made herself a sandwich, and then she filled her glass with water from the faucet. Sliding her bottom onto the stool at the counter, she felt more stable and confident that she could finish her sandwich without fainting. She ate in silence while Calida stared off into the distance. Halima rocked back and forth behind Deyanira in a dining chair, her arms folded across her chest, whimpering in grief.

With the last bite of her sandwich in her mouth, Deyanira took a deep breath to prepare for the next steps. She got up from the table and walked over to Calida, cupping her daughter's face in her hands, "Oh, *mija*, I am so sorry."

Calida snapped out of her daze with Deyanira's acknowledgment. There were no words or sounds to match the trauma Calida had expelled from her young body. Her mouth opened, and her spirit screamed silent, torturous screams. Her face was wet without defined tears, just a glisten of sweat and tears from forehead to chin. She wept silently while her empath mother did the only thing she could. Deyanira spiritually pulled those emotions out and filtered them for her. Calida and her mother were so connected that everything around them slowly melted away.

Just then, in the peace and silence, came a shout, dragging them from their exchange and thrusting them into the present reality. "I cannot comfort my daughter because she is dead! And it is all your fault!" Halima shouted.

Deyanira, exhausted from the spiritual exchange, blinked her eyes to regain a clear vision of the present. Just as her eyes regained focus of the room, Deyanira saw a vase fly across the kitchen, towards the wall by the dining room table, smashing into three pieces.

Deyanira roared, "You dumb bitch! Your daughter is dead,

your husband is dead, and we almost died because you are dumb! I gave you instructions. You were told to grieve. You didn't want to feel your emotions, so you tried to parent my daughter while I was gone. Did you think they wouldn't show me what happened? Did you really think you could come into my home, receive my safety and protection, and then blame me for your own actions? I was going to be gentle and kind to you. I had empathy for your humanity. I understood, but you sit in my house, in the safety of my covering, and attack me? I should throw you outside the gate to be tortured by those zealots. Make no mistakes. You are allowed to grieve, but if you displace that burden on me again, you will feel the wrath of a hundred Gods."

The thick Chicago accent and ear-piercing authoritative octave set the tone that this was not a conversation, but rather a declaration. Humbled, Halima had no words and retreated back to her chair with tears. Deyanira, after finding herself a seat, took a deep breath to calm herself. She understood Halima's humanity and confusion. Deyanira was a nurturer by nature, and when she wasn't in mama bear mode about her daughter's traumatic near-death experience, she did, at her core, have immense empathy for Halima.

Deyanira stood up and walked towards her shelving on the wall. Without making eye contact with Calida, she told Calida to take a salt shower to help release all that extra energy. Searching the jars on the shelf, Deyanira asked the Orisha, Osain, to guide her to the right blends. "I will make us some tea and explain what happened and who those people are. I am terribly sorry for the loss you have experienced. I can imagine. You cannot eat yet. Too many emotions and grief have filled your belly. My tea will help." Deyanira placed a tea kettle full of water on the stove.

"What are you?" Halima asked.

The undertone of the question was rooted in fear, amazement, and bewilderment. Deyanira could sense all of Halima's feelings and thoughts swirling around her head. "Depends on who you ask," Deyanira smirked, forgetting the circumstances of their tea time. "I am the Oracle."

Halima was annoyed with her response and replied, "I don't know what that means."

Deyanira realized she was going to have to start at the beginning. Halima had to be the only *Boricua* on the island with no knowledge or connection to psychic readings or to Santería. "Oh, of course. I am going to have to start at the very beginning for you to understand who those people are. First, you know who Yahweh is, right?"

Halima nodded, but her ancestors said not really.

Deyanira poured the hot water over the herbs in the cups and reached into her lower cabinet for honey. "Yahweh is the original Jewish version of your Christian God. Your God is loosely derived from a higher, original being. So when you say praise God as a Christian, that is who you are talking about. Follow me?"

Halima nodded with confirmation, so Deyanira moved on. "Okay, so Gods, Goddesses, Loa, Orishas, Semis, they are all beings that we, as humans, breathe life into with our belief. Humans don't understand that belief is a huge energy force. If they truly believe that they can move a mountain, they would be able to. That is one of the few things the Bible gets right. You following?"

Halima paused to determine if she should lie. "What is an Orisha?"

Deyanira thought to herself, *Wow she really is indoctrinated in whiteness.* "Okay, Orishas were the first beings. Most of them walked the Earth just like us. They are complex, just like us. Orisha learned lessons and grew spiritually, just like us, and they all have gifts. We are their children. Most of us on this island have ancestors from Africa who worshiped them, so we are connected to the Orisha by bloodline."

"So there are more Gods than God?" Halima asked.

Deyanira scoffed, "This is exactly why Yahweh is so dangerous, but I have skipped ahead. Yahweh is one of the youngest manifestations of beliefs that exists. There are some low-level beliefs that never quite took root, but I don't want to go too far off-topic. So most manifestations of belief—"

"Wait, why do you keep saying that? Why don't you say Gods?"

Deyanira leaned in and looked Halima in the eye. "Because the word God, by design, is a box of control and oppression. It was designed kind of as a trap to entice the ego of the deity. The word lures deities in with the promise of followers and belief. However, the ideology then traps them only providing tiny spurts of energy from their believers and shifting the rest of the energy to be used for nefarious purposes—but I can tell from your glazed-over look that you don't understand a thing I am saying. So in terms, you understand: manifestations of belief aren't Gods, because the word was designed to steal limit a deity, and keep them small never gaining too much power. Because if they did they could fight against the things on Earth that are wrong."

Halima was grateful that Deyanira realized nothing she said had made sense to her. Just moments ago, in her world, there was only one true God.

"Okay, so here's the shorthand version, to give you a basic understanding. Most manifestations of belief derive from an original, ancient being. As word of mouth traveled about these beings, their stories changed a little here and there. Different tribes created different names for these beings, based on their own languages, and thus, a pseudo-being was birthed. But they weren't completely separated from the original being. Like a mother with an umbilical cord, they were connected by an energetic umbilical cord. They are always connected. When a new being forms, it looks like they are all connected by their backs, all symbiotic and thriving on each other's wisdom, power, and experience. Remember, energy can never really die, but it can be transferred, transformed, or transmuted. When I said some beings didn't make it, it is because the belief in them was transferred to a new being, and the people who believed in them either died or converted to another belief. So the energy of belief was transferred from them to elsewhere. I am getting off-topic from the questions you asked. Back to Yahweh. Like, Yahweh has several pseudo beings."

Halima excitedly interrupted, "Oh, the holy trinity, the Father, Son, and Holy Spirit, right?"

Deyanira sighed. "Lady, listen, you're pissing me off. Just assume everything you have ever been taught is wrong, a half-truth, or bullshit altogether. Listen to me, and when I am all done, you can go through your belief system on your own time and pull apart the bullshit. You're thinking small. Not global. The different sides of Yahweh are the Jewish, the evangelical, the Catholic, and the Lutheran. Basically, if a church system has enough followers, it births a different side of the original being. The Jewish sides of Yahweh each have their own side, and the original side of Yahweh is a branch off of El which is another being, but I don't have time to walk you through that. Same with African Orishas and African Lao. Yemaya and Mami Water come from the same manifestation of belief, and so on, and so on. The key here to note is that each being is, in fact, their own. If you told Yemaya that you wanted to call her Mami Water, she'd probably drown you. They are connected like family. So when you were young, people saying you were just like your cousin angered you because, although you were related, you were still very much an individual, it is like that, you follow?" Deyanira took a sip of the hot tea and savored the warm feeling in her throat.

"How did you know that about my cousin?" Halima asked.

"HELLO, Oracle remember?" Deyanira pointed to herself. "Keep up. So now you have the basis that there are many manifestations of belief, and they are connected to their original forms. Okay well, Yahweh is a mutation. A corruption of divine order and balance. A young man in the time of Jesus took the teaching and used Yahweh as a guise to hate women, all things spiritual, and magic. He started killing magical beings as offerings to his Yahweh, but his Yahweh is just a vessel. Maybe at some point, he was a deity with emotions and empathy but I doubt it. His version was never given a belief on his personality just all the negative controlling aspects of the other Yahwehs. The ritual he performed made his version of Yahweh the ultimate source. Which means any praise, belief, or offering to any version of Yahweh flows directly to him. This version of Yahweh has been hiding in plain sight, and his followers have been controlling the world for some time. Mass genocides as offerings, oppression of women, black and brown people— his followers are behind it all. They are called the Brotherhood."

Chapter 28

"Lottie would never leave the girls. Ever. Especially in Chicago. She doesn't know anyone here, Falah," Deyanira said in a panic after Maribel called her from the theater.

Falah knew in his heart she was right, but also that his Aunt Lottie was weird and unpredictable. He was not too convinced that Lottie had any maternal instincts. Deyanira asked Falah to go pick up the girls so she could meditate and feel for Lottie's energy. Deyanira mastered her empathic gifts with Lottie during the summer after her sixteenth birthday.

When Deyanira mediated, she could seek a person's energy and feel their presence. Unfortunately, she was filled with panic and rage, and her emotions clouded her gift. Her fear was an enormous block. Deyanira knew she needed to release the anger and ground herself if she wanted to feel Lottie's energy. Deyanira screamed and kicked over the rocking chair and ottoman. She grabbed the end of the coffee table and flipped it over onto its top.

Deyanira fell to her knees and cried out, "I've lost so much. Don't take Lottie from me, please. I need her. I don't know how to do this. I need help. I need someone to show me how to be an Oracle and a mom to my sisters."

Deyanira's exhaustive cries turned to whimpers, and she

drifted into sleep, searching for Lottie's spirit, her essence; her energy. She felt nothing. It was just a void, as if Lottie didn't exist anymore. "ARGGHH, must be that damn charm of hers!"

Lottie was always so cautious. She made a charm that shielded herself, a protection spell similar to the boundary around New Orleans. Deyanira gave up and walked to the kitchen. She paced the kitchen in frustration and fear. Her sweater snagged the top of the dining chair, and she stumbled. Deyanira's anger rose and bursted. "ARGHHH!!"

She grabbed the chair and threw it to the other side of the room.

Falah brought the girls home. They were full of fear and confusion. Maribel, in her confusion, became hostile. "Maybe she left us because we weren't as special as her precious Deyanira."

From across the room, Deyanira's heart sunk. With a deep sigh, she tucked her own emotions away. "Lottie loved all of us the same. I just had a need. She had to help me with something. Aunt Lottie may have been a complicated woman, but you know who she loves. You know deep down she loves you. You're just upset."

Maribel was torn between sitting with her emotions and projecting her anger onto her sister. "You can knock it off with that wise, old owl shit. You're not that much older than me. You're only in charge because I'm under eighteen. You're not that fucking smart." She knocked a pile of papers off the table and stormed upstairs.

Falah spoke through a chuckle, "Big Mama was always good about letting people express their emotions. Bet she wasn't ready for y'all."

His attempt to lighten her mood did not amuse Deyanira.

"We need to call the police, Falah! Your auntie is missing."

Falah rubbed his head from back to front and over his brow. "Little sis, you know I am just as worried as you are. Auntie isn't a child. She has to be missing for some time before the police will go looking for her. I already made some calls and got some people out there. I got people checking the local hospitals. She would never leave, not like this, not right after Mama passed. Something happened, and I'm scared for her too, but I also know you girls' hearts are aching, and seeing my big ass freaked out isn't going to help."

Deyanira laid down on the couch with her head in her big brother's lap and drifted asleep. She was all out of tears. Deyanira floated outside of her body while she drifted into darkness. She felt like a balloon released by a small child. Deyanira was traveling to a space that still felt very much like her imagination. Deyanira stood at a door, trying to feel if it was safe, but her exhaustion had seeped into her bones and settled in her spirit.

Behind the door, Deyanira could hear people. Chatter and movement. She entered the room but didn't remember opening the door. Deyanira wasn't a part of the scene; she was more of an observer. She felt like she had entered a story, a play, or a movie, but the characters were unknown. The home was modest and clearly from the past, an ancient past. There was a mother with her two children. A son played on the floor and an older daughter sat on a stool, speaking to her mother who was stirring a cauldron over fire. "Mama, do we have fresh water for when the woman arrives?"

Her mother nodded and told the boy to fetch fresh water. Deyanira watched the scene unfold, taking in her surroundings. Her fingers touched the clay walls, and she felt connected to the land. The land felt foreign, but very much alive and powerful. Gentle and fierce all at the same time. Emotions overwhelmed Deyanira when the energy of the room connected to her. A woman came shortly after to visit the girl. From what Deyanira gathered, the girl was an oracle, like herself. Although she didn't stumble through her gifts and her channeling as Deyanira had. She clearly had ancient training. When the woman received the messages from the young girl, she praised her and left treasures for the family. Deyanira was almost jealous of this young oracle. The energy of the room shifted. It felt dark and thick suddenly.

Deyanira searched for a seed or root. Dark energy could be balanced if it was just a seed, but not a root. Roots only grow and extend into branches that flower. Those flowers spread seeds of evil everywhere within its reach. Lottie taught Deyanira that when feeling energy, it was important to understand the difference between dense, poisonous energy and powerful emotions. As an empath, Deyanira could filter pain, grief, and anger, because despite what society said, those feelings were natural. She could even pluck out seeds of jealousy, anguish, resentment, and envy to be transmuted for healing. Once energetic seeds took root in someone's spirit, they could not be transmuted. The seeds would poison her and they often became a root poisoning several lifetimes for that person's spirit.

The brother was in the corner of the room, filled with malice and jealousy. His sights locked onto her with a seething gaze. Their mother's maternal instincts felt the energy as well. "Ariarathes, come here, my love. What troubles you?"

The boy ran and jumped onto his mother's lap. "Everyone thinks Cyra is special because she has powers. I want powers.

It is not fair, Mother. I want to be special too."

The mother lifted the boy towards her chest for a tight embrace. She kissed his forehead and then all over his face. Her affection loosened the energy of the room. It was lighter and less dense, but the energy was, however, still a root. Deyanira felt so much pity for the boy. How could someone so young already be so corrupted? Just then, the room spun to another moment when Ariarathes was younger and alone in the room with a man. Deyanira watched with the assumption that the man was his father. She watched for what felt like hours. The room spun to different moments and different places, all while the man spoke awful things about women and women who had magical gifts. He was furious when Cyra was born gifted. Her little infant arm adorned the birthmark of the stars. Once Ariarathes was born, he'd poisoned Ariarathes against his sister day by day. Their father also complicated Ariarathes's feelings for his mother as well. Deyanira finally understood how he was so full of hate at such a young age. Her acknowledgment of his seed taking root, once again, made the room spin again.

Ariarathes was older, a young man with facial hair. He sat outside a temple, on the stoop, with his head in his hands.

"Ari!" An older Cyra cried out in glee from the temple's doorway.

Her veil was a beautiful shade of blue, embellished with gold, and her jewelry was extravagant. She ran up and embraced her brother. "Ari, I missed you so much! Tell me, what have you been up to? Tell me, have you found a bride? Will I have nieces and nephews soon?"

Cyra kissed Ariarathes all over his face, as their mother used to. He squirmed and ran hot with frustration. Ariarathes wiggled away and wiped his face. "Why do you do that?"

Cyra just laughed, "Oh you silly boy, you will always be my little Ari. Now tell me of all the things you have been up to."

Ariarathes cleared his throat. "I have been traveling, and I met a man named Bartholomew. He spoke of another man with powers. Powers greater than yours. He was the son of a God. He walked on water and healed people with just his touch. His name was Jesus. He fed five thousand people with just a basket of fish and bread. He even brought a man back from the dead. Jesus was a great man, greater than any woman, oracle, or healer we have." Ariarathes spoke with enthusiasm, and his eyes lit with delight.

"Oh, Ari! That is amazing. You must tell me all about this man and his life! Tell me all about the man that spoke of him. Where did you meet him? Can you bring him here? I would love to meet him and hear his stories. I want to hear all about the man with powers. Can he bring the man with him?"

Ariarathes's delight faded from his eyes. Rage replaced it. His mind swirled with confusion and jumbled thoughts. Why was she not jealous? Why was she not mad to hear that men had powers now too? The words flew in the wind of his thoughts and swirled like debris in a tornado. "Bartholomew is a great man. I am sure he has powers, too. All the men that follow Jesus do."

Cyra was always naturally curious. She thrived in areas of new theory and knowledge. Ariarathes traveled for over thirty days to chastise his sister that he met a man more powerful than her. Cyra gave him no satisfaction. Her curiosity devastated him. Ariarathes wanted her to feel what he had felt his whole life: growing up in her shadow. The normal and average little brother to the great oracle, the son of, his mother, the great healer. Just an ordinary boy who grew into an ordinary man. Extraordinary only by the travels and knowledge he consumed. He just wanted to give a glimpse of how he felt.

"Ari, stop."

He heard a struggling and gagging voice plead. The voice pulled him out of his thoughts and back into reality. His eyes focused and he saw he was standing over Cyra with his hands around Cyra's throat. Her eyes were wide with confusion and pain; tears escaped the corners of her eyes and ran into her ears under her veil. That was a crossroads for him. He could stop and bear his burdens and pains to his sister. Ariarathes briefly paused. His hands stopped squeezing, but they did not release her throat. At that crossroads of healing or hate, his spirit turned towards hate, and that root grew into a vine. A vine that wove around his heart, its thorns sinking into Ariarathes's heart energy. The fuel of his heart caused the vine to bud. Ariarathes walked away from the temple, hooded and in the shadows. Cyra's lifeless body laid on the steps of the temple. Bells rang and a search for Ariarathes would begin soon.

Ariarathes traveled through the backstreets and out of the city as a hooded man to a village two days journey from the city. He stood in the market and began telling stories of Jesus, the powerful man, and Jesus's father, the one true God, and the miracles and adventures he had with Jesus. He exclaimed he was a disciple named Bartholomew. He was never called Ariarathes again. Years later historians will document conflicting data that the disciple Bartholomew was in two different regions at the same time. His popularity grew, and soon, men, women, and children gathered to hear him speak daily.

Once his followers started bringing offerings and gifts,

the vine around his heart bloomed with poisonous flowers. Deyanira was watching the poison spread at a rapid rate. He started asking the men to stay behind for a separate meeting. The private meetings of men happened behind closed doors in spaces away from the ears and hearts of women. Talk of men being the true bearer of power charged the room. The vine's blossoms reached from the fake Bartholomew's heart into the men's heart space, the energy spreading poisonous seeds. Talks and plans contorted the lessons of Jesus into power, oppression, and greed. A secret society of men formed and grew. They designed a system that elevated men, consumed everything in its path, and suppressed magic. The small group turned into a large gathering, and then these followers made pilgrimages to other countries to spread their message. There were two faces of this movement. On the surface, a passionate flame burned people's heart space with the hope and love of Jesus, who was the son of the one true God. Then, in the shadows, the movement also fueled greed and oppression.

Deyanira watched everything unravel at a physically and energetically rapid pace. Then, in the corner of her eye, she had a vision of Yahweh. Off his side, there began a birthing of a new faction of belief. It started young and weak, but the belief grew strong, and then stronger than Yahweh himself. The faction began tormenting the original Yahweh, and the original Yahweh grew brittle and weak. When Deyanira returned her focus to Bartholomew, Bartholomew was in a dark and musty room. He had five followers in the room with him. "Oh, Yahweh, we are your chosen. We are the men of power. We offer you this sacrifice so that you are honored and fed, and we are protected and elevated in your name."

In the corner, Deyanira saw a young woman cowering.

"We offer you this *kakhard*, who was practicing the old ways and denying you as her God."

Bartholomew waved his hand in the woman's direction. The followers grabbed her as she fought, crying out and begging to be released. On the cold slab of stone, the four men held her down, one man on each limb. Bartholomew stood at her head with a knife. He paused for a long time, watching his followers' faces and demeanor. Deyanira was frightened by the malevolent strategies within him. She watched with a hand over her mouth, as she knew what he was doing. "You, come forward. God wants you to give this offering, and he will bless you with riches and notoriety."

He pointed to the man holding her left arm. He was struggling to hold her down, but not because he didn't have the strength. He radiated the energy of fear and dripped with the energy of doubt. Bartholomew put the blade on the floor and grabbed the woman's left arm. "Go, my son. Show your God you love Him. Show Him that He is the one true God, and anyone who doesn't believe Him is evil."

The man dragged his feet, shifting his position to the woman's head. He lifted the knife above his head, his eyes filled with tears, and plunged it into the woman's heart. Deyanira turned her head in horror. She couldn't bear to watch. She heard the woman choking and gasping, drowning in the blood pooling in her slit throat.

Deyanira's line of sight was drawn to the twisted new faction of Yahweh. He grew large and muscular, still connected to the older, original faction of Yahweh. He now towered over the original Yahweh, breathing deep and admiring his new power. He looked around the spirit realm. The new Yahweh realized other beings had fewer followers, or they had smaller offerings that were average and not powerful. The other beings were less than him through his skewed view.

Ariarathes assumed Bartholomew's name and station with the man called Christ. Deyanira realized Ariarathes's vine of evil and hatred managed to not only create a new God connected to Yahweh but also to corrupt and poison that God.

Yahweh himself was a young God. Yahweh's ego was easily enticed by Ariarathes's promises of worship and offerings. This new being that Ariarathes created was all the worst parts of Yahweh concentrated. This new version was unlike any manifestation of belief that existed before. Yahweh did not offer guidance, balance, and life lessons to his followers; he only wanted energy. He could transmute their vitality into his own dominance and power. Yahweh let his followers mold him into whatever they wanted, as long as they fed him energy. He started pouring that energy into the protection of their cause of domination, ushering in opportunities and great fortunes. Ariarathes mapped strategies out for generations in that small, damp candle-lit room, with the blessing of his new Yahweh. The plans Bartholomew set forth in that room would be the same strategies enacted over history, throughout Europe, invading and colonizing countries and households throughout the world. The vine energetically reached most of the world by the time Deyanira was born. Bartholomew's poisonous vine birthed the Brotherhood, and Deyanira realized she had just received a peek into the past of the Brotherhood.

Deyanira woke up around noon the next day, exhausted, feeling hungover and sore from the couch. She heard Falah in the kitchen cooking for their sisters. In her state of grogginess, she wondered if Lottie was actually missing or if it was all a dream. She heard a spirit's voice say, *You're asking the wrong* questions. *Is it real? Where is Lottie? How do I get her back? The right questions are what you have to seek. Why did they take her? What is their plan? How can I stop them? Can I be patient and train myself to stop them?* Then, the loud voice faded, and a chill ran down her back and up her arms.

Chapter 29

Over dinner one night at Deyanira's house, Maribel announced she was running for mayor of Arecibo. The sisters jumped up to celebrate and congratulate her. Deyanira broke out the rum to make a toast. As the family broke into random conversations, Deyanira stepped outside to start the fire. Maribel's quiet approach to her sister startled Deyanira. She jumped and the two women had a good laugh. Maribel stumbled with her words. "Dey, can I ask you a question?"

Deyanira didn't look up from the firepit, she just spit it out. "Should you do it or will you win?"

Maribel kicked her foot in her sister's direction playfully. "This is bigger than organizing protests or helping the community. I don't know if I'll be good at compromising with politicians. I don't know how to even work with them. What if I try and I fail? What if I do a terrible job? What if all I do is make enemies?"

Deyanira stopped messing with the fire and embraced her sister. "Come here. You were born for this. You're going to be and do great. You know they won't let me see your life or the girls' much with my gifts, right? But your ancestors showed me big plans for you leading the people of the island. I know that much. Compromise enough to go further and higher, but not too much. Boricuas have had enough people compromising on their behalf. They need someone who will burn it all down for them. That is you. They'll respect you for it."

She kissed the side of Maribel's face. Maribel smiled and then pushed her sister's mushy advances away.

Maribel's husband was a gentle and soft-spoken man. He fell in love with Maribel's passion for the Puerto Rican people and her passion for the island. He courted her in college by following her around campus and supporting every petition, protest, and demonstration she built. When she finally agreed to date him, she informed him that she was not interested in marriage and that she would always put the cause first. He nodded and carried the signs from the trunk to the capital. When he finally proposed, he dropped to a knee and said, "I'll follow you to the end of the earth if that is what you need. You lift up the people, and I'll lift you up."

He grew up with a father who was a Santero and it came down in a reading from the Babalawo that he would marry an exceptionally powerful woman that would change everything. However, his father often tried to fight that narrative and tell his son that as a man, he was to do great things, and his wife should be the one supporting him. That was the proper order. Maribel's husband's spirit never quite accepted that narrative, and he got comfortable with the idea he was going to marry a woman who would shake everything he had known.

Maribel's community party for her mayoral candidacy had a large turnout. Many people from all over came to eat, dance, and support her. She walked the lot, hugging and conversing with every single person there, except Deyanira. Once the people dispersed and the sun faded into the east, Maribel's adrenaline bottomed out, and she almost fell over.

"I am not sure what to do when she gets like this," Maribel's husband whispered to Deyanira.

Deyanira placed a hand on his shoulder. She knew he was just worried about her. "She will never stop. It is part of her destiny. Her ancestors will push her to the brink. Just give her all the love you have in you to give. Be a place that is safe for her to be tender and vulnerable. She is out there fighting wars, but all Maribel's stubborn ass ever needs was cuddles and tenderness, even when she was sick of us and our shit."

Deyanira and her brother-in-law let out a collective laugh that echoed through the vacant lot. Maribel approached them out of curiosity, with a side-eye. "Are you two talking about me?"

Her arms were folded and her body was weary. Deyanira turned around and threw her arms around Maribel, squeezing her tightly. "We were just commenting on how we don't know how you do it, and all we can do is try to keep up and stay out of your way because you'll get sick of our shit." Deyanira swayed back and forth slightly as she spoke. "We're just so proud of you. This really is an amazing thing you are doing. You're doing a great job, *Hermana*."

Maribel wanted to break down crying in her sister's arms. Deyanira always knew how to make her feel loved and seen. At least, when she wasn't making Maribel want to punch her in the face. "You go on home. We'll clean up out here, Mayor Diaz," Deyanira said with a wink.

Maribel collapsed on her couch while her husband walked to the kitchen and filled a basin with warm, soapy water. He put two scoops of coconut oil in a bowl and then put it in the microwave for about fifteen seconds. When the microwave dinged, he gave the bowl a stir and grabbed a rag from under the kitchen sink. He walked into the living room with a basin in one hand and the bowl of oil in the other. He dipped the rag in the soapy water and wiped his wife's feet down. Once they were clean, he dipped his hand in the oil and rubbed her feet with the perfect amount of pressure and tenderness. Maribel sunk deeper into the couch as her whole body relaxed. She muttered, "I don't deserve you."

He stopped rubbing her feet and waited for her to open her eyes. Maribel looked at her husband, only for him to say, "Don't say things like that. I am rubbing some feet and you are on the way to freeing a nation. I appreciate you honoring me, but find words that honor me without shrinking you."

He leaned over and kissed her softly. Whispering "Mayor Diaz" with a smile.

Chapter 30

Deyanira sat quietly sipping her tea, watching Halima process all the information she just given her. Deyanira felt pity for Halima. Halima was thrust into learning all of these heavy things at once *and* amidst tragedy. It had taken Deyanira over twenty years to grasp the concepts she was dumping on Halima in one night. Deyanira stood up to get more tea but then fell over to the floor. Deyanira felt drugged, almost. She remembered her wound and lifted her sleeve. As Halima and Calida ran to her aid, she saw that her arm was black as tar. Her arm was spiritually poisoned and dying. The wound spread to her shoulder, and soon, her neck. Halima and Calida got Deyanira to her feet, and Deyanira whimpered, "I need to rest and see how to stop the poisonous wound from spreading. Take me to bed and don't do anything. Call no one and stay inside." The words were raspy, weak whispers as they left her lips. Halima nodded and helped Deyanira to bed.

Once in bed, Deyanira was pulled immediately to the table of her guides and ancestors. Deyanira had felt nothing like this before. The poison was like a separation, and in the spirit realm, Deyanira felt like a knife was severing her spirit from her physical body. She was hunched over in pain, even in the spirit. She cried out, "What is happening to me, Abuela?"

Abuela's face was filled with fear and concern. Deyanira had never seen Abuela scared. Her guides parted left to right, and a native man small in stature stood at the end of the parted sea of spirits. He had different features than her Taino ancestors. His spirit glowed unlike any of her other ancestors. It was the oddest thing she had ever seen. He walked towards her and held out his hand. "I am Balam." She realized she found herself on the floor in pain. When she touched his hand, it took her to a point in time when he was on a boat.

He was with a group traveling across the sea. Then, the time changed to his feet touching land. She wiggled her toes in the sand and recognized the energy. "This is Puerto Rico," she said out loud.

Balam nodded and pulled her to the tree line of the beach. From there, they watched him and his companions unload the goods they had brought on their boat. Women soon emerged from further down the beach. Then the men carrying the goods trailed behind them. This time, the walk was different for Deyanira because she was walking as Balam instead of herself. She felt all his emotions. His fatigue from the trip, his joy of the safe journey, and then lust. It pulled her focus to one of the Taino women. She was beautiful and had a laugh that filled the air and woke everyone around her. He was in love. She felt his heart race and his whole body light up at the sight of her. He moved around his voyage companions to get closer to her. Once he found himself close to her, he tried to tell her, without words, that the ocean was no match for her beauty. Deyanira chuckled and mumbled, "Okay, Casanova, I see you."

Deyanira followed them around for about a week. There were flirty hand touches and nonverbal affirmations of love. When it was time for Balam to return home, he begged the beautiful

Taino woman to come with him, but she refused. She brought him to her home instead, where her mother's mother lay old and frail. Balam left the Taino woman in her home with her grandmother.

He started walking uphill. Once he reached the bigger mountain peak, he felt a shift in his energy; Balam sat down. He took many deep breaths and cried. He looked out from the peak to the lush land and the ocean. Balam felt the breeze on his skin. The heat was thick at this point of the day, and so beads of sweat formed on his forehead. He heard the spirit of his people calling. He knew the ancestors had answered his inquiry as he climbed the hills.

Deyanira, in the distance, watched him beg his ancestors to stay on the island with the woman he fell in love with. Deyanira turned to him, and they faded back into the room with her team. "Wait. Ancestors cannot tell you what to do. They can only suggest. How did your ancestors tell you no?"

The man held his head in shame. "They didn't tell me no. They reminded me that I was the descendant of a Deity and the son of a healer. I had a great destiny on our land. My mother was a great healer visited by the Jaguar spirit many times in the form of a man. Then she became pregnant with me. I am half God. I am Balam. The spirit of the Jaguar is within me. I didn't just stay because I was in love, I stayed because I feared my power. I didn't want to have an entire village depend on me and my gifts. I feared myself. They sent me on the journey not because I was trading goods, but because I was their protection. The idea of all those people on that boat looking up to me and my gifts was scary. When I used my gifts, I felt the power of the Jaguar spirit course through my body, and I was scared to wield it. I chose to stay.

"The boat never made it back to my people. I owed their ancestors a great debt. I stayed, and because my spirit's power was absent on the boat when the storms came, the spirit of the Jaguar was not with them and the sea took them. That didn't matter. I ignored it. I lived happily for some time with Karaya, my wife. I turned my back on my training and my gifts. I had a simple life working in the village. My inner connection to the Jaguar spirit faded. I often found myself at the peak of the hills, searching for it within. I told myself it left and returned to my land. Soon after, the white men came to the island, and they brought sickness. Karaya was pregnant with our daughter when she caught the sickness. I tried to call on my ancestors and the spirit of the Jaguar, but everything was quiet and out of reach. I thought I was being punished. I thought my ancestors were killing my love and my child because I didn't return home with my people. Karaya went into labor and died giving birth to our daughter. I named her Tanama, after Karaya's favorite river. I felt like our child was a butterfly.

"The white men started capturing and killing everyone. I knew I was being punished for staying. I hated the island and regretted my choice. I hated Karaya, and I hated my daughter Tanama. I beat her often. As often as I could, and when a white man wanted to buy her, I gave her to him. Finally, I could leave and return to my land. Before I left, a white man killed me for stealing a boat. When I died, I ran from crossing over. I did not live a fulfilling life. I was a coward, filled with anger. I sold my daughter to a man, and I couldn't face that. I walked the island for lifetimes as a spirit. Avoiding any time the underworld called for me. Then, you were born. I felt your power the day you were born. For the first time, I felt the Jaguar and it was within you. The Jaguar spirit didn't leave me for my land because it was in me and my ancestors. It lay within our bloodline, for the one who would heal things. The land of my people could only strengthen the Jaguar spirit. I decided I needed to cross over and take my place as an ancestor."

Deyanira looked down at her arms. They were gray and fading. She didn't realize she was so weakened. Her spirit was being pulled away from her body at a rapid rate. She looked up and saw Abuela crying with a hand over her mouth in terror. Balam crouched down next to Deyanira as she lay on the floor of her team's meeting room. In her weakened fading state, she was now completely on her back. "The Jaguar is you. It is not within you. Become the Jaguar. Stop fearing your power! You have felt it your whole life inside of you like the power of the sun bursting and thrashing within. You are meant to walk with Gods. You are the descendant of a God. If you want to live, you have to embrace your true nature. Be the Jaguar."

Deyanira whispered faintly, "But how?"

Chapter 31

The Puerto Rican Day parade in Chicago was always a good time. Everyone was outside at the park eating and drinking, rocking their Puerto Rican flag. Maribel loved to paint tiny flags on her sisters' cheeks with makeup. It was the one time Deyanira let loose and let the girls drink. They walked around with Gatorade bottles, laughing and dancing. Alma was coming out of her shell. The parade tucked her shyness away. She borrowed a red halter top from Camila; Alma embraced the music. Her sisters couldn't tell if she was growing up or if the "Gatorade" loosened her up. Boys walked by, grabbing Alma's hand and twirling her to the music. She felt beautiful and lively. Alma didn't want to be the quiet sister anymore, hiding behind Camila as her mouthpiece. She danced salsa and decided that night she would be adventurous.

Alma wasn't sure how she was going to execute being adventurous, but it needed to happen. She listened to her sisters' stories about college on the island, and college sounded so fun. Deyanira frowned when their stories got too wild. She wasn't judging them; she was just worried about their safety. The girls would laugh and poke her in the side when they noticed her frowns. "Hey old lady, lighten up. We're young, and we're supposed to have fun."

During the parade, Deyanira was tipsy and laughing freely at Camila's story of a drunk salsa night with some hot guy on a roof. She waved her hand in Alma's direction. "You should apply there. It would be fun for you, I bet."

All the sisters fell silent and looked at each other in disbelief before laughing and demanding Deyanira stop drinking because she was clearly drunk. Deyanira just *pfft'd* them and sipped her "Gatorade." As the day got cooler and the sun faded, Deyanira sobered up to watch the girls. Chicago at night required a distinct set of rules and Deyanira preferred to go home than follow them. They were making their way back to Deyanira's car when they ran into a large Puerto Rican man wearing a pastor collar.

Deyanira apologized and realized he was staring at her sister Alma. He was young– Maribel's age, at best. Alma froze in place with fear in her eyes. Deyanira's attention went towards her sister. She touched her arm and saw it all. Alma had dated him during high school. Deyanira saw he had shaken Alma, and threw her to the ground once. Alma only stopped seeing him after he had punched his car and dented it. He was always angry with Alma, telling her she was dumb and never listened to him. It took Deyanira a while to realize that everything she saw was real. Her many gifts, like time walking or reading people's thoughts, were still blocked from her on demand, so only occasionally did she get a taste of them. Deyanira released her sister's arm. She turned towards the large man in the collar. Her eyes lit up golden as she spoke. "Luis, you hurt my sister?"

His brow furrowed, and his shoulders squared up and out addressing Alma and ignoring Deyanira's question, "You've become exactly what I knew you would be: a drunk, barely clothed ho. You should call me, Alma. I am a pastor of a church.

I can help you get saved."

Alma immediately hung her head in shame while Camila and Maribel tried to understand what the hell was happening. They kept looking at Alma for an explanation but she provided no words. Deyanira reached into her purse and pulled out a flask. This action only furthered Luis's confidence, so he laughed and leaned back to fold his arms. "See Alma, your sister can't even stop drinking to conversate with me. I told you. I can take care of you. You don't have to live like this. I can get you out of the streets. You can come live with me."

Each word he spoke triggered Alma to shrink further and further into herself. Deyanira took a large swig of rum from her flask and spat it on the ground in front of him. It startled everyone. Everyone stopped to see where the altercation was going to lead. Deyanira used the rum on the ground to draw a symbol. "I curse you today, let all the karma from collective lifetimes fall on your head in this lifetime. You will feel the weight of your actions now, and you will have no peace."

His eyes grew large, and then they quickly changed to anger as he pulled a cross out of his shirt. "I rebuke you in the name of Jesus, *bruja*."

Deyanira doubled down and laughed. "Your white Jesus has no power here, abuser. Enjoy the rest of your tortured life." Deyanira dusted her hands together as if to say, *well, that's that.* She locked arms with Alma and walked away. "Come on, I decided we need some food to go."

They ordered some more food at a kiosk. They sat and ate in awkward avoidance while Deyanira tried to busy her sisters with mundane topics of conversation as if she hadn't just sentenced a man to his death in front of them. Finally Maribel, as usual, interrupted Deyanira's monologue of nothingness.

"So we are just going to act like you didn't sentence some random guy that our sister apparently dated to death?"

Deyanira choked a little on her drink. "I didn't sentence him to death, and I'm not a *bruja*. During lifetimes, you can create karmic debts, and it is your responsibility and your bloodline's responsibility to balance them. So if you're a shitty human in one lifetime, you may get six lifetimes of repayment and discomfort to balance the debts owed from the past. So all I did to him was cram the six lifetimes of repayment into one lifetime, creating more of a painful, treacherous life. It is highly unlikely he will learn any lessons from my curse, but if he does, I technically would be doing him and his bloodline a favor. I know he won't learn anything though. He isn't the type. He will waste the rest of his life crying about how he is cursed, and its awfulness."

Her sisters listened intently while she talked. When Maribel was sure Deyanira was finished speaking, she said, "I don't believe in that shit. You're not going to tell me that the oppression of women, Puerto Ricans, and Black people is because, in another life, they oppressed someone else and created a debt for their bloodline. Fuck outa here with that."

Deyanira felt awful. "Oh, no. Oppression is man-made. It is an evil construct. The spirit world has been trying hard to combat it for generations. I might not know everything about oppression or the people who made it, but I know it was created here on this plane. Oppression poisons the spiritual plane. Repayment depends on what you and the ancestors of your bloodlines did in previous lives. Our bloodline is pretty powerful and feisty, so I am sure our ancestors will burn his church down or some shit."

Maribel was dissatisfied with her sister's answer. She knew

not to press too hard for too much insight. Deyanira rarely discussed spirituality with them. She was still learning. It wouldn't be fair for her to share things with them and then later have to correct herself like, *sorry guys, I misheard it, and actually shit is not like that at all.*

The sisters headed back to the car as the night's frigidity blanketed their bodies, causing them to shiver in unison. They never quite got used to the cold of Chicago that other Chicagoans called "nice." They approached a commotion on Ashland. Lots of people were crying and yelling. A circle of people had formed in the middle of the street, stopping traffic.

"I hope everyone is okay, and there isn't a terrible accident," Alma added.

As they approached the crowd, Deyanira could see a delivery truck stopped in the middle of the lane, and on the ground, lying still was Luis.

"Shit!" Deyanira yelled out with a gasp, worried; maybe she did kill him. She pushed through the people and got down on the ground next to him.

He was breathing but barely conscious. "Please, I'm sorry. Please take it back. I can't move anything."

Deyanira saw the ambulance in the distance working through the traffic jam. "Oh, good. The curse did what it was supposed to. I thought it killed you, I was so worried. I can't take it back, silly, what's done is done. Now you are paralyzed from the neck down, and your family will put you in a state home. You won't feel pain, you're welcome. You will be left to yourself and your mind. There may be moments where you are abused or neglected by staff, but if you are smart, you will reflect on what you have done to Alma and to anyone else you hurt." She patted the top of his head and smiled as she got to her feet.

The sea of people parted for her as she worked her way back to her sisters. Many of the people surrounding him were witnesses to Deyanira cursing Luis. As people moved out of Deyanira's way, the sisters got a clear picture of who was on the ground and what had happened. Their hearts collectively sank. Alma gripped Maribel's arm tighter when she saw Luis lying on the ground. Deyanira bopped through the crowd and exclaimed, "He'll be fine. He's alive."

When they got in the car, Alma burst into tears. Deyanira started apologizing immediately. "I'm so sorry. I really am. I could see what he did to you. I saw him make you cry. I had to make him pay."

Alma nodded her head and wiped her tears. "No no, I know you love me and did it for me. I just feel so bad he is in pain."

Maribel, at this point, couldn't take it. With her eyes rolling, she took a deep breath and said, "Oh, for fuck's sake. I didn't see what Dey saw, but I know *this*– he's a piece of shit. Alma, you're the sweetest, and anyone who makes you feel bad is a shitty human. If he did more things than make you feel bad, he deserved everything he got. Fuck him. We are not going to sit in this car and cry for that piece of shit. In war, people die. He went to war with the wrong family and lost. He's lucky he didn't die, and he's lucky he got the sister that curses people and *not* the sister that cuts them. Because I'd be locked up and you would miss my witty personality. Enough of this shit; today was a good day."

They all got quiet, and Deyanira drove home in silence. They pulled up to the house and Deyanira announced that she had forgotten to grab milk. The sisters piled out of the car, and Deyanira left for Walgreens. She cried in the parking lot. *What kind of person curses someone? I'm a monster,* she thought as tears poured out over the steering wheel.

Chapter 32

Deyanira faded out of consciousness on the floor in the meeting room of her team of guides. As she fell victim to the fatigue, she questioned how her spirit could lose consciousness. Her eyes blinked, and Balam became fuzzy. His words echoed in her mind, *Embrace that you are the Jaguar.*

She was transported to nothing, the place in between cross-roads and death. There was no more pain, only a tug to go towards something. Her intuition said that the tug would become a drastic pull, like what Solanine had experienced. *How can I embrace the Jaguar within me?* Deyanira sat down with her legs crossed. "Okay, what is blocking me from embracing the Jaguar?"

She remembered the day she cursed Luis. The emotions from that day came rushing back. The shame she felt that night at Walgreens. That was the first time she had shown her sisters her gifts, and she scared them. She stepped into her power unapologetically and her sisters' reaction made her feel dirty. In the car, she rubbed her arms while she cried as if she was rubbing away the shame. In the darkness of nothing, she wept again. She wept for release. Deyanira needed to shed her shame and accept her power. When she felt lighter, she stood up, "I trust myself with myself."

Each time, she repeated it louder and louder. A light shone over to the left of the darkness. She repeated it louder, and the light got brighter. Deyanira got on all fours and started slinking toward the light, like a cat. Her spirit morphed into the shape of the Jaguar while she continuously repeated, "I trust myself with myself." The words became roars as the light enveloped her body.

Deyanira sat up in her bed and let out a powerful roar, making the shelves on the walls shake. The Jaguar spirit surrounded her with an energetic light, similar to a smoke ring in the shape of the enormous cat. The blackened coloring of her arm dissipated as she roared.

Calida was crying in Halima's arms when Deyanira sat up. Halima's mouth agape. Deyanira could feel large amounts of raw energy pulsating through her body, pushing out the poison and healing the large scratch. Calida typically would run to embrace her mother however, she could see the Jaguar spirit, and she didn't know if it was safe.

"*Mija*, it is okay," Deyanira said as she waved her arms for Calida to come closer.

Calida wiggled away from Halima and walked towards her mother slowly. Once she was at the side of the bed, Calida took two of her fingers and traced Deyanira's face slowly. "Mami, is that you in there? I saw a tiger."

Deyanira scooped Calida in her arms. "Oh *Bébé*, it is the Jaguar and yes, it's me. The Jaguar helped heal me. Whatever ritual the Brotherhood did on Solanine at Halima's house, it sent her to pull me out of my body to serve them. She planted the connection in the wound to poison and separate my spirit from my body. The Jaguar destroyed the connection from the ritual, removed the poison, and healed me. The Jaguar is a part of me and will protect us. Now we have much to do."

Deyanira sprung from her bed, full of energy, and walked into the hall, ushering Halima and Calida to follow. "Now Halima, you stay here. There's plenty of food and just feed the animals. Stay away from the fence. They will eventually realize I have left and will leave the gate. Finding me will take precedence over killing you. You staying here without calling the police will convince them it is okay to let you live. When things die down, I will have my sister work on getting you a new name."

Deyanira opened the door to her altar room, grabbed a lockbox off the bottom shelf, and brought it into the kitchen, still talking to Calida and Halima. "Once my sister gets you a new name, you'll be safe because they will be more focused on finding psychics and mediums. You must stay here for at least a month."

Deyanira opened the lockbox. It revealed three burner phones, a Canadian, Portuguese, and Guamanian passport, three stacks of cash, and three prepaid visa cards. She handed one of the money stacks and one of the burner phones to Halima. Halima looked at the money and phone, confused. "How are you going to get out of the house with them out there? How will I get to my family to bury their bodies?"

Deyanira paused and braced herself for her answers. "I'm so sorry. The Brotherhood has gotten a lot better at covering their tracks than when I was a kid. I can assure you that they took your family's bodies and cleaned up your house. I imagine the Brotherhood forged a text or letter to the police saying that your husband was taking your daughter. So now, no one will believe your claims. If they can't kill you, the Brotherhood will discredit you. When my Aunt Lottie disappeared and I reported her missing, the police said that there was a text about her finding some man and them eloping together. But I knew that was a lie because Aunt Lottie was old and didn't know how to text. I am so sorry. You will have to do a memorial for them without their bodies. The important thing to do while you're here grieving is to stay safe."

Halima was speechless and only could nod her head in understanding.

Deyanira walked to Calida's bedroom and pulled out a backpack. She started rolling clothes and packing them into the bag. "The perk of this land I bought is that there is a lot of forest and vegetation that I blessed and asked for protection. I purchased it with the idea that one day, I may have to slip out. I designed it that way. Calida and I will take the trail in the back of the home after I do a shielding to hide our energy from any empaths working with them."

Deyanira tucked in Calida's Teddy Bear named Best Friend. She had had Best Friend since her first heart surgery at six weeks old. She wouldn't sleep or go to most places without him. He was a necessity because Deyanira was not sure when they would return. Halima left for the bathroom because she was scared for them. She wanted to pray for their safety, but when she closed the door, she realized she didn't know who to pray to. Out of frustration, she knocked everything off the counter and slid down to the floor.

"Mami, where are we going? I'm scared." Calida asked as she followed Deyanira into the master bedroom. Deyanira stopped and got down on Calida's level, placing her hands on Calida's shoulders, replying in a whisper, "We are going to Mexico, Mija. I have to find a Maya healer to help me work with the Jaguar. Don't be scared when we get away from the house. I am going to call Uncle Falah to take us there safely. I don't want

Halima to know because if she leaves and gets captured, I don't want her to have information about where we are going. If she listens to me, she'll be safe Mija, I promise, sshhh." She kissed Calida's forehead and resumed packing her things in her own backpack.

In the kitchen, Deyanira was making food for their journey when Halima joined her. Deyanira said, "After three days, do the ritual with salt water, using the basket on the front porch. Do you remember the ritual we did when you first came? Right now, you need to feel your emotions, so I do not suggest doing it now. Don't avoid your emotions, but you're allowed to take breaks. The basket ritual will help you feel lighter and not be consumed by depression during this isolation."

Halima nodded. Deyanira walked over and placed her hand on top of Halima's hands. "I am so sorry for your loss and that you were thrust into this life. The grief will get lighter, but it will never leave, and I am so sorry you're hurting."

Deyanira returned to making their food for the journey. She felt genuine empathy for Halima. The consequences of her actions were crippling. Deyanira did not have the heart to tell Halima that Solanine was probably a spirit trapped in servitude of the Brotherhood without rest. Deyanira made a silent promise to free the girl from the Brotherhood, so she may rest and ease her mother's pain.

In the altar room, Deyanira grabbed a photo of her and Calida and wrapped it around a ginger root with *romero* sprigs. Ginger was spiritually as strong and pungent as it was in meals. It served as a cloak to their energy against the empaths working with the Brotherhood. Romero had long been Deyanira's herb of choice for protection. She had felt a long connection to its use and essence. She placed the photo in her bag and prepared for their exit. Calida had her backpack on, and she pleaded with her mom to bring Bassat. "Mami, I can't leave Bassat."

Deyanira's heart ached, as she had a hard time telling Calida no. "Bassat, come."

Deyanira beckoned the cat to the front room. Bassat came and sat in front of Deyanira like a soldier, awaiting her orders. "Go to Camila's house, *amor*. You go there and protect them until we return."

The cat meowed in reply, and Deyanira told Calida to say goodbye. "Mija, I promise Bassat will be safe if we leave her. I cannot promise she will be safe if we bring her with us."

Calida cried and squeezed Bassat uncomfortably tight. "I love you. I'm sorry you can't come. Please be safe, I need you."

Deyanira opened the back sliding door and signaled Bassat. "Now get going." With that, Bassat was out the door, into the dark of night.

Moments later, they were saying their goodbyes to Halima and leaving. "Now tomorrow, you are going to call this number. It is my sister Camila. You are going to explain everything, and she will probably act like you are exaggerating about magic or the Brotherhood. Eventually, get mad and hang up on her. Understand she is doing that to throw off the Brotherhood, in case they tapped the phone. What is important is to tell her I left—"

"Where should I tell her you went?"

Deyanira clarified. "You won't. You will say I acted erratically. Keep telling her that I kept saying the spirits of El Yunque would protect me."

Halima still had questions. "So you're going to El Yungue? There are spirits there?"

Deyanira grew tired of Halima's interruptions. "Just say

it that way. My sister will understand. It is not for you to understand."

Out the door and into the veil of night they went. At the edge of the yard, Deyanira kneeled down and placed tobacco leaves at the base of a tree. "Grant us safe passage, please." Deyanira drew her machete, and they walked carefully through the trees and down the hill.

"Mami, are we going to El Yungue?"

Deyanira was listening to the energy and land, so without eye contact, she responded, "No *Mija*, that was for the Brotherhood, if they are listening. They don't know who or what I am, and I would like to keep it that way as long as I can. If they think I dragged you to the rainforest and I suffered from delusions, they are more likely to give up on me. At least, I am hopeful they will. They are arrogant. The Brotherhood murdered all the powerful mediums according to their records. Other than Halima and us there are no witnesses to what I did at her house. I am hoping they will all assume Soldanine was the powerful one and their ritual for her went awry killing their agents."

Calida, being still young and limited, shocked Deyanira when she replied, "They had a house full of dead people with no wounds. Don't be a fool, they will not leave you alone."

Deyanira paused and looked back at Calida. "Get out of my baby."

Calida laughed. "Mami, I heard them. They aren't in me." Just then, there was a rustling of leaves off in the distance. "What was that?" Calida asked.

"I believe the *duendes* accepted my offering and the task of keeping us safe." At the top of the hill towards her property, she could hear a man scream. "Come, we have to hurry." Deyanira did not have time for the million questions Calida had about

Deyanira's trust in the *duendes*. She loved her child, but Calida often had a rigid way of thinking. Once it was established one way, another way is not an option.

They reached a home at the bottom of the hill, and Deyanira knocked on the door. An elderly man answered the door, rubbing his eyes. "*Perdon, mi amor*, remember I said one day I would come for the car? Today is the day. May I have the keys? Remember, tell no one. If asked where the car went, remember what I said? You finally sold it."

She reached into her bag and handed him two thousand dollars. He shook his head and retreated into the home to retrieve the keys. Deyanira took Calida's hand, and they walked around to the back of his home where a small car hid under a tarp. Deyanira pulled back the tarp, which revealed the dusty, older model Honda.

Calida's face scrunched up. "Ew, so many spiders."

Deyanira smiled, "Anansi's protection *amor*, now get in."

They drove to the coast and parked near a beach as the sun rose. Calida had dozed off. Deyanira grabbed the burner phone out of her bag to call Falah. She quietly stepped out of the car to let Calida sleep.

"Hello?" Falah answered the phone.

"Falah," Deyanira said, then paused. She realized she was about to ask him to put himself in danger for her. They had previous conversations about this day, and although Falah was very clear about helping and protecting Deyanira and her child, there was so much he didn't know or understand.

"Lil sis. Is that you? What can I do to help?" He knew that if she was calling from an unknown number, it was time.

"We need to get off the island, but we can't fly, Falah."

Falah was out of bed, packing a bag and sending out texts.

"It is okay lil' sis. I'll fly down and get us a boat. We'll take it to Turks and Caicos. We can fly out from there to somewhere."

Deyanira was crying. "Okay, thank you." She placed her hand over her mouth to control her cries.

"We'll work it out, I promise. Don't cry, I got you. Meet you in Aguadilla, okay? Can you find yourself a place to hide out until tomorrow morning?"

Deyanira wiped her eyes, "Yes, I'll be okay. See you then." Once she hung up, she broke the burner phone and tossed it into the bushes.

Deyanira started driving the long way through Ponce towards the west coast of the island. Once Calida was awake, they stopped at a roadside kiosk for a huge *bacalaito*. Calida could forget they were on the run, and it felt like a fun road trip. They pulled into a hotel, and the exhaustion hit Deyanira. She leaned back in her chair and closed her eyes for a split second. "Mami, will Uncle Falah know where to find us?" Calida asked.

"Yes, baby. He knows we will meet here, but to keep us safe, he won't tell anyone where we are. Let's get a room. I need to sleep."

Chapter 33

"Go potty, amor. Uncle Falah is on his way upstairs."

There was a knock on the hotel door as Calida closed the bathroom door. As Deyanira opened the room door, Bassat sprinted into the room, and Falah laughed his infamous full-bodied laugh. "Look who I found in the parking lot under an old Honda," he said as he closed the door.

Bassat jumped up on the bed and meowed in disapproval at Deyanira.

Deyanira folded her arms. "You sneaky brat! What did you do, climb in the back of the car when I wasn't looking? Argh."

Calida came running out of the bathroom and squished her kitty.

On the boat, Calida, Bassat, and Deyanira napped on and off while Falah navigated to Haiti. Falah had contacts there and decided it was the safest route. Once docked, Deyanira had to argue with the cat about hiding in her giant purse. "You could've stayed with Camila, but you came here, and I do not have a carrier, so get in my bag or you will get left behind."

Falah and Calida laughed as Bassat climbed into Deyanira's bag. They were walking with their bags down the street. Falah was holding Calida's hand, and chatting with her.

A woman grabbed Deyanira's arm. "Papa Legba told me you

and your brother would be here. Come with me. I have a lot to share with him."

Falah grew up around Lottie, so he didn't shake easily, but the idea of a woman who knew he was coming to Haiti before he knew he would even be in Haiti stunned him. "Close your mouth, *Cheri*. I have many answers to your questions." The woman crouched down to Calida's level with a smile and booped her nose. "Oh my *Doudou*, you are something powerful, aren't you? Papa told me your secret."

Calida smiled at the woman. The woman held Deyanira's hand tightly. "You come with me. We have much to discuss before you go to Mexico."

They entered her home, and she immediately went straight to business. "I'm Esther. Papa Legba hid your grandfather Charles's plans from your *Tati*. She gets lots of information with her gifts, but sometimes, she hears something and tries to change it, or she hears something wrong entirely. She loves hard and sometimes that means trying to control things she sees. So Papa hides things from her, or he tells her something else. You understand?"

Falah rubbed his bald head and furrowed his brow. "Who is my *Tati*?"

Esther laughed and patted his hand. "Lottie. Tati is like an aunt in Haitian. Lottie doesn't know everything about you or your bloodline because Papa needed to ensure she didn't meddle. You know Lottie and your family practice Voodoo, right?"

Falah nodded, and she continued. "You know theirs differs from ours, but the same. Just like how Christians have Catholics and Lutherans we have African Vudu, Haitian Vodou, and Lousiana Voodoo. Your father was a Haitian bloodline. He was from our lands. Well, his family was. You are of Haitian descent. You have a lot of favor in Vodou from your bloodlines."

Falah's eyes got big. He had given up on meeting his father, but the mention of him caused his inner child to cry out. "What about my father?"

Esther took a drink of water. "Your father loved you and had planned to meet up with you and your mother after he finished college. He never made it to college. He was struck by a drunk driver and passed. You felt it that night. Your mother thought you were sick because you cried so hard as a boy. You didn't stop crying until his spirit came into your room and sang you a lullaby. He's been watching over you as an ancestor this whole time. He is so proud of you."

Falah wept uncontrollably. Deyanira tried to comfort him, but she knew he had to get it out. Esther reached over and placed her hand on Falah's. "You have to tell her. Tell the Oracle what you have been working on all these years for your Papa Charles." She placed her other hand on Deyanira's. "You have to tell your brother you're the Oracle. The ancestors brought you to this family on purpose. You and Falah have been fighting battles separately and preparing for the war you will wage together. Falah in the mundane and you in the spirit. Your sisters all have a part, too." Esther winked at Calida. "And you *doudou*, you'll carry the war to the heights it needs to put an end to the Brotherhood if we're lucky."

Deyanira choked on her water. Hope filled her eyes. Thoughts raced through her mind. *Esther knows about the Brotherhood. She is here to train me and Calida for this war. There is so much I don't know yet or understand. I need help.* "You know about the Brotherhood?"

"Oh *Cheri*, we ran them off during our revolt against the

French. Since then, they have spent their days trying to destroy us."

Deyanira asked, "So can you help me? Train me and Calida for this war? There is so much I don't know."

Esther shook her head. "You have instructions on where to go for your training. You think you aren't trained or prepared, but you are, and you are passing it on to Calida. I already gave you what I was supposed to give. Talk to your brother and trust him ." She looked at Falah. "Talk to your sister and trust her." Esther got up and held out her hand to Calida. "Come on, let's get you a treat." She led Calida to the kitchen.

"So I guess we have a lot to talk about. We need to decide on where to go," Deyanira said, with her eyebrows up. "I am the Oracle who has a lot of powers. I have more power than any medium born in a long time. I make Aunt Lottie look like a normal human without gifts. I have to get to Yucatán. There's someone there I need to meet who can train me in the spirit of the Jaguar."

Falah chuckled as he responded, "Well, there it is. I'll make the arrangements to go. We can have a long conversation about who I am as well. For starters, I am not a drug dealer and I never have been."